69° NORTH

69° NORTH

Robert Jackson

The Book Guild Ltd
Sussex, England

First published in Great Britain in 2003 by
The Book Guild Ltd
25 High Street
Lewes, Sussex
BN7 2LU

Typesetting in New Century Schoolbook by
Keyboard Services, Luton, Bedfordshire

Printed in Great Britain by
Bookcraft (Bath) Ltd, Avon

A catalogue record for this book is available from
The British Library

ISBN 1 85776 767 5

For Em

ACKNOWLEDGEMENTS

This is a first novel and without the support, encouragement, and in some cases active discouragement, of friends, it would never have reached completion and publication. I am deeply indebted to the following people. Nigel Mackenzie, Richenda Todd, Jane Rasch, Wil Garfit, Chris Davies, Tim Hextall, Nina Osipova, Carol Biss, Joanna Bentley, Clare Frances, Robin Buchanan, Nick Milligan, Bumble Ogilvy-Wedderburn, Sam Badrick, John Tanner, Beat Guttinger, Eve Bonham, Tony Bertram, Jacques Redon, Fred Dovaston, Guy Rasch, Anthony Tryon, John Illsley, Ailie Collins, Dan Maynard-Taylor, Piers Fletcher, Claerwen Green, Graham Walker, Leicester Le Seuer, San Plowman, Harry Edmonds, Ian Mackie, John Gibb, Brian Fratell, Rory Pilkington, Michael Mann, Lochy and, throughout it all, Em.

Chapter One

The bulbs on the console flashed rhythmically, red-yellow, red-yellow. Glowing dully, their muted warning barely penetrated the smoke-laden air of the office. A klaxon perched high on the treatment plant's roof trumpeted the alert. The wail drifted into the teeth of the Arctic gale and down the fjord to Murmansk.

Admiral Alexander Bodanin stood by his desk stooped over a music score, seemingly unaware of the urgent signals from the console. He had long since disconnected the wires to the sound alarm; the small speaker now served as a perch for a family photograph. He peered through his glasses at the intricate mesh of staves, crotchets and semi-quavers. He had left his audio-cassette at home, and was beginning to regret demanding to conduct the final piece in the choral concert. He tapped the beat with the biro in his right hand and tried to hum the melody, which had eluded him for most of the morning. His humming faded as he walked over to a nearby table and poured tea from a thermos flask into his half-empty cup. He sipped the unsweetened brew and returned to his desk, to find that he had let his cigarette burn down to the filter. A wisp of smoke drifted from a line of ash in the metal ashtray. He groaned inwardly: it was the third he had wasted this morning. He reached in his pockets. The beginning of the ritual of finding and lighting another that could take up to five minutes.

His eyes scanned the clutter of his desk aimlessly. The active part of his brain was still trying to unravel the finale. He patted the pockets of his coat and opened a drawer that he had searched already, all to no avail. His efforts moved a loose page from his newspaper against the console, causing a section of print illuminated by the flashing lights to appear ominously skeletal. His attention was drawn to a photograph on the wall and he

1

viewed the black and white image with a hazy smile. It was of a young Captain being handed his first command – only fifteen years ago – but it could have been his son. The subject had hair and even a chin discernible above his starched collar. He noticed the dark brows, arched over pale eyes. He recollected just how close to tears those eyes had been brought by the proud emotion of it all. He did not refer to the mirror on the opposite wall for a contemporary comparison; his decline into late middle age had been swift and thorough and he did not need reminding. Instead, he looked through the window, down into the shipyard and out across the bay, where thirty-five nuclear submarines lay tethered.

Once the pride of the Northern Fleet, they lay rafted together in pods of five, rotting in the freezing water. In their midst lay the hulk which he had commanded, the icebreaker *Polyanaris*, now the guardian of their waste. Full to over-brimming with spent nuclear fuel, rusting chain anchored her amongst the submarines. He scanned the old shipyard, which in the past had been the scene of so much activity. When he first took command the shore crews had worked around the clock, crawling like ants over the vast docks, provisioning, bunkering and arming the fleet. All that remained now were the rows of cranes, which stood frozen and suppliant, their heads bowed to their fate. They provided a sinister backdrop to the concrete tanks that lay in orderly ranks along the docks. These contained the nuclear waste garnered from regional power stations. When combined with the deadly cargo in the *Polyanaris*, their contents represented an unsettlingly high proportion of the world's nuclear waste. It lay morbidly dormant, awaiting treatment: treatment for which there was no money and little incentive for the country to provide. The tanks were left to the ravages of the Arctic's weather and guarded by a desultory band of conscripts, who gradually became immune to the regular leaks and alarms. Theirs was an emotional immunity, for time alone would tell what effects the radiation would have on their health.

The Admiral saw a vehicle pull up at one of the tanks with its lights flashing. He decided to focus instead on a solitary seagull hovering in the snow-laden gale – it should join its friends sheltering behind the wharf. He turned to the desk that had been his command for the last three years, and pushed aside the score to find, at last, the packet of cigarettes. His relief was tainted

2

by the absence of matches. Another search would now ensue. Beyond it, his anxiety now stretched to his biro and the concert. The familiar round of forgetful determination and mild frustration would continue until lunch. The afternoon would find him asleep at his desk. His pension beckoned.

He heard the sound of studded leather against iced metal and sighed in anticipation of the knock.

'Come in.' The words were unwelcoming.

The door opened, accompanied by a flurry of wind-driven snow, which lifted the papers on the desk and rattled the photographs on the wall. The Admiral's displeasure was alleviated by a glimpse of his biro and matches beneath the restless sprawl of paper. A young sailor, his pale face still bearing the final traces of acne, interrupted his thoughts.

'Sir, we have an alarm at vessel Number Five.'

The Admiral lifted the biro from his desk and shuffled the score into order. 'I'm sorry?'

'Sir, we have a leak from Number Five vessel. Captain Osipov has recommended evacuation of the immediate area, until we have quantified the radiation level.'

The rating looked over to the console where, beneath the report on last night's ice hockey game, the flashing lights could be clearly seen. The Admiral signalled for the rating to join him as he walked to the window. 'Oh well.' He placed his face close to the glass and pointed with his nose. 'What do you see out there?'

'Sir?' The rating stood nervously to attention. His Admiral was only a few paces away.

'What do you see out there?' He gestured for the sailor to stand at ease but without success.

'The storage ship *Polyanaris*, Sir!'

The Admiral scratched the side of his nose with the back of a finger, the corners of his mouth drooped in resignation. 'Yes, I suppose that is all you see.' He turned his back on the window and asked, 'Well, will you be singing with us on Saturday?'

The sailor stood to attention. He was confused, but persevered with his task.

'Sir, the alarm. It went off ten minutes ago.' The rating pointed at the flashing lights. The Captain had warned him that he might find the Admiral difficult to move.

'Baritones, that's we need. Russian baritones, full-blooded, their voices sweetened by mother's milk and the richest of honey.' The Admiral waved his biro at a framed photograph of uniformed mariners, tiered like a wedding cake, each immaculate in their uniforms, their mouths agape: seventy baby starlings receiving the worm. 'The Northern Fleet Choir, without compare.' He turned to the rating, 'So, do you sing?'

'No, Sir.' The young sailor eyed the console nervously. He had only recently been posted to Andreeva and this was his first alarm. Engineers looking like threadbare astronauts had driven past him as he had run to the Admiral's office.

'Well, if you are going to be with us for a while, I recommend it. The choir provides a worthwhile and satisfying interest. That, and companionship too. There's not much else goes on up here.'

He waved a large, white hand in the general direction of the console and the flashing lights. 'Obviously, we should be attentive at all times, but you shouldn't worry too much about those things. We have alerts from time to time but usually nothing too serious, the odd leak or cracked cylinder, that sort of thing. You'll soon get used to them.' The sailor was trying to remain calm, but his recently completed training had taught him there was no such thing as a minor leak, and that even a small dosage of radiation could prove fatal. The Admiral continued. 'That's just the start of it. The rest of our day will be in turmoil. We'll have the men from the Nuclear Agency and their green friends from Medina putting their noses where they aren't wanted.'

His plan for the afternoon was in tatters. The Navy had begrudgingly agreed some while ago that the Central Nuclear Agency should be informed of all leaks, and that the international environmental group, Medina, should also be consulted. The afternoon would be spent sparring fruitlessly over more safety measures and the access to information: both sides would be vociferous but effectively powerless to make any changes.

The Admiral shook his head and gestured for the boy to look out of the window again. They could now barely make out the *Polyanaris* through the hurtling snow. 'She used to be my command. We kept Siberia open for the country. This is a summer's day compared to what I've seen. And now look at her – the Navy's dustbin. Full from stem to stern with nuclear waste. We used to take that stuff out to sea and sink it, but not any more. Oh no, we are all very internationally aware now. So, we fill our ships

4

with it and let them rot next to our submarine fleet.' He slapped the back of one hand into the palm of the other. 'But there it is. A malignant hen amongst so many sick chickens.' Since coining the phrase he had used it a hundred times.

He turned to look at the rating, who was still standing uncertainly to attention. The Admiral walked over to him, held his arm, and smiling, said, 'You run along and tell the Captain that I will not be joining him in the evacuation. He'll understand. I stick to my post in times of danger. And as for you, think about the choir. We always need young blood.'

The rating saluted an unreturned salute, spun on his heels and opened the door to leave. A blast of wind, even stronger than on his arrival, lifted the papers on the desk. The Admiral, to his consternation, could no longer see his biro or matches.

'Oh damn it!'

The rating could just hear the words, as his feet rattled down the staircase. The Admiral set about tidying his desk and finding his briefcase and the all-important incident file. His preparations for the concert would have to wait until tomorrow.

Chapter Two

Genia had left the path on the frozen river some hours earlier and set out across the wilderness to find the tell-tale signs that would lead him to his quarry. The Arctic winter was bleak and cold – the sun was near the end of its hibernation, and so was the bear that was Genia's prey on this late March morning. As he worked his way through the scrubby trees, he was looking for subtle changes in light and shade. An unusual mound, a depression or hollow, broken or strange angles in the branches of the birches – any of these could lead him to the air-hole and the underground den of the bear.

Genia made his way steadily and softly for a man of his size. His rifle was slung over his shoulder, benign against the bulk of his shoulders. A leather belt was wrapped around his waist, and from it hung his skinning knife. The only colour in the white gloom was the flash of red in his fox-fur hat. His breathing was even, misting through a full moustache flecked with grey, the first signs of middle age. His eyes were alert and, unusually for Genia, cold and menacing. He was close; he knew it.

He leant against his stick as he peered into a sheltered bowl beside a hillock. The evenness of the ground had been disturbed. He sensed the bear and stood, frozen in the silence of the forest. A small gust of wind agitated the branches which, quivering, dusted his hat with snow. He remained motionless; he could just make out a black line in the snow, a wisp of condensation seeping from it. He worked out what to do.

Below him lay a mature adult, nine feet in length, weighing over 350 pounds, who had delivered two cubs three years ago. She had reared them, trained them to hunt and fend for themselves and then, in the way of the bear, deserted them, as she set about preparing for hibernation. Gorging on moss, grass, berries – anything she could find to garnish her fat store for the months of torpor – she now lay calmly unaware of the mortal danger that stood a few feet away.

Surprise and her anaesthetised state were on his side, but he could not know exactly where she lay, how deep and in what position. His bolt-action rifle was loaded with three rounds; reloading at close quarters with a crazed bear lurching towards him required all the skill, calmness and determination that his years in the Kola Peninsula had taught him.

He had two options. To creep up to the hole and fire randomly into the dark space hoping to inflict a fatal shot, or to disturb her, let her rise from her hole and then shoot her in the open. The first option, whilst tempting, had several disadvantages. His early shots might only do slight damage or, worse still, miss completely. He chose the second option. There was a time when he would have taken his dogs to stir the bear from its den, but one had been badly wounded when a bear's paw tore open its flank. Genia had stitched the wound himself.

He stood for a while, his face emotionless. Then he exhaled – almost a sigh.

Lowering himself onto his knees he removed his gloves, lifted his rifle off his shoulder, and worked a bullet into the chamber. With his rifle in one hand and his stick in the other, he crawled towards the entrance. He neared the hole; another soft gust wafted snow crystals across the mouth of the den towards him. Something unsettled him. He looked around, but there was no movement anywhere. He lay on his stomach and, lifting the flaps of his hat from his ears, listened again. 'You are getting old, Genia,' he thought as he slowly edged to the lip.

He pushed his stick slowly into the hole and moved the tip in a circular motion, lowering it inch by inch until it met with some resistance. He raised himself to his knees and then lifted onto one foot like an ungainly sprinter and, not moving the stick, he edged his nose over the hole. He could just see – about three feet down – brown fur. He started to prod the mound gently. He stopped, listened and looked for any movement. There was none. He pushed harder and heard a deep breathy snore and, rising to his feet, he now rammed his stick hard into the fur and roared for all his might. This time, the bear stirred.

The ground underneath Genia exploded. He was flung to the

7

ground and, in the confusion, he lost his grip on the rifle. The immense head and shoulders of the bear burst through the mat of roots, branches and dead leaves. Genia caught the sweet smell of the den at the same time as the bear's nostrils were filled with his man scent. She bellowed in anger and alarm.

For a second they stared at each other and then a cub emerged drawing their attention from the hole. This was the brown mound that had been on the receiving end of Genia's stick. The mother roared again as she struggled to free herself from the den.

Genia scrabbled to his feet and his eyes searched frantically for his rifle. He saw it, embedded in the snow, near the bear. He had no option but to flee. He scrambled away, stumbling and gasping through the snow and branches as the bear finally freed herself and charged after him. In the summer he would not have stood a chance. Now she was torpid and fat she may choose to return to her cub; the chances were even. He ran for five minutes, a zigzag path over fallen trees and clumps of undergrowth, his face scratched and battered by the frozen branches. Only when he was certain the bear had given up the pursuit, he stopped, leaning his blood-smeared face against the cold bark of a tree. He was panting heavily. 'You are too old for this, Genia.' He said it out loud this time.

He returned to the frozen river and trudged back to the camp. He was greeted by the sound of barking that could be heard above the solid crunch of his footfall and, as he drew closer, the hum from the generator filled the air. A door opened in one of the huts and a shaft of light spilled across the flattened snow. The yellow glow was soon filled with shadows. Valery, the camp's other guide, stood in the doorway and Genia's dog, Pana, bounded out to greet his master, eagerly sniffing Genia's legs as he walked. He flicked the dog over with the back of a hand; Pana rolled in the snow and growled with pleasure at the customary greeting. Seeing that Genia had returned without fur or rifle, Valery gestured a question to him. Genia shook his head and made an open handed reply as he neared the hut.

'How about you?' Genia asked, as he climbed the steps to the cabin.

'No luck. We must have walked miles, though. What's happened to your face?'

Genia had forgotten the damage and wiped some congealed

blood from his cheek. 'I found one, but I made mess of it.' He removed his hat, to reveal a sweat-lined brow and matted hair above a face that, despite the blood and bruising, retained its latent kindness. He told Valery the story as he removed his bulky clothing. 'You don't fancy going to get my rifle do you? I'm sure she'll have gone back to bed by now,' he asked as he finished the tale.

Valery smiled. 'You sort your own problems out.'

'I think I'll leave it a few days.' Genia reached down to untie his bootlaces. 'How have they been?' He referred to the two German men who had paid to shoot bears. During the winter months, the camp for salmon fishermen was used as a base for hunting. The local collective retained Genia as head guide. The job also allowed him to keep his own hut further up river. When he was not taking out dollar-paying foreigners, Genia would spend the majority of his time there. His customer on this occasion had found the conditions too severe, and Genia had decided to go out alone. He would share the dollars with the Collective, and the furs provided him with a solid income in the winter.

Valery dropped onto the sofa. Beside him lay a mound of outdoor clothes in pooling snowmelt. 'Yours is still grumbling about the cold and the food. He's in bed, sleeping off what he drank this morning.' He yawned and continued, 'Mine's OK, but I won't be sad to see the back of them.'

Genia looked at Valery, nearly twenty years his junior, and wondered whether he had possessed such self-confidence at that age. Genia hung his quilted coat and leggings on the hooks near the door, and then padded his feet, wrapped in sea socks, to the chair in front of the fire. The faded grey wool was a patchwork of darning that showed a delicate hand. He looked down the length of his body and wriggled warmth back into his toes. He gazed at the fire and thought of the last time he had been separated from his rifle – eighteen years ago in Afghanistan, during a Mujahideen ambush. It seemed a lifetime away. The fire shed a warm light that flickered in his eyes and illuminated the crow's-feet around his eyes. As he remembered the past, the wrinkles became more pronounced. Slowly, he shook his head from side to side. A pine log crackled and spat a glowing ember. It landed on his foot.

Shaking off the offending spark, he grunted '...Mmhh? Yes, me too. I've had enough of it.'

He examined his foot to see whether his sewing skills would be required later, and was almost disappointed that the wool was only barely singed. The sock's repair would have been a welcome addition to his job-list back at his hut. Genia had decided to let Valery return with the hunters to the city. He would spend another week in his hut by himself; he wasn't ready for Murmansk just yet.

He was thirsty and thought about going to the kitchen to find a drink, but the fire's coaxing warmth held him in his chair. He sat reflecting, his arms across his chest and his legs outstretched, unaware of Pana, who had crawled under his knees.

He gazed at the fire and, after a few minutes, asked Valery, 'Has it ever occurred to you, that we spend the winters trying to kill everything in sight, while in the summer, we tenderly release every salmon we catch back into the river?'

But Valery had fallen asleep on the battered sofa, his mouth agape. Genia did not turn to seek an answer or repeat the question, for he had dozed off as well.

A week later Genia cadged a lift in a supplies truck returning to Murmansk. He had sat cramped in the cab with two others, the journey taking nearly a day and he was weary from the jaw-rattling bounce of the truck's suspension. The heaters had been at full blast with the windows closed. This, combined with chain-smoked Marlboros and vodka, had made it impossible for him to sleep, despite the monotony of the chatter. The journey had left him with a headache that even the cold of Murmansk could not penetrate. The truck dropped him near his father's apartment. He stretched his arms, shook his head and stamped his feet before setting off across the square. As he turned the corner into Chekova Prospekt, screwing up his eyes against the sleet, he saw against the wall what looked like a tree-stump. He looked again as he got closer, and this time could make out the shape of a beggar kneeling hunched and plaintive against the flaking paint. Her head was wrapped in a woollen shawl. Her arm levered out her hand; a single coin nestled in the ragged woollen sock that served as a glove.

'A few *kopecks*...' the voice trailed off, void of expectation.

He walked past and then turning towards her said, 'It's late for you old lady.'

He searched in his pockets. She grasped his hand as he offered the coins; he could see her eyes through a gap in her shawl, mournful yet with the ghost of a smile. He could picture the cheekbones and the toothless mouth, feel the ache in her bones. He knew her cold existence: the cot in a basement, the leaks from the pipes, the scraps of food in a cardboard box, the wrinkled photos of a son in the army and a husband long gone. 'Welcome home, Genia', he thought, as he added another coin to the meagre pile. Her muffled appreciation escaped through her scarf and across the windswept square where his boots made solid prints amongst the shuffling trails of the pensioners.

He had been born in a similar building over forty years ago. They had lived closer to the centre but all these blocks were the same, and the echo from the concrete as he climbed the staircase filled him with a sense of sad resignation. He smelt cooking and heard the sounds of a half-tuned radio; with each step, disjointed images from his youth filtered through his mind. He automatically listened for the cry of a baby, but this was a pensioner's block and the static from the radio was the only sound. It was as if he had never been away. He approached the door to the flat and turned the key in the lock.

The room was dark and the warm current of air sucked out of the door by the cold of the corridor brought with it the smell of his father and the hospital soap that, even now, he managed somehow to obtain. Genia smiled, but on seeing the darkness in the apartment, his heart sank. It was too early for his father to be asleep. Switching on the light he found everything in its usual immaculate order and was relieved to see some of his sister's belongings on the table. They would be visiting a neighbour. He dropped his bag on the floor in the tiny hall and set about unravelling the many layers of clothes. Like a bear in a telephone box he struggled to free himself from his coats and pullovers, without shedding snow in the main room – he knew how that would offend his father's sense of tidiness.

He found in his rucksack the slabs of dried fish that he had brought from the camp and put them on the kitchen table. He went to the sideboard and saw there the photographs that he knew so well, black and white and as fresh as the day they were

11

printed, the glass shielding them from the wear they would otherwise have received from loving lips and fingertips. He reached to
touch the frame around his mother's face as the front door
opened. He pulled his hand away as he turned to greet his
family.

'Genia? Where have you been? We thought you were coming
last week.' Nadia's voice was warm with surprise.

The two hugged and then he looked into her face. He was
pleased to see his sister's sad smile, her eyes accentuated by the
paleness of her skin. He lifted her off her feet and swung her
from side to side.

'Ah, my darling Nadyusha!' Her hair straggled across his face
as he breathed in her soft warmth.

She pushed him away in mock disgust. 'Ugh! You smell like a
polecat! When did you last wash?'

'I had a *bania* a week ago,' adding to cover his embarrassment,
in imitation of his father, 'that's more than enough for any man.'

He put her down but she still clasped his hand, 'So how long
have we got you?'

He didn't reply. He looked over her shoulder and saw his father
removing his coat and boots in the corridor. He went to help the
tall, frail figure as he leant against the wall, his fine profile
defaced by a cold-induced dribble, which wobbled precariously at
the end of his nose.

His smile lacked warmth, his face was weaker. 'He's aged,'
Genia thought, as he put his hand to his father's elbow to assist
him.

'You can stop that!' This was the normal reaction from his
father, as he brushed away the helping hand. Brother and sister
glanced at each other as their father stood erect, and offered his
face to be kissed. His son brushed his lips across his father's
cheek, feeling the coarseness of bristle and loose skin. They patted shoulders. Genia remembered the times when his father had
towered over him, cuffing him across the head and wrapping his
arms so tightly around him that he could hardly breathe.

'So, he returns.' The irony was intentional and sister looked at
brother again and shrugged.

'Let me get you something to eat,' Nadia said to defuse the
comment, just as her mother would have done.

'How easily we fall into these roles,' Genia thought as they went about the family rituals, brushing crumbs from the table-cloth, laying out cutlery and glasses. They chattered and patted each other as they fussed over the commonplace acts of domestic life. In this room they had shared so much happiness, so much laughter, but recent suffering and grief had taken their toll.

'Where's Viktor?' Genia asked.

Nadia wiped hear hands on her apron. 'Oh, he's away in Amsterdam. He'll be back tomorrow.'

Genia paused before asking, 'So, where's my nephew, the brave Volodia? I have a present for him.'

'I'm afraid he has had to go back to hospital...' He could see in her eyes that it was serious. He glanced at his father who shook his head and Genia braced himself for what was about to come.

His father was bitter. 'They should have spotted the signs sooner. Half this city is falling apart with cancer. We've been told "It's not looking that bad", but I'm afraid I've heard all this before.' He was referring to his wife's wasting illness. 'What are these professionals up to?'

'Papa...' Nadia pleaded softly.

He waved his hand dismissively at Genia. 'The poor mite is currently on some form of drip in a ward full of dying children. That's how your brave Volodia is. And, while you hide away in the forest and his father cavorts around the world, your sister suffers for us all.'

Genia went to Nadia, held her shoulders in his outstretched hands and dipped his head to look into her tear-filled eyes.

'When did all this happen?' Genia asked, but he only half took in the reply. He felt his stomach churn and his breath grow heavy.

'I'm here now, Nadyusha, I won't leave...'

She drew him to her and sobbed into his chest. He stroked her hair and patted her back until, after a few minutes he murmured into her ear, 'Nadyusha, you'd better let this old polecat wash himself.' She almost smiled.

On his way to the bathroom, Genia went over to his father who was fiddling with the tuning control on the radio. Genia put his hand out to touch him but pulled back; there was nothing he could say. They had been through all of this before. His mother, always able to coax and cajole her husband out of his moods, had kept the peace between them.

13

Without her, his father sat reminiscing and thinking of what might have been. He hated his life without her. Nadia visited as often as she could and he took delight in Volodia, but even that pleasure was tempered by the sad thought that his wife had not lived to see the boy. He had watched her decay and now everything he held dear was also decaying. Murmansk, Russia, his grandson; everything was falling apart around him. He sat in his chair as the announcer made way for the music that heralded the news bulletin. Genia tried to escape to the bathroom, but the wave of a veined hand shepherded him back into the room. Everything stopped in the Sukhov household for the news; tonight would be no exception.

'So, do you hear this? Our new national anthem. Huh! The only thing that's new about it is the words.' He turned up the volume for the report. 'And have you heard them?' He turned to Genia. 'I imagine the news doesn't reach you out there in the Kola. It's unspeakable, an insult to everyone who lived and died for that song. How can they change the words?'

Nadia stood behind her father and gave a conspiratorial shrug to her brother. 'Well at least they've revived the music. It can only unite.'

Their father was not to be persuaded. 'What's the point? They take the soul out of the anthem and all you are left with is an empty husk.' He strained to listen. 'There – can you hear it? "God will preserve us." How did He get in there? What was wrong with Lenin – he used to be our saviour!' He turned off the radio abruptly and brother and sister waited in silence. The news usually prompted discussion, but on topics only of their father's choosing. It had always been that way.

'So how long before you return to your hideout in the forest?' This was old ground and Genia looked wearily at his father as he replied.

'I work there, father.'

Normally a lecture on wasted potential and shirking responsibility would have followed, but the news of Volodia's deterioration had dampened his father's spirit. He simply replied, 'Yes I suppose you do.' As he stood up from his chair, he added, 'At least you're not a *biznizman* or working for that mob that masquerades as our bureaucracy. I suppose I should be happy that I don't have a *Novy Ruskiy* for a son. There is that to say for you.'

14

Nadia smiled at Genia. 'Come on Papa, it's getting late. I'll warm up some soup and we can eat before I take Genia back to our apartment. You must be hungry.'

The old man nodded in agreement. As he turned to his son, a glimmer of a smile brought warmth to his eyes. 'I'm glad you are home with us, Genia. A family should be together in difficult times.'

Genia nodded, and held his father's hand.

Chapter Three

Nadia and Genia stood side by side on the bus. The city's transport service was one of the few pieces of infrastructure that had withstood the economic ravages of recent years. The bus was full to over-brimming as this was the hospital's visiting hour. Old ladies clasped paper-wrapped parcels, children swung from their parent's hands and sad, solitary figures stared out into the gloom. The bus ploughed its way through the slush and up the hill that led to the District Children's Hospital. Genia and Nadia were silent. Nadia hadn't been permitted to visit Volodia for nearly a week, and her anxiety was etched on her face. Viktor had been called away to an alarm at the docks. He was likely to miss the one hour visit altogether.

Visiting hospitals was never easy for Genia. Once the pride of Murmansk, in their day the hospitals could boast to be amongst the finest in the Soviet Union. His father had practised there and had been fiercely proud that Genia was going to follow in his footsteps. But it was there, too, that Genia had decided he was not going to pursue a medical career after all. The only thing he regretted now was the way he had let it happen. He had realised after two years that it wasn't right for him, but instead of telling his father outright, he maintained the pretence. His attendance record deteriorated and his exam performance slumped. His father's disappointment had turned to anger when he realised that Genia was going to give it all up and join the army.

The bus pulled up. Nadia looped her arm through her brother's as they walked through the double doors with the throng of other visitors, shuffling the slush off their boots onto the flattened cardboard boxes that acted as mats. The once pristine white flooring had become grey-black from years of wear, the bleakness accentuated by a few brightly-coloured children's paintings, which hung, half-glued, to the walls and blinds. Genia remembered his brief time in the children's hospital. He braced himself as he recalled the frightened sobs which soothing words could not calm, and the brave smiles that fell part-trusted. He had known how dire Volodia's illness was the moment he'd seen the shake of his father's head. He shivered, wishing he was back in his hut, safe and secure. They could just send him a letter to let him to know when it was all over. His increasing panic was disturbed by a voice he had not heard for a long time.

'Genia?'

He turned to greet a face that he had known so well. It was Irina, fifteen years older, but still with that strong warm smile, that fine profile, her hair piled on her head, and a biro absent-mindedly acting as a hairpin. She crossed the corridor, grasped his arms and beamed openly into his face.

'Where have you been? I hardly recognised you with that moustache!'

Genia shrugged and scratched his face self-consciously. 'It's my winter wear, Irina.' He looked happily at her and turned to his sister. 'I don't think you ever met my sister, Nadia?' Nadia approached and the two women introduced themselves.

'We are visiting my nephew Volodia Kharkov. He's undergoing chemotherapy at the moment. Is he one of yours?'

'I'm still mending broken bones. But why don't you go and see him? I'll find out what I can for you and come and find you in the ward. Kharkov you said?'

'Yes. That would be great. Thank you.'

Nadia led the way and Genia took a deep breath as they rounded the corner into the ward. The beds were further apart than in the standard wards, although they still managed to fit fifteen into what was a relatively cramped space. Inhaling through his mouth, he kept his eyes on a point somewhere in the middle distance. He listened only to the click and squeak of his feet on the linoleum. He wanted to appear to Volodia as if he had just walked out of the forest. He knew that if he let the place get to him, the boy would see through him.

'Here he is! Ha! Volodia, what are you doing lying in bed at this time of day?'

'Uncle Genia!'

A smile spread across the child's ashen face – sunken eyes found laughter. Strands of hair wisped over his scalp; his once-firm body barely filled the hospital robe. A drip hung menacingly from a stand next to his bed, and beside it stood a sick bowl covered with a towel. Genia watched a drop form in the transparent bag, roll slowly into the plastic tube and down into the boy's arm. 'Sand through an hourglass,' he thought.

'Volodia, you look terrible! What have you been up to?' Nadia felt her son's brow and kissed his cheek, but Volodia nudged her away, his eyes on Genia, the uncle he adored.

'Well, whatever it is you had better sort yourself out. We've got bears to hunt and fish to catch, and you're not going to be much use to me trussed up like this. I bet you smell of soap too.' He leant over the boy and took an exaggerated sniff. He immediately wished he hadn't. 'Achh! Just as I thought! I've told you that they can smell a clean man five kilometres away!' The child smelt of death.

Volodia was aching to ask for the present that his uncle always carved him, but was too much in awe to say anything. Genia sensed that he shouldn't tease him any more and pulled from his coat a small cloth-wrapped parcel, tied with string.

'Here we are, my brave little man. Something to add to your collection.'

The boy carefully untied the string and unwrapped the parcel. He held the carving in his wasted hands: a rough-hewn figure of a bear, raised on its hind legs and roaring.

'There you are, whittled by the master himself and all for you.'

'Thank you Uncle. It's smashing.'

'You should have seen the original. Three metres in her stockinged feet and as wild as a cut snake...' he heard himself embellish the tale, holding the boy spellbound. As long as he kept talking Genia knew that he would be all right.

The swing doors to the ward opened and in rushed Viktor, his anorak flapping as he strode towards the bed. Middle-age had softened his once hard frame and mellowed the sternness of his expression. Genia remembered how in Viktor's student days it was a face that had intimidated opposing ice hockey players on the rink and, in later life, the intimidation had been felt by the authoritarian bodies who refused to listen to his reasoning.

'I'm sorry! I was delayed up at Andreeva, Nadia, I'm sorry,' he said as he kissed her. He shook Genia's hand. 'So how are you today, Lodda? Is the food as bad as ever?' His concern showed through the pretence he was displaying for his son.

'I'm not feeling very hungry Daddy.'

'Well, when you do I have this for you.' Viktor produced a huge bar of Toblerone from his coat.

'What is it?' Volodia peered at the triangular shape, intrigued.

'It's chocolate, with honey and nuts. I bought it at Amsterdam airport and it looked so good I nearly ate it myself. In fact I think I will now.' Viktor made as if to take it away from him but Volodia clasped it to his chest, along with the bear.

As the family talked Genia looked around the ward for the first time and saw hunched figures clustered around other beds. The first words and smiles of greeting had evaporated to leave the fear and awe that made up the hush only found in hospitals. Theirs was the only laughter in the ward. Genia shivered as he saw the condition of the other children and was relieved when Irina came into the room. She gestured for him to join her and they walked out of the ward so as not to be heard.

'Why don't these people smile and talk properly to those kids? They're not dead yet, for God's sake.'

'It's obviously been some time since you've been in a hospital, Genia. I've talked to Volodia's doctor. His leukaemia is treatable and it seems that so far it is responding.'

'Are you sure? He looks dreadful.'

'You know as well as I that we wouldn't be able to treat him unless there was a fair chance of recovery. He's had a rough ride, though. As you can see he is very weak, the chemo is giving him a real bashing.'

'I know, just look at the poor mite...' Genia looked across the ward to see Nadia wiping the boy's brow.

'If you can find the money you could help by buying a different treatment which would ease the side effects. The hospital has run out but it's available from Norway. The hospital gets a delivery of additional drugs once a month. I can arrange that for you if it can be afforded. That would help; he wouldn't feel so nauseous.'

Genia looked across the ward, only partially comforted by Irina's reply. 'Why does this country treat its children so poorly?' The words were more a sad declaration than a question, and one that Irina had heard too many times before.

19

'Genia, I've told you what I know. They think they've got it going into remission but the boy has got to have the strength to cope with the cure. Those additional drugs can only help. Why don't you go and tell your sister?'

'No, I'll leave it to the doctor. It's her story. She can't have many opportunities to give encouraging news.'

'She's just started her round. I'll make sure she visits your nephew first.' Genia watched her as she walked over to the doctor. She had aged well. Her features were more Scandinavian than Russian, and he remembered how he used to tease her about it. She caught him looking at her and smiled. The years fell away as she walked back over to him.

Genia asked, 'Are you working now or can we talk?'

She took his hand and was shocked by its coarseness. 'You wouldn't make much of a surgeon with this.' She lifted it to reveal a scarred, leathery palm. It wasn't the hand that she used to know so well. 'What have you been up to, Genia?'

Genia withdrew his hand slowly and smiled. 'It will take a while to tell you...'

'Well, it can't be now, I'm afraid. I, too, have parents visiting, and I'm late. But another time?'

'Yes, I understand. Look, I'll...'

'Don't say you'll phone me. Those were the last words you said to me. Other people have managed to get through. It would be nice to see you again. A lot has changed. I live alone now.'

'I'll walk with you to your ward.'

'Yes, that would be nice.'

She held his arm, the first time in public, for theirs had been a clandestine relationship. She had been a married doctor, ten years older than the medical student with whom she had fallen in love. As they walked, old emotions tumbled from recesses that had been sealed over for a long time. The memories of guilt, recklessness and eventual heartbreak simmered in their minds as they talked about the mundane. Reluctantly, he left her to return to his family and the grim reality of Volodia's illness.

He stayed a short while with Nadia and Viktor before returning to his father's flat. He walked out into the night where the earlier hard frost had brought the temperature to just below freezing. Fluffy wet flakes swirled in beams of the streetlights. He took a slow, deep breath and noticed the milder air through his scarf-covered mouth. He could hear a police siren as he wandered the empty road. It took him nearly half an hour to return to his father's building. He turned the corner into Chekova Prospekt and there, in the corner, he could see what looked like a log, the freshly fallen snow heaped up against one side. His heart sank. He knelt beside the frozen figure. He gently lifted the scarf from her face and sighed, 'You should have gone home earlier, old lady.' He tried to close her eyes but they had frozen open. He covered her face with the threadbare shawl. For the want of something else to do, he brushed the snow from her dead body.

Jody Lucas sat on the grass bank beside the tennis court. It was four minutes past eleven and the other courts were in play and rang with the sounds of family tennis. The light 'thwack' of serve met by the solid 'chock' of return were a constant background to occasional groans and laughter. She twisted a racket in her hand as she talked to the couple sitting with her. She looked towards the car park waiting for the arrival of her husband. The courts lay next to the clubhouse that sat on a knoll overlooking Lake Tuxedo. A solid red brick building with long shuttered windows, it was the social hub of one of America's most exclusive residential estates. A sail-like Stars and Stripes rippled in the breeze from a white flag staff. Uniformed stewards prepared for lunch on the terrace, while nannies looked after their charges by the heated, outdoor pool. Monied America going about its Sunday morning in comfort and ease.

The group by the court looked restless. It was now five past eleven, and Sunday courts were at a premium. They had already turned away a couple of polite teenagers who were hoping for a no show. Had they been older they would have got the court.

'Look, why don't you guys get started? He's obviously stuck on the phone or something,'

Jody picked at some grass as she spoke. 'I knew it was a mistake to let him meet us here.'

'We'll just have a knock until the great man shows, Jody.' The couple walked onto the court.

Bright fluorescent balls fell from newly opened tubes, and dust from the court powdered their shoes as they knocked-up.

Greg's arrival was announced by the throb of eight litres of

Chrysler engine that nestled under the Cobra's bonnet. He only used this machine for driving around the park; occasionally he would take guests for a spin but most of the time it lay under covers next to the other toys in his garage. The car draw to a halt, one last blip on the accelerator to make sure everybody had seen him, and the club returned to normality.

'Just do it!' A black wire connected his ear to his mobile and to some poor unfortunate on the other side of the world. 'You've told me that already... Do me a favour? Don't think – just do it! Look, I'm late... I got to go... Yeah, yeah – we'll speak later.' He unplugged the earpiece, picked up three rackets from the passenger seat and climbed out of the vehicle.

'Sorry honey! Hi Tommy... Meg!' His smile broke across the tan of his face to reveal the standard of dentistry that only big money can buy. His was a slight figure, even in the bulk of his tracksuit.

Tommy looked at the pile of rackets under his arm. 'Jesus, Greg! This isn't Flushing Meadows!' Greg ignored him and tested each one in turn against his ear. Satisfied, he threw the chosen weapon into the air. 'Rough or smooth?' he snapped. He took short quick steps as he went to join Jody, who had been collecting balls from the back of the court.

'Right, I'll serve. All you've got to do is stand back to Tommy and play to Meg – preferably at her,' Greg instructed.

In one elegant motion, Jody scooped up a ball using her racket against the side of her foot. 'Honey, this is a friendly hit. Remember we're having brunch with them afterwards.' It was pointless, for Greg Lucas was a man who did not know the meaning of the word relaxation.

As she walked to the net she tucked a strand of fine golden hair into her cap, whilst Greg prepared to serve. 'Everybody ready?' he asked and without waiting for a reply fired a service at a startled Meg. 'Fifteen love!' He grinned as he strode to the other service court. Tommy, in an attempt to lighten the atmosphere, shouted across the court, 'Come on Greg – speed it up! We've only got the court for an hour.' Greg's reply was a grunt-laden serve that ricocheted off the court and into the back netting. 'Out!' yelled Meg, failing to disguise the delight in her voice.

The second serve was in and the game proceeded. The couples were evenly matched in talent but Greg's competitiveness gave the husband and wife team the edge. He had a natural ability to cause friction in any activity. Jody had long since given up pleading with him to relax, and she was still acutely aware of the discomfort and irritation he aroused in others. There were many times when she should have apologised for his behaviour – she would have felt better if she had – but her inbred sense of loyalty prevented her. During the five years of their marriage she had seen their once large circle of friends dwindle. They were still high profile at the major charity and club events but invitations for weekends and quiet suppers became less frequent. The friends of her youth were less prepared to put up with him, as they were distressed to see her natural grace treated so roughly. On the increasingly rare occasions when they were invited, he was openly ignored, the only effective weapon against him, but it was Jody who paid the price. These evenings ended in a silent drive home, Greg vowing never to see those 'assholes' again, and Jody laying awake into the early hours.

Greg and Jody won the first set six four and they agreed to play the best of five as time was short. Tommy served a fast, deep, skidding serve that Greg missed completely.

'I'm sure that bastard's foot-faulting,' Greg muttered, and Jody winced. She knew what was coming.

Tommy sliced a serve to Jody, which kicked wide. She covered it well and a long rally ensued, Greg yelling 'Mine!' and grunting with each strike now, sweating heavily. They lost the point and Tommy started to serve, but was stopped as he uncoiled by Greg's raised hand.

'Tommy, I hate to say this, but I think you're dragging your foot.'

Tommy was incredulous. 'What...?'

'I'm serious, Tommy. I think your foot is brushing the line and you need to know it. That's all.' He shrugged and prepared to receive, but Tommy was not amused. Jody and Meg looked at each other and agreed through their glances that this was for the boys to sort out.

'Greg you can't foot-fault me from that end of the court. That's just dumb.'

'Where else can I call it from?'

'Well, thank you. I'll bear it in mind.' Making a huge effort to remain composed, Tommy looked at Meg. 'Why do we put up with the little jerk?' She smiled. He answered his own question. 'I know – because of Jody.'

His next two serves rocketed into the net and Greg congratulated himself on a job well done.

A table had been laid out on the deck and Greg was in the kitchen busily making the Bloody Mary, his only act of domesticity. The once pristine work surface had been laid waste with the by-product of his toils. Tommy came in, his hair still wet from the shower, a towel in his hand. 'I needed that! Hey, will the victor share some of that with the vanquished?' Greg liked the way that Tommy ingratiated himself. 'Why sure! Rosita, bring the long glasses. These are useless.' The maid appeared from the scullery with a tray and ice-bucket and started to clear up the mess.

Greg and Tommy walked out on to the deck, glasses in hand. Below them sprawled the woodland of Tuxedo Park, off to the right the lake and the clubhouse. They leant against the hard-wood rail. A large maple shaded them from the sun. It was Sunday, Greg reflected. He had just closed a deal and had something big in the pipeline. Life was good; he was going to LA for a few days where he could catch up on some old friends. But he was uneasy.

'You've been to Russia haven't you?' Tommy was pleasantly surprised. Greg hardly ever asked anyone about anything unless he needed something.

'Yeah, just after the Berlin Wall came down we did about $1 billion worth of long-term debt in Moscow. I go back every year to renegotiate the repayment schedule. Basically the place sucks. I'm always glad to see the back of it. Why, have you got something going down?'

'We're joining a fishing trip with Mike Cummings. I've done a lot with him over the last few years. He's taken a week on a river somewhere up in the Arctic Circle. It was hard to say no. He's got the hots for Jody and he asked her when we had dinner with him in London, just after Thanksgiving.'

'Well, they don't come much bigger than Cummings. It sounds great. You like salmon fishing don't you?'

'Yeah, but not that much. We go for a few days each year to Jody's family's place on the Miramichi.'

'So what's holding you back?'

24

'Well it's a week and it's Mike's show.' He paused, uncomfortable at sharing his confidences. This was unusual territory for him. 'We're committed now. I just don't feel that great about it, that's all.' He stared pensively into his glass and then rallied. 'Hell, Mike's laying on the Lear – the whole package – and I must make one and a half a year out of him!' He perked up, sucked the remains of his drink through the ice and grabbed Tommy's glass. 'Here, give me that. You can't fly on one engine!'

Jody stood in front of the mirror, a huge towel wrapped around her. The freckles on her back had started blending into the tan that would see her through the summer. Her hair was slicked against her skull, down the nape of her neck to the tops of her shoulders. Swimmer's shoulders, her father had called them, and as a teenager she had taken it as a compliment. But as the attraction of boys other than her two brothers developed she became more self-conscious. At five feet eleven she preferred to pad around in heel-less loafers or, even better, barefoot. In the early days, Greg used to buy her black stilettos that made her tower over him. He stopped her from wearing them when an old friend they ran into at a party told Greg how good it was to see her in 'that trashy stuff again'.

She looked at her reflection as she picked up the hairdryer. Meg emerged from the bathroom and the two women set about preparing themselves for brunch. Meg and Jody had known each other since college and they enjoyed an easy, uncomplicated relationship.

Meg had at first been charmed by Greg, but once he had exhausted his first spurt of attention, the veneer faded and what was left was much the same as most men that they knew. Hard working, but more money-obsessed and with a belligerence that seemed to be out of proportion to his success. Jody deserved better.

Jody was never a girlfriend in the true sense. She wasn't particularly interested in girls' things. 'My problem is that as I never had any sisters,' she would say, 'I was virtually brought up by my brothers and, as a result...' she would drift into a southern drawl, 'I don't have no gurl-tawk.' Getting her into a shop was virtually impossible, but she took a childish delight in mail-order, getting giggly and excited at the arrival of the delivery truck, anticipating the thrill of opening each parcel as if it were Christmas.

She was open and welcoming, and showed a natural interest in people that would be seen simply as charm in someone else. With Jody it was more. Her father had brought his children up on Kipling's theory of being nature's gentlemen. Jody gave 'If' her own interpretation; a feminine sensitivity to male affability that immediately put people at their ease.

Meg wrapped a towel turban-like around her head and walked over to the table. Jody had finished drying her hair.

'So how's it going?'

'I guess you mean am I pregnant? Well the answer is – after two days of PMT – no. At least I now understand how Greg feels all the time.'

'Hell, I'm sorry.'

'Yeah well. It'll happen. He's got me on every remedy known to man, and some more besides. I thought we women were meant to be the goofy ones. He's got every article written over the last decade downloaded off the web, and we're booked in to see some new *fertility-meister* when he gets back from LA. He's become obsessive.' Meg started to say something, but Jody continued. 'Yeah, I know. The point is he's become really determined about it, and he's made it clear that adoption is not an option. "I'm not giving the Lucas name to some Mexican half-breed," as he says. He's missing the point entirely.'

'But you still want children don't you?'

'Sure I do. I just wish it could be more...' she paused, 'more natural, more relaxed. He reckons that he's as potent as a buffalo, which kinda puts the pressure on me. It'll sort itself out.'

Jody walked over to the bed where her clothes had been laid out. She quickly slipped into her underwear and wriggled a pair of jeans over her hips. 'Where would I be without Gap Easifit?' she said, looking at the $2,000 of silk day dress that Meg had left draped over a chair.

'You're just a tramp Jody. My, is that the J.C. Penny summer collection sweatshirt that Mrs Lucas is wearing today?'

'Last year's, actually.' She gave a twirl. 'Did I tell you about Russia?'

Meg made a look as if she had just sucked a lemon. 'Urgh! It's my idea of hell. You're meant to leave all that stuff to the men.

Were you denied the oestrogen option as a child? Most of us gals get on pretty well with it you know. You lay on a beach, get horny in the sun, pamper your body, read a book, drink a few cocktails, hang out in the spa, pat 'em on the back when they come back from the golf course and pig out on lobster. You come from a seriously dysfunctional family.'

'Have you ever heard of anyone coming from a *functional* family?' Jody balanced precariously as she squeezed her feet into her loafers, the heels showing years of wear as a result of her refusal to put them on sitting down.

'I just adore Michael Cummings. He was one of Pa's best friends. We spent a week with him every year on the Spey before he died.'

'"On the Spey"? Is that like being on the booze?'

'Don't be crass. The Spey is one of Scotland's finest rivers, although, sure we did drink a lot. It goes with the turf. So does wading up to your armpits in water, waving a sixteen-foot rod about in the pouring rain. The only cream you apply is Jungle Formula and you can enjoy the uniquely horny sensation of playing a fresh-run, twenty-five-pound salmon as the sun sets over the hills. Have I sold you?'

'You need therapy.'

'Fishing is my therapy.'

'Which proves my point.'

Jody laughed and left Meg sitting in front of the mirror applying various unguents to her arms, legs and face.

She bounced downstairs and out on to the deck.

'Now will you look at that? You've got to admit, Tommy, my wife is the best-looking broad in the park. And it's all her own. Not a cent of cosmetic work on Mrs Lucas. Come over here darlin' and give your man a kiss.'

Jody drifted over to him and, avoiding his lips, kissed his cheek, pulling away as he grasped a handful of buttock. His public compliments were always designed to reflect on him; in private he was usually critical of her appearance.

'Is this "virgin"?' she asked, picking up the jug of Bloody Mary.

'No, I eased some vodka into it to help Tommy get over his defeat. It has to be one of my best-ever mixes. Give it a try.'

She poured a glass, took a gulp and nodded in appreciation. 'At least Dad taught you something useful. You're still overdoing the horseradish though, and a hint more lemon juice would get you in the zone.'

'You're one hell of a bitch to please, you know. Tommy, what do you think?'

Tommy wagged a finger. 'Oh no, I'm not getting involved in this one.'

'A wise move. It's pretty hard to argue with a girl who was taught how to make these things at eighth grade.' He went over to Jody and rattled the final remnants of ice and mix into her glass. 'I'll make another jug. This one will knock your socks off!'

Jody was glad to see Greg in a good mood. He never usually took criticism that easily; perhaps it was the vodka or the anticipation of his trip. The phone rang and Greg yelled from the kitchen, 'Whoever it is, I'm not in. Don't they know its Sunday?'

Tommy whispered to Jody, 'Christ! What's got into to him?'

'Search me!' was the reply.

Chapter Four

The office of Cummings and Associates was a discreet double-fronted house in Hans Place just behind Harrods. It was from here that Michael Cummings ran the hedge funds that had made lifelong friends of his investors and enemies of several European finance ministers. It was from here that he ruled his empire with a benevolent efficiency. Michael worked on the maxim that it was better to appear slightly more stupid than you actually were, a luxury that was not permitted to many and certainly one that he had not employed in his early years. The benefits of a sound provincial background, five years at Stowe, followed by three years in the Welsh Guards, presented to the world a young man full of confidence, able to capitalise on the 'open goal' of opportunities that were the late sixties.

Now nearing his sixtieth birthday he smiled at his own good fortune. Michael had done pretty well anything and everything in the city, from bill broking to gilt trading, from jobbing to derivatives. His geniality and an unusual attention to detail had seen him through; when Big Bang came he found himself an unwitting but delighted partner in a firm of stockbrokers who were taken over by an American bank. 1975 saw him £15 million better off with a greedy City at his feet.

He had just returned from lunch. The table at the end of his office had three files waiting all with large white labels with 'Kola 2000' printed in bold.

Michael bustled into the room. 'Right let's get going. We've got some important business to attend to.' He took off his jacket, handing it to the steward revealing a mustard-coloured silk lining, his Brigade braces stretched over an off-white silk shirt. Pippa, his PA, sat to his left. To his right was Steve Newman, Head of Security and Logistics. Michael liked this meeting more

than most and was prepared to give up part of his day to pre-
side over the detailed planning of his annual fishing trip. It was
his sixth year and he couldn't wait to get there.

'This year we're going to fish eight rods, I think we were a bit
light with six last time. There'll be Ginny and me, her sister
Sandra and Sandra's husband Gary, as well as Greg and Jody
Lucas. Steve, I'd be delighted if you'd like to fish this year, as
there's bugger all else for you to do out there. And the son and
heir, if I can tear him away from Paris.

'Have they got a proper cook? That cretin they shipped out last
year was a complete waste of space – far too "evolved" for my liking. I prefer a girl cook – this is a fishing lodge not the Gavroche!'

'I spoke to *Touch the Wild*, and they told me that they had
booked a Scottish girl called Bumble.'

'Make sure you contact her before she heads off, and let her
know what additional supplies she can expect from us. The veni-
son fillet was popular last year – and could you make sure we
get some proper eggs? Those Russian jobs are completely
anaemic. You'd better check up with Greg Lucas's office to see if
he has any peculiar eating habits. What about transport?'

Steve opened his file and pulled out a schedule. 'Mr and Mrs
Lucas will arrive the day before. They'll stay with you in London
that evening. We've got clearance from Northolt on the Saturday
but I'm afraid it's an early start – seven-thirty take-off.'

'That's fine by me, the earlier the better. I like to have a fish
on the bank before dinner on the first night. The low cloud at
Murmansk ruined it last year. What about communications? Can
we reduce the number of aerials bristling from your cabin this
year? You looked more like Tony Hancock than the trained killer
I pay so much for.'

Michael occasionally referred to Steve as his trained killer. He
was the first person to have the job who wasn't ex-SAS. When
asked at the final interview whether he was really cut out
for the job coming from 14 Intelligence Corps he replied, over-
defensively, that whilst his speciality was surveillance and communications, 'rest assured I am a fully trained killer, if that was
what the question implied'. He got the job but had regretted the
statement ever since.

'I have contacted Mr Lucas's office regarding his requirements.
He plans to be quite active I think.'

30

'Ah well, at least we won't have Bloomberg in the hut.'

'They have asked whether that would be possible?' Steve added, knowing what the response would be.

'This is a fishing trip not G8. I only let you bring all that kit last time to give you something to do. Try and head them off a bit will you? Problems with satellites – something like that. Now my birthday...' The trip coincided with Michael's birthday and he usually threw a party for the whole camp.

'Michael, I would like to discuss additional local back-up first.' Steve looked earnestly at Michael.

'The answer is still no. We had that five years ago when we first went out there. It takes the edge off the day to have Kalashnikovs waving about. It also put the local Collective's nose out of joint – they pride themselves in being the law out there. Besides there's nothing up there but a few poachers, and the village sorts them out. You should have seen the poor bugger they left tied to a tree for a day. He lost the taste for poaching after the mosquitoes had been at him.'

'I'd still like to lay something on at Murmansk airport. We're pretty high profile when we go through there...'

'Look there's about a hundred fishermen from around the globe who arrive on scheduled airlines every Saturday throughout the summer; in our pioneering days we had the dubious delight of being amongst them. There has never been any hint of any trouble. They've had everything from Royalty to rockstars out there. Why should anyone bother an impecunious financier and his entourage as they arrive in the Edward?' (He always referred to his Lear Jet as 'the Edward'.) Michael realised he was letting his rhetoric run away with a genuine concern. 'If it'll make you feel any better, lay on something for the transfers at Murmansk; we're only there for thirty minutes. But for God's sake, no leather jackets, dark glasses and machine guns! It creates an air of tension. I'm on holiday, remember? Now can we get onto my little event?' He rubbed his hands with glee.

Steve returned to his office, took off his jacket and brushed its shoulders with the back of his hand before introducing a wooden hanger and burying it into the dark recess of the wardrobe. He had worked for Michael for nearly three years, and from 'a lukewarm start they had developed an understanding and closeness for each other. Michael would have preferred Steve to be more of a character; he found it hard to break through his reserve. He once had a competition with his son to see who could describe five noticeable facial features. They both got stuck on two, and both had included his glasses.

Steve was serious about his job, which was the nature of 14 Intelligence. He had served a total of twelve years, reaching the rank of Major, but was never destined for further promotion. He was too much of a loner – even in a world that celebrated the loner. He had served in most of the hot spots in Northern Ireland, the Gulf and Yugoslavia, and more recently had worked alongside the Americans in anti-narcotics and money laundering activities. He was decorated for one of his tours of duty in Omagh when he had infiltrated the IRA cell that had been responsible for a bombing campaign that had seen three RUC men and fifteen innocents blown to pieces.

When he first arrived at Hans Place he had carried out a complete review of his predecessor's activities. He had concluded that the strategy was more appropriate for a movie star seeking to draw attention to himself than for a low profile figure such as Michael Cummings. There had been too much attention to bundling into cars, and not enough time trying to work out just what the likely risks were, and how they were going to manifest themselves. Michael's power lay in his knowledge and his ability to decide the short-term fate of global currencies. What was at risk was his information, not his person. Michael warmed to Steve's approach, as he too had become uncomfortable at the daily pantomime that involved him going around London.

Steve set about protecting Cummings and Associates' sensitive information. He had recruited a small team to work with him, ensuring that there was not an e-mail, phone call, fax, photocopy, letter or – as Michael joked – carrier pigeon that left his premises without it being logged and available for retrieval.

Finally, Steve set about creating their own information gathering system; this was the area about which Michael needed most persuasion. 'Look Steve, when I first started in the City we read annual reports, had the odd lunch and kept a pretty girl with big tits and a pair of scissors to take press cuttings. That was "intelligence gathering". Rules are rules and I will not overstep the mark.' Within a year, one floor of Hans Place was given over to External Operations and Michael was one of its more frequent visitors.

A phone rang and Steve picked up one of two handsets as he walked around his desk to his chair. 'Newman.'

'I've got Mr Lucas's PA on the line for you who's insisted on talking to you directly. *His* name is Tracey...'

'Put him through please.'

'Er... Mr Newman?

'Yes that's right. How can I help you?'

'Mr Lucas has got one or two items he would like me to go over with you regarding the Russian trip. Would you be kind enough to copy your proposals regarding security to us, so that we can have an input?'

A frown formed between Steve's eyebrows. 'Americans. It's always the bloody Americans.' he thought as he replied, 'We are in the process of finalising arrangements at the moment. What might be easier would be you could let me know if Mr and Mrs Lucas have any specific requirements or concerns, and I could address these directly. Basically this is an annual family fishing trip and we maintain a low presence on all fronts. We will have robust communications systems and I will e-mail the manifest to you this afternoon. With regards to security, we see the remoteness of our location and our low profile as our main blanket. We do lay on extra cover at key times, but not at the camp. Has Mr Lucas had any specific threats or problems in the past?'

'No, its just that we're kinda uneasy at this end over what's going on in Russia at the moment – kidnapping, extortion, bombings, you know.' A waspish edge had appeared in Tracey's voice.

Steve was about to say 'you make it sound like downtown LA', but instead replied, 'These are all valid concerns and I assure you that we monitor the situation on a daily basis. If it gives you any comfort, the main crimes that you refer to take place in the larger cities such as Moscow and St Petersburg. Where we are going we are supported by the local Collective who see us as a benefit to the community. Mr Cummings' party has been going for five years, and the locals even have a photograph of him in their offices. We are treated as friends.'

'So is that it?' Tracey snapped. 'Look, Mr Newman. My boss is a high profile, high net worth individual, well known in Wall

Street and married to P H Harrison's only surviving great grand-daughter. Together they are about to visit the largest Mafia state in the world.'

'Now that's a slight exaggeration.'

'That's how Boris Yeltsin described his country – I'm only quoting him. We have genuine concerns at this end. By the way, do you mind if I call you Steve?'

'Not in the least. I apologise for not asking you to do so earlier, Tracey.'

'We've been in touch with Washington, we've searched the web and all we get is bad news about this place. No one is advised to travel from here unless it's absolutely essential and fully covered. Haven't they just dropped another nuclear sub to the bottom near Murmansk? If that's not a bearpit what is?'

'I think that's being a bit unfair,' Steve added, full of reason.

'I gotta tell you Steve, Mr Lucas is serious about this, and I'm afraid nothing you have told me gives me any of the answers that I need. Let me ask you a question. How would you feel if we were to organise some local support in addition to what you've got planned?'

Steve slumped in his chair. 'Well, let me answer your question Tracey. We have only just finished a meeting with Mr Cummings, and he was uncomfortable with the idea of additional support on the ground. Whilst he recognises the real concerns there are in a trip of this nature, he insists that we maintain a stress-free environment. This is his fishing holiday.'

'OK. One final item – side-arms. I presume there will be some on tap once they get out there?'

'Tracey, I'm not trying to be difficult but I assure you we plan in detail and have never had any hint of a problem in the past. The plan stays open until departure and if we need to add features we can easily do it at the time. Mr Lucas really should take up the general safety issues of travel in Russia with Mr Cummings in person.'

'Steve, I'm just doing my job here. I've been given a list and now you have it. I'll report back and let's see what happens.' The phone went dead.

'Lucas will want a .45. They always do, although he won't be able to hit a cow's arse with it,' Steve muttered as he got up and walked to the window and looked down onto the square. A girl was laying out a towel to benefit from the spring sun's early rays. He wasn't happy though. Nearly everything that Tracey had said was true; he had worked through it all a year ago.

Chapter Five

Genia was encouraged by the reflection that greeted him in the mirror; Nadia's haircut had been one of her more successful efforts. He stroked the surface of his upper lip and took comfort from its new-found smoothness. He noticed for the first time in a long while the scars that had been a legacy from Kabul. They had become part of his facial topography and usually went unnoticed. One cut a track through his right eyebrow, the other was a fine white streak that followed his jaw line from his ear to halfway down his face.

He examined his palms. He hoped that it was the eyes, not the hands, which were the windows of this particular soul. Irina's remark had bruised an ego that he thought he had buried long ago. His reaction to it intrigued him. He was a tall, fit man who enjoyed the physical self-confidence that went with these attributes. His appearance wasn't something that usually concerned him. But tonight he was inspecting his hands. The oil from the camp's generator had ground its way deep into the pores. A palmist would not need a lamp to assist in interpretation, as the lines of divination were darkly etched; there were additional bumps and ridges that had more to do with the past than the future. He had managed to tidy up one set of nails, but found working on the other impossible, and had been forced to ask Nadia's assistance. She had teased him unmercifully.

He went to his room, opened the drawer in his cupboard and pulled out a white shirt. He savoured the sweet scent of camphor as he wrapped the shirt around his shoulders, although moths would be unlikely inhabitants of the totally man-made fabric. He fumbled for a while with a tie, but after a few unsuccessful attempts decided to abandon it. His collar, buttoned to

the neck, would be his only gesture to the grandeur of the restaurant at the Arctic Hotel.

'So you're off then?' His father stood in the doorway. He had
taken the phone call from Sergei who had left instructions for
where Genia was to meet him.

His father disliked the man who ran the Volna Collective, the
organisation that controlled the trawlers and the licences for
hunting and fishing on the southern coast of the Kola Peninsula.
In the old days the head of the Collective was a prestigious politi-
cal appointment, awarded to a citizen of long-standing merit.
Genia's father saw the appointment of someone he described as
'an inarticulate thug' as just another nail in the coffin of his once
proud nation. Worse still he was his son's paymaster. Genia did
not share this view. He saw Sergei as an honest man tackling
an increasingly complex task of balancing the competing interests that *perestroika* had brought about. The Collective, which
had been created under Stalin, was a bureaucracy and, like all
bureaucracies, had been the early prey of profiteers and crimi-
nals. Senior military personnel and state officials had always
milked the old system. But it was organised crime, in all its
various guises, which had ultimate control over the New Russian
society. It was different people who were 'more equal than others'
now, and Sergei was part of the new order.

'Yes, I've got to make plans for the summer and settle up for
the last few months. Did anyone else phone?' Genia hoped that
Irina would have tried to contact him, but his father had disappeared into the kitchen and didn't answer. 'I'll most probably
stay with Viktor and Nadia if it turns any worse.' There was still
no response.

He decided to go to the station; a first drink there would be
far cheaper than at the Arctic Hotel. He walked down the long
flight of steps that ran from the row of flats to the ones below.
The descent would take him fifteen minutes, and a good deal
longer on the way back, particularly if Sergei was in a drinking
mood. Murky pools of light from the few functioning street lamps
filtered through the thickening mist. On the snow-covered steps
he passed an old man who had paused for breath, his frail lungs
searching for oxygen in the acrid air. Genia issued a greeting to
the man as he trotted down the steps. Soon he reached Five
Cornered Square, an unintentionally humorous legacy of Stalin's

big plan for the city. Its humour was lost on the city's inhabitants, but for Genia it was the most appropriate way to describe the city that was his home.

A dog trotted up alongside him as he waited at the traffic lights, one of the thousands of strays that ran around the city. 'What a curious fellow you are!' Genia mused. The dog seemed to be half-standard poodle, half-German shepherd, but happily unaware of his uncertain pedigree. He clearly had a healthy regard for the city's drivers or a distant memory of obedience training, for he waited with Genia, crossing the road only when the lights had changed. They parted company once they had safely reached the other side.

The station was one of the few parts of the city that Genia liked. It was the advent of the railway that saw the creation of this city and subsequently the port. The large blue building presided over the city's brief history, and had witnessed more than its share of joy and sorrow. The passengers for the Moscow sleeper were about to embark; Genia leant against a pillar watching the clutches of people preparing for their farewells. Many of the flower kiosks were still open; bouquets of roses tied with white ribbon lay in vases, bright splashes of colour in the misty gloom. Sailors from incoming vessels who were making their final leg home, nursing hangovers from the first night ashore, were searching through bags to ensure that they had not lost the gifts for their children. Young women, their eyes heavy with mascara, carrying their worldly possessions in one bag, set off for a new uncertain life in the capital city. They may have made a living in Murmansk, but Moscow was a different proposition. Anxiety lurked beneath the make-up.

Genia noticed the nervous-looking conscripts in over-sized uniforms embraced by crying mothers, their fathers standing impassively by; a stern handshake would be good enough for them. He remembered his own farewell as he left to join his regiment, nearly twenty years earlier. His father had been too angry to go to the station and had forbidden his wife to go. Nadia had been the only person to say goodbye. Genia had never seen his mother again.

Soon steam from the station's leaking heating pipes mixed with diesel fumes from the train's mighty engines as they spluttered noisily into life. The leaden mixture swirled into the city's sulphurous mist and into Genia's lungs. He had been used to the clear air of the peninsula and coughed involuntarily. He decided that his health was worth the price of an expensive drink, and went to the hotel.

Genia walked past the men in black leather coats who were the hotel's private security force, and handed his coat to the wardrobe attendant. He went upstairs to the bar. It was still early, and a group of Finnish businessmen were unwinding from a day's work. He ordered a beer and winced at the charge of 150 roubles, nearly a week's pension for most of the population; he had indeed put a high price on his respiratory system. He sat down and waited for Sergei, watching a television, one of many dotted around the bar, all tuned to MTV. A black boy band gesticulated mechanically and sang about 'attitude' and 'respect', the words lost on Genia. The music was irretrievable.

'Genia! I didn't recognise you without your moustache.' It was Sergei – short, barrel-round, be-whiskered Sergei. 'Are you in love or something?' he said, clasping Genia's hand in his own bear-like paw. 'God, what a journey I've had! We had to land twice. There was a moment when I thought we would be spending the night out there.'

The Collective had access to a number of ex-military heli-copters. In the winter they were used for supplies and in the summer they ferried fishermen from the airport to the various camps. Although the pilots had thousands of hours of experience, they relied on good visibility to negotiate their way round the mountain ranges that lay between the Volna and Murmansk.

'You would have hated it, you old woman!' Genia's fear of fly-ing was a constant source of amusement, particularly as he had to spend many hours taking guests to the more remote stretches of the river. His expression, set in what was often interpreted as stony indifference, was in fact fixed by pure fear. His experiences in Afghanistan had left more than physical scarring. 'Now let's have a proper drink,' Sergei added, pointing to Genia's beer and, collapsing into a seat next to him, he summoned a waitress.

The two men hadn't seen each other for a while. Sergei had dropped in with the German hunters but only stayed for few hours. He was always on the move. Genia told him about his experience with the bear and her cub and Sergei shook with laughter. 'What do you expect if you don't use dogs? You wait until I tell the others. Too much brain not enough common sense – that's our Genia. You most probably wanted to have a chat. I would, after all that time out there by myself. I can't see why you do it. Did you stop to talk?'

'I ran like hell! I tell you Sergei, my heart was going like a trip hammer. I waited a week before going back to get my rifle. That was the worst bit. To complicate matters, there was an extra half-metre of snow and I was crawling around in the dark trying to find it. I didn't know if the old lady had gone back to her hole or was still lurking around. I crawled round a stump and put up a hare and I nearly died of fright! I've never been so happy to get back to my hut.'

'We should get you a proper job – we're going to lose you one day if you carry on like this.' Sergei paused for a moment and then added, 'We may anyway – ' Genia looked at him and leant uneasily back into his chair as he watched Sergei run a finger between collar and neck. 'It's money.'

Genia had known that the Collective was experiencing financial difficulties.

'How bad is it?'

Sergei leant forward, his elbows on his knees, the buttons of his shirt stretched tight across his stomach. His eyes searched Genia's face for understanding, but found none. 'Look, I've got the people I sell the hunting permits to telling me they are being squeezed because other places are dropping their prices. The people who buy the netted salmon are saying they can only pay less because there's an over-supply of farmed fish from Europe. And to complete this happy scene, I have some young buck, Oscar – I think you know him? – digging the ground from under me saying he's got friends in Moscow who could get the additional revenue. A few years ago I would have swatted him, but they all see dollar signs, and he's got more support than I find good. So what do I do?'

'Welcome to the market economy.' Genia patted his pockets and, finding them empty, resisted the temptation to ask for a cigarette. 'If you let the Muscovites in, they'll net the rivers empty and shoot the place clean. It would all be over in ten years. But you know that. We're almost netting too much already; the runs of salmon are flattening out, and I seem to run into more poachers than bear.'

The bar was filling with more people; Sergei and Genia were the only Russian customers. The waitress delivered their drinks and offered to pour them, but Sergei gestured her away.

Genia continued, 'The only reason I was out there dancing with that bear was to keep the quota you set me for skins. I wasn't doing it for my health. The rod fishing must make money; they pay through the nose to be there. But if there are no salmon, you've killed your goose.'

There was sweat on Sergei's brow now as he replied. 'But it will take some time and you know how the Collective thinks – jam today. The salmon run is still the best in the world and we could build more camps. In five years time I could be sunning myself by the Black Sea and the river would still be packed with fishermen paying more than they are now.'

'It sounds like you've made your mind up – I have a feeling that you are about to tell me you can't pay me.' As he finished the sentence he noticed Sergei shuffle his feet beneath the glass table-top. 'I'll tell you about my position Sergei, because I'm not in the mood to be messed about. I have my nephew in hospital and he needs medicine from Norway. I need a lot of dollars and fast.' He leant forward in his chair. 'So please – just pay me what I'm owed.'

Sergei shrugged and opened his hands in a 'what can I do about it?' manner. Genia looked away. Both men sat in silence. Sergei pulled on his cigarette. 'We've had to pay out more dollars than we wanted, everyone's hurting. Trust me when I say there is a real problem, I'm not just trying to screw you.'

'Sergei this isn't about trust. It's not going to change what I've got to do, and the money I need to do it with. I have no option.'

'I'm sorry about your nephew. Was that the fair-haired kid that sat on the pilot's lap a couple of years ago? You were in the back puking!' The remark was intended to bring a touch of levity, but Genia's expression let him know he wasn't getting away with it. 'What's he got?'

'Leukaemia. They've got him up at the children's hospital in Noyenka.'

'We still haven't sold your skins, I wanted to see you first. I owed you that.' Genia stared at the carpet. 'What I can do is organise a trip to Kirkenes for you, if you feel up to it. I'm meeting Kim, the old boy's son, here later.'

41

There was a risk of a jail sentence if he were caught with skins on the run into Norway. He didn't relish three years in Murmash prison. He searched for other solutions

'Why don't you put my skins on a trawler docking at Kirkenes, or one of the other ports?'

'Everyone wants their cut, and it'll take some time to get them there. The best value you'll get is with the bus. It's your best option. I'll only need a bit of notice for the driver to be ill. The good news is that they haven't been checking the bus recently. How long will it take to order the medicine?'

'I'm going to find out tomorrow, but I imagine three or four days. Sergei, I will have to get the cash when I get there, so I can go to the hospital before the return. Kim had better be straight.'

Genia had done the four-hour run to the Norwegian border once before, several years ago and had vowed never again. He could already recall the sweat in the small of his back as he approached the Russian Customs Post.

'Let me tell you about Kim. He's not his father's son...' Genia shook his head, it was getting worse. 'Your other option is to take $250 a skin from us. I can give it to you now. Would that be enough?' Genia usually got $500 from the Collective. If he ran the risk of smuggling the four skins into Norway he should get even more.

'I'll need more than a thousand Sergei. Can you pay more?'

Sergei shrugged his shoulders. Genia knew he had to yield to the inevitable. At least he'd been given an option: other employees would have been given the price, probably less, and would have been told to take it or leave it. Hunters were easy to find.

'Well, it looks like I'll be driving the bus.'

Sergei ambled off to the bar. Large patches of sweat had accumulated under each armpit; he shook his hips as he rescued his trouser belt from below his belly. Genia looked at him as he waddled his goose-like way back to the table, carrying glasses and a packet of cigarettes. Genia grudgingly admired the man. He was such an unlikely figure; the power and respect that he wielded were in inverse proportion to the physical and intellectual attributes bestowed upon him. He had also learnt not to be deceived by Sergei's unlikely build. Genia had, several years ago, seen him turn on a guide who had been in the pay of some poachers. The guide towered over Sergei but the confrontation, when it came, was over and done with in seconds. Sergei simply charged at the guide with fists flailing like a character in a cartoon. The outcome was far from comical. The startled victim suffered a broken nose and lost a few teeth before being hurled into the river. It was typical of Sergei that the guide kept his job; he had learnt his lesson and the performance, which was in front of a collection of other guides, established law and order for the new season.

'Why don't you be Camp Manager this year? There's more money, better tips, an easier life. You know the river better than anyone and all the clients like you. You can't like being told what to do by the Englishmen *Touch The Wild* provide. Why don't you take it?'

'I'm happy as I am, Sergei.'

'Think about it, Genia. *Touch the Wild* have asked you do to it and I can make sure you get a dollar payment from them. Look, if we are going to open up more camps we need you and your English. It would be a wise move for you. The skins are going to get more difficult, and I can pay an old man half of what I'm paying you to keep the camp in mothballs over the winter. You'll become a luxury I can't afford. Everything's changing Genia. Think, please.'

'Maybe next year Sergei. Thank you – really, I appreciate it.'

'If it would make any difference I would slap you for being the fool you are. Don't say no tonight. Give me your answer next week, I'll need to know by then.' Genia gave an exaggerated Sergei-like shrug and broad smile, and in return he received a light cuff round his head. Sergei laughed. 'You deserved a slap anyway. You think hard, Genia Sukov. Who knows where it could lead?'

'You've chosen a strange place for staff discipline, Sergei.' Kim appeared from behind them. Genia eyed him and saw at once that Sergei was right. He wasn't like his father. The old boy was from Uzbekistan, a smuggler who ran most of the illegal exports from the port of Murmansk. Nearly sixty, he had been ill for some time now and his eldest son, Kim, was destined to fill his shoes. Kim was dressed in expensively modest clothing, his short-cropped hair framed a face that had many of his mother's soft Taiwanese features, although he retained the latent malevolence of his father. He was a New Russian from head to foot but more

43

immaculate, more feline. He showed a confidence that belied his thirty-two years of age. He treated Sergei with quiet insolence, and ignored Genia completely.

'Kim, this is my good friend Genia. What would you like to drink?'

'I'll have a Pepsi.'

'I've got a table booked so we can have some food.'

'No... I can't do dinner.'

Sergei ordered the drinks and an uneasy silence descended on the table. Genia decided he wasn't going to ingratiate himself with Kim and fixed his attention on a television screen. MTV was showing another group of gesticulating youths, their nodding heads covered in flowerpot hats, wobbling as if on springs. A young woman sat at a table with two Russian men, a working girl being delivered to the hotel for the night. She too gazed blankly at the screen, sucking her drink through a straw; a well-manicured hand tapping the side of her glass, uninvolved in the men's conversation.

Sergei broke the silence. 'We've decided to split this year's furs. Genia will be doing a run to Kirkenes with four, the remainder we'll do as usual.'

'Sure.'

'We'll need to arrange some dollars on delivery in Norway. The balance can be added to the main settlement.'

'Sure.'

Genia was getting irritated. The boy was treating Sergei with contempt and he found himself becoming angered by the indifference he too, was receiving. 'Sergei, I'll leave you two to your business. I'll phone you in the morning when I know about which day. It's been a pleasure to meet you Kim. Give your father my good wishes.'

'Yeah, sure.'

'I'll see you out.' Sergei got up. He knew that Genia was about to say something that they might all regret. Kim sensed it too and stood up. 'We're in the middle of converting the floor of our apartment block. We've got the suppliers from Finland over. It will be a huge area when we've finished.'

'However big you make it just remember that we all end up with a plot four metres by two.' Genia's referral to the state entitlement for burial sites had the desired effect on Kim.

'I don't understand,' Kim retorted.

Genia smiled. 'Tell your father. He will.'

Genia felt Sergei's grip on his elbow; the two made an unlikely pair as they walked down the stairs.

'Times are changing Genia – times are changing,' Sergei urged.

'Yes, but didn't your father say that to you? Mine always did – still does when he decides to talk to me.' They stopped at the bottom of the stairs and Genia stood close to his friend. 'That boy is neither wise nor foolish. He's out of his depth, Sergei, and dangerous; you watch your back, my friend. He's a natural ally for Oscar.'

'Well if he is, you haven't helped my cause tonight.'

'Sergei, what would you have done?'

'In the old days I'd have torn his head off. Times are changing.' He said it more to himself than to Genia as he patted him on the back and turned to the stairs. Sergei looked at the red-carpeted incline and decided to take the lift instead. 'I said you wouldn't like him. I'll speak to you tomorrow.' His voice echoed off the marble as he pushed the button.

Genia went to the lavatories. He needed to empty his bladder before going out into the cold night air. As he was washing his hands he looked at the mirror. 'Well, what are you – a New Russian or a hunter?' he asked of the suited but uneasy figure that looked back at him. 'A poor excuse for either...'

He went to collect his coat but halted as he searched in his pockets for the scrap of paper that he had been given by Irina at the hospital. He looked at his watch; it was still early and he didn't want to go home just yet. He went to a phone booth and inserted a coin. The phone rang for about thirty seconds; he was in two minds about whether to put it down when a sleepy voice answered.

'Have I woken you up? You're doing an early shift aren't you?'

'What does it sound like? I had fallen asleep on the sofa. What time is it?' He could almost feel her stretch, see her head lean back, her face crumpled with sleep.

'It's just after nine. I'll leave you to it. I'm sorry. I shouldn't have disturbed you...'

'No it's all right, I would only have given myself a stiff neck. I needed to get to bed.'

It was good to hear her voice again. The phone had played a

leading role in their relationship with daily conversations on the hospital system just to talk and laugh, and night calls when her husband was still at work when they had both ached with the frustration of not being able to see each other. The hours they must have spent apart, their love and intimacy made real by the frozen wires of the Murmansk exchange. All that wasted time apart.

She had detected the slur in his voice, Genia was, at the end of the day, like any other man.

'Should I be reaching for my diary?'

'Well, I'm not far from your flat and I thought it would be nice to talk.'

'Genia it's always nice to talk, but I'm exhausted and I've got a bitch of a day tomorrow. Where are you?'

'I'm at the Arctic Hotel. I'm due to stay with my sister tonight, and I thought I'd just give you a call...' He could feel embarrassment blister the boldness that the alcohol had given him. Why was he still so reluctant just to say what he meant? He wiped his hand through his hair from forehead back, and grabbed the last shreds of confidence before it eroded completely.

'No, the truth is I wanted to see you, I wanted to come round – but it's not the right night, is it?'

He lifted a hand to his mouth to chew a nail but his recent manicure had deprived him of any comfort from that source.

'It was really nice to see you the other day, it was good. Sure, if you want to talk on the phone tonight then let's do that. Whose phone are you calling from?'

'A phone box at the hotel. I've paid my rouble – we've got all night. Please see me?'

'Genia, I haven't seen you for over fifteen years. Ten years ago you could have breezed into my life and I would have welcomed you. I'm getting older Genia – we all are. And I know you – you haven't thought about the consequences of this call, have you?'

'No. I saw you, looked at you as you talked to that doctor, and it all came flooding back. I've got your number, and I'm here now. I've shaved my moustache off.'

She could hear the warmth in his voice, anticipate his tenderness and was sorely tempted. 'If you were unhappy or in trouble I'd see you Genia, I always would. But just because you're nearby and have had a few drinks is not a good enough reason now. I deserve more than a call on the off-chance.'

46

'Yes, you're right. Look, Irina, I'm sorry. It was wrong of me to call like this, but it – it just felt right.'

'I know.'

'I'll call you, I promise. Sleep well and I'll phone you at work tomorrow.'

'You get home safely and if you call that will be nice.'

Genia put down the phone and collected his coat from the cloakroom. More girls were arriving with their minders as he approached the main door. 'Where do they get their confidence from?' he thought as he looked at the brittle, gum-chewing beauty of their faces. He went outside to the traffic lights; hanging from them was the street-sign Five Cornered Square. His friend the stray joined him as he waited for the lights. Genia lifted his face into the sleet that, somehow, managed to penetrate the polluted fog. He shouted at the crescent moon that he knew lay beyond.

'Murmansk!'

The Central Regional Library was set back from the road behind the statues of St Cyril and St Matthew who, in partnership, were responsible for creating the bones of the alphabet upon which was hung the Russian language. Dressed in their classical robes they were a token gesture to learning in a city of sailors and warriors. The pair were unusual companions for the rest of the town's statues of seamen and bosomy matriarchs.

Genia opened the second of the double doors and when he saw the length of queue stretching to the cloakroom he regretted not bringing a book. It would be at least a two-hour wait until he got to the medical library on the third floor. The building was full of students. They looked young, and upon reflection, could have been his children. Earnest, tidy and well dressed, they waited patiently in this immaculate hothouse of reference and learning. He thought of the months that he had spent bent over a desk, scribbling notes from the medical archive in pursuit of a qualification. Now his function was simple reference to help ease suffering; it would still be a two-hour wait.

He reached for his library card. Without it he would not exist in this building and he had a memory of tucking it into his top pocket as he left his father's apartment, but was not entirely sure. He found it and as he did so noticed the phone that was bolted to the wall. He phoned Irina at the hospital. He was bounced from department to department but finally made contact.

'I'm sorry about last night.'

'It's OK. It was nice to hear from you.'

The queue moved on and Genia asked a girl, 'Will you keep my place while I'm on the phone?' The girl smiled in agreement.

'Where are you?'

'The library. I'm getting some more information for Volodia. Your doctor friend was pretty sure, but thought that we should come here before ordering the drugs.'

'It's a cold day – it must be full.' There was sympathy in her voice.

'Yes, I forgot what it was like to be a student.' He repeated his apology, 'I'm sorry about last night, it was wrong.'

'Don't say that. It was just the wrong time. Have you really shaved your moustache off?'

'Yes.' He touched his upper lip, a rasp of bristle emerging now. He could hear voices in the background.

'Genia, I've got to go. Phone again won't you?'

'Yes, I want to see you.'

'Me too.'

He felt a longing that he hadn't felt for many years and he realised how alone he had been. But Irina was right: he hadn't thought it through. He hadn't set about finding her; he had simply bumped into her by chance. It would be letting coincidence drive his life yet again, but he knew that fate had been a more reliable master than his self-determination of old.

He became aware of a minor commotion behind him. Viktor, late as ever, was trying to work his way through the crush of students lining the staircase. His efforts were getting him nowhere. 'How did he ever become an activist?' Genia thought before whistling loudly to gain his attention – a conspicuous gesture that succeeded in not only attracting Viktor's attention, but everyone else's as well. A sea of faces looked up to where Genia was beckoning Viktor to join him. The action labelled Genia as a troublemaker and he knew he would be reprimanded by the entry librarian when he eventually reached her. The signal was crude but effective and the crowds parted reluctantly allowing Viktor to climb to Genia, accompanying his progress with exaggerated thanks and apologies.

'You really didn't have to do that,' Viktor said loudly.

'Viktor, you are too old to be socially embarrassed. We are both entering an age when we do as we please.'

'Have you ever considered setting an example? You could learn a lot from these people.' His voice still loud, he was clearly embarrassed.

'Have you ever considered being on time? We said ten o'clock. If you'd arrived on time it wouldn't have happened.' Genia's voice was as loud as Viktor's now and some students smiled in amusement at the pantomime unfolding in front of them

'Well there is that of course. I'm sorry I'm late, Genia.' Viktor bowed his head.

'And I'm sorry that I made you *think* that you looked a fool, Viktor. That's far more unsettling than actually being one.' He bowed in return. 'If anyone is in the wrong it can only be me.'

'Think nothing of it.'

They patted each other's backs and peace returned to the staircase.

Their combined search through the medical pamphlets confirmed the doctor's recommendation and they found an alternative should it be in short supply. Volodia was weakening and time was of the essence. The two men then waited in the queue outside of the computer room so that they could access the Internet and the Norwegian Health Service. It looked as if it would take at least an hour, so they chatted in the corridor having put their names on the list.

'Did you recognise the face on that poster in the computer room?' Viktor asked.

'Balding, glasses, beady-eyed. He looks like an *intellectual* to me.' Genia used his father's voice.

'He's the world's wealthiest man. He created the operating systems that drive over half the world's computers. It's Bill Gates.'

Genia paused and thought for a moment.

'Thank God Dad's not here to see this. Sergei was right – everything is changing. You know it shows my ignorance. Because Bill Gates is so famous I assumed he must be dead. Is that a recent picture of him? He hardly looks a leader of the people.'

'He's our age Genia. It's quite a thought isn't it?'

'Is my father actually right? Has it all been too swift or am I just acting middle-aged?' Viktor let Genia ramble for a while: he knew his mood. 'If I were him, I'd be worried. What can he do with the other half of his life that can possibly achieve as much? Success and failure usually come in equal measure. I'd hate to have to have his burden.'

'I doubt if he has many anxieties.'

Genia looked at the poster. 'You know Viktor I was thinking, while I was waiting for you, looking at those students. They are in bleak limbo; one foot in a flawed past and the other in an uncertain future. Look into that *bizniz* studies room. It used to be part of the science section. What real impact are Mr Gates and his friends going to have on the daily lives of these students, other than making them short sighted? Who was that Hungarian who said, "Revolution needs three essential ingredients. A bullet, a twinkle in the eye and twenty five years"?'

'I haven't heard it before. Are you sure you didn't make it up?'

'It was certainly a Hungarian – it will come to me. The point is we were toppled not by a bullet but by a grinding war of attrition that we couldn't afford to win, let alone lose. The children that were born when the wall came down are now only eleven years old, so there are fourteen years of instability ahead of us, if my Hungarian friend is right.'

Viktor pointed through the glass door where three rows of students worked at their desks in silence. 'Look, there are more students here today because of the cold, but they are here working. It was always like this. There is true quality in these people. I'm always told by the other scientists that I meet how impressed foreigners are with our capacity for learning. We take it for granted. We don't absorb subjects, they absorb us. If that remains the case and more resources become available, then you and I have nothing to fear for the future Genia.'

Genia peered through the double windows out onto the street below. The sun had reached its highest point barely lifting the greyness. More students were arriving and were shufffling the snow off their boots and clothing.

He responded, gazing at the students. 'In the meantime, instead of people dying in the Gulags under lock and key, they remain there voluntarily; they have nowhere else to go. Volodia is ill in hospital and the state can't afford his medicine, and I'm forced to break the law to provide the dollars to pay for it...'

50

Viktor was horrified. 'Genia, I thought you had the dollars. We wouldn't ask you to do anything...'

'I thought a lot before telling you, but there is a risk I may get caught, in which case there will be no money. I didn't want you to build your hopes up before we had the drugs back in the hospital. You don't need any more disappointments. You had to know that's all. I've made my mind up, so lets not talk about it any more.'

'But Genia what have you got to do? For God's sake tell me! This can't be right. Nadia wouldn't want this. Volodia wouldn't want this. We must talk about this.'

Genia put a hand on Viktor's shoulder. 'It involves me driving some skins to Norway in a bus and being paid in dollars there. I've done the trip before and I'm still here to tell the tale. Think of me as a highly paid delivery driver. I've made my mind up and I don't want a lecture on the subject.'

Viktor pushed Genia's hand from his shoulder. 'Genia no – absolutely no!'

'Allow me the satisfaction of doing something to help my nephew. I promise you that if there were too big a risk I wouldn't be doing it. It wouldn't be worth it.' Genia wished he was as convinced as he sounded. 'We've got to see whether we can get the medicine first of all. Are you any good on the Internet? I've never driven one of those machines. When are you next away?' He was keen to change the subject.

'Oslo, next month... Genia, this doesn't feel right. Let me talk to Nadia about this.'

'Of course, but you tell my little sister that I've made my mind up. Come on. Where's your goggles? It's nearly our turn to go gliding.'

'Surfing, Genia, surfing.'

'I knew it was something stupid like that.' Genia lead Viktor through the doors, his voice breaking the silence of the room. Thirty heads swung to face the men. Genia put his finger to his lips and issued a hissing 'Sshhhh...' at Viktor.

Chapter Six

Six hundred garages crested the hill beside the main cemetery. They lay in three orderly, rusting rows. Genia fumbled with the keys to the padlocks as he trudged up the slope, dodging sideways to avoid a taxi that was lurching down the muddy incline, half pushed, half driven by its owner who was trying to bump start the engine. The car started on the first attempt and then partially disappeared in a haze of exhaust fumes and muddy spray. The driver managed to juggle his foot inside the door and close it well before reaching the bottom of the slope and the perils of the main road beyond.

Genia trudged up the hill to Garage Number 422 and the doors that he had hoped he would never see again. It was seven o'clock and he had been awake most of the night. He had initially decided to approach the trip as a normal relief driver would – no concerns, nothing to worry about – just a simple twelve-hour return trip. But late that night it occurred to him that he might not be returning for a while, and he should put his simple affairs in order. He also packed a small survival kit which he put in his knapsack. If he was caught he certainly wouldn't give up without trying to escape, but there was no point even trying unless he was prepared. Dried fish and fruit, matches and paper were packed in a billycan, then wrapped in a plastic bag, along with his knife.

He sweltered in spite of the frozen morning. He was wearing several more layers of clothing than usual. A trickle of sweat ran down a sideburn to his neck. He'd been drinking too much and was getting out of condition. He would not put up much of a contest to any pursuers in his current state.

'422' had been splashed onto the door in blue paint with an unruly brush. Genia paused before wrestling with the straggle of bars, chains and padlocks that kept thieves at bay. Sergei had confirmed the instructions on the phone last night. The vehicle would be waiting loaded, fuelled and ready to go. All he had to do was turn the key and drive it away. It had all sounded so simple. The Mercedes bus was nearly fifteen years old but started first time, and Genia relaxed as he drove the vehicle down the track, keeping the front wheels either side of the central drainage ditch that flowed with a gleaming mixture of snowmelt, oil and anti-freeze.

He turned onto the main road and down the hill to the Polyanari Hotel where he would meet his passengers. The fan heaters were working – something he hadn't counted on – and whoever was the usual driver was clearly a man who liked his creature comforts. The battered seat had been robustly repaired, the radio worked and a prancing horse emblem was fixed to the steering wheel.

The clear sky held a thin layer of solid cloud, which lay like an enormous sheepskin along the length of the estuary and over the city of Murmansk. To his right the vast cement head and torso of the statue of Alyosha the Hero emerged like a doom-laden lighthouse through the ripples of cloud that formed in this sea of white. Ghostly wavelets nudged the unyielding features as they glistened in the grey light. The statue's emotionless eyes looked out over Murmansk and away to the Tundra beyond. To his left, the vast red and white striped columns of the central heating chimneys pierced the climatic membrane. Billowing smoke and steam lay sideways along the cloud, unable to penetrate the inversion layer.

Genia followed the road down the hill and through the cloud layer into comparative darkness. It was a descent into the underworld. A dull coppery light reflected from a hundred window-panes in each of a thousand blocks of flats. The light stuck like oil to every illuminated surface. The piles of coal stood like burnished pyramids beside the mighty heating plants, which ceaselessly pumped hot water to the citizens throughout the winter. This man-made, three-dimensional tableau was more forbidding than any canvas.

He was due to collect his passengers at eight, but was early in order to arrange the paperwork. This half-coach, half-van had distributed passengers and goods up and down the length of

Norway for many years before being sold to the Murmansk Company which had acquired the licence to run these twice-weekly trips to the border at Kirkenes. Genia had six passengers this morning, some spare parts for a trawler stranded at Kirkenes, and his own unlisted contraband, which was buried at the bottom of the storage hold. Any serious check would reveal the bulky skins. It was chance that would determine the outcome of the day. He had done his worrying and planning last night, it was now time to let events unfold.

He pulled up in front of the hotel and was greeted by a small huddle of people. Two girls were saying farewells to their families, before departing to Norway for a sponsored degree course. These girls would have been the cream of their year and were now entering into the unknown. Their parents, once so proud, realised that they were losing their children, probably forever, for what attraction would Murmansk hold after a year in Norway? Their mothers' tears were laced with bitterness. Nearby four men smoked, round-shouldered in the cold, nursing hangovers from the night before. They talked, their breath misting in the cold air: a teasing question from one caused a sheepish smile from another and knowing grins to the remainder; they would return to their families in a shabby state.

Genia moved amongst these people, diverted from his own particular concerns and tried to load his fellow travellers and their luggage on the bus. He checked their tickets and their other paperwork to make sure there would be no hitches at the border. The men sprawled over the seats at the back and the girls sat upright in the front seats, handkerchiefs to their eyes. Outside their mothers held each other, and their fathers shuffled uncomfortably alongside. Genia closed the door and took his coat off before settling into the driver's seat. His, 'Right, is everybody ready?' was greeted by an affirming silence and he started the engine and pulled away. The girls sobbed, and he turned the radio on to blanket his ears from their sadness.

The first hour passed swiftly. The bus climbed once more out of the cloud layer shortly after they had crossed the Kola River and headed west over the suspension bridge. The sky had brightened in the intervening hour and Genia enjoyed the spread of long shadows over the land and the music mixed with occasional chat from the radio. The coach bounced and swung its way down hills and round corners, his passengers silent now; the men comatose, the girls, too tired to cry any more, had fallen asleep on each other's shoulders. His skins lay dormant in the hold.

Well into the second hour the signal from the radio weakened and the Spice Girls' song that Genia had been tapping his fingers to against the wheel faded into a blur of static. He tried several times to retune to other stations and, not finding anything to his liking, turned off the set. The vehicle made steady progress towards the halfway point, rumbling past the many cemeteries and commemorative statues that lined the road. The road from Kirkenes to Murmansk was littered with the graves of soldiers. In 1941 the Germans had seen their capture of Murmansk as crucial to the defeat of the Russian army. They first captured Kirkenes, then landed tanks and troops and started the slow grind forward to Murmansk. His father had brought him on several occasions as a child to the memorial to his uncle's regiment. He remembered being sent off with Nadia by his mother to collect mushrooms and berries, returning to find his father sitting on the stone steps with a photograph in his hand, mourning his brother, an uncle that they had never known. His family's sacrifice in the defence of Murmansk was a cornerstone of his upbringing. Genia's eventual rejection of the Soviet dream was always taken by his father as an insult to the blood that had been spilt on the road to Kirkenes helping to achieve it.

Genia was musing on how this road was looming once again into their family history as the bus rattled down the hill into the outskirts of Nickel and the huge open cast mine that gave the town its name. A vast, flat-topped, snow-covered slagheap the size and appearance of Table Mountain dwarfed the town. It was a landlocked Murmansk – rows of apartment blocks, a central heating plant billowing steam and a railway line that was its lifeline to the outside world. Kilometre-long trains bearing ore rumbled slowly to far off destinations, the wailing of the trains' hooters, strong and mournful, cut the air and echoed around the valley. Genia had once been snowed up in this town for three days. It was a grim uncompromising place, where people laboured hard for their wages and eventual pension. The miners shared the town with retired soldiers and guards from the camps that were situated nearby, unmarked on any map. People were born, lived and died here, but it was a tough, bleak, unrelenting existence. A harsh cycle of life under a slagheap's shadow.

As they weaved up the hill away from the town they passed the cemetery. Here families had paid for and maintained each plot. The painted railings delivered the first true colour since leaving Murmansk. Bright reds, greens, yellows and blues glossed the ironwork, and flowers were changed regularly. The State instructed that no god or Messiah received the dead. They were returned with civic and state formality to the earth that had provided them with a living, their soul and spirit, it was decreed, dying with them. In his youth Genia had been to many of these funerals and seen women throw caution away in their sadness and grief, by crossing themselves in public.

His silent anger rose as he left the cemetery behind him. He battled with it as he drove the next hour. He had long ago recognised a greater being and his belief carried him through every day.

He was brought back to the task in hand with the appearance of a barbed wire fence, three metres high, that lined the road. His thoughts had not been wasted, as his contemplation had renewed his sense of purpose and steeled his determination. He would need it, for they had arrived at the border.

They reached a long, undulating stretch of road that ran parallel to the border fence, the coach's wheels throwing up glistening crystals of ice which hissed and swirled in the wind that blew across the surface. To his right he saw a myriad of lakes and streams; to his left the three-metre high, twenty-four stranded, once-electrified, barbed wire barrier that separated Russia from its neighbours.

He thought about the hundreds of thousands of miles of wire that girdled his country and its subjects. He saw the watch towers, evenly spread on every vantage point, and thought of those desolate eyries and the years, totalling thousands of lifetimes, wasted by the soldiers who manned them. The barbed wire also made him think of prison; in a few minutes when he reached the Russian side of the border, he would find out if his home for the next three years would come equipped with electrified wire and searchlights. He finally questioned his motives for embarking on this venture. Murmansk and Volodia seemed a long way away.

He rounded a corner and he was at the barrier. Behind it he could see the compound that was the Russian border. A solitary guard barred his way and signalled for the vehicle to stop, waving everyone out.

'We all have to get out,' Genia said as he lifted himself out of his seat.

One of the men with a headache and mood to match shouted from the back, the last dregs of alcohol still with him, 'Tell him to come in here, it's freezing out there. We don't have to show our papers until we get to the building.'

The last thing that Genia needed was an obstinate passenger and a border guard who had as much time as he wanted to make life difficult for them. The guard banged his hand on the side of the bus and repeated his order more forcefully. Genia bustled the two girls out and went to the back to talk to the men.

'I've come across this guard before. He'll keep us here all day if we mess him around. Come on, let's do what he says.' Three of them got up, but the fourth crossed his arms and looked out of the window. Genia ushered the three to the front, and when they were out of the way, leant over to the man.

'You've got to get out now or we'll all suffer.' There was urgency in his voice.

It had no effect. 'You tell your Russian brother I'll show my papers when I have to. I'm staying put, and that's it.' The words were as welcome to Genia as the stale breath they travelled on.

The situation was getting out of control. He went back out and took one of the other men to one side and whispered harshly. 'Look, I haven't got the time to be messed around by that idiot today. You get him out now or I'll boot him out.' In an effort to persuade him, Genia added, 'I've only got two hours to see a woman in Kirkenes, and we're late already. I don't care what you say but get him out – now!'

The man nodded and went to speak to his colleague, leaving Genia to take his papers to the guard. He stamped the circulation back into his feet and tried to calm his nerves. It hadn't started well.

The two men eventually walked forward from the bus. His tormentor winked and tapped his nose, 'I hope you'll give her one for me!' he said. Genia climbed back into the cab and started the engine, shaking his head and muttering something unspeakable.

He parked the vehicle behind a van, the wheels straddling the inspection pit that ran for fifty metres along the length of the building. He was encouraged to see that the examination lights were switched off. He turned off the ignition and led his passengers to the passport control.

'Where's the usual driver?' asked the woman behind the desk after examining his papers.

'His child's playing up. I was called in at the last moment. I tell you I could have done without it today.'

She looked up at him and smiled as she stamped his passport. 'How many have you got?' In his paranoia he thought she was referring to the furs, but her smile proved otherwise.

'Six passengers in all. Please don't give them any trouble. I want to see the back of them.' She nodded him through saying nothing. He handed his customs declaration form to an official who gave it a cursory glance, and then waved him through. He walked across the line into the Customs section. He would soon find out if they were going to check the luggage hold.

His vehicle stood in isolation. Two guards leant against it next to the luggage compartment, the skins and his freedom. He looked back. One of the Norwegians was arguing about the rouble exchange rate at the moneychanger's counter, and the rest of the party were waiting at the passport desk. It was going to take at least ten minutes for them to be cleared. He needed a cigarette and started to pace up and down. His future lay in the hands of the two soldiers by the truck. If they decided to do their job, life was going to be very different.

Self-conscious and vulnerable in the stark brightness of the waiting room, he decided to sit down and feign sleep. He found a wooden bench and ignored the pain in his back as he stretched his legs out in front of him and closed his eyes. He reminded himself to keep thinking that this was just an ordinary trip, and took increasing comfort in the metallic clack and thump of the rubber stamp used by the officials on his passengers' papers. It was still a long ten minutes.

The door opened and a cold draught swept into the room.

'Who's the driver?'

Genia leapt to his feet and walked stiffly to the guard who ushered him outside. It wasn't one of the soldiers he'd seen earlier – it was their Sergeant, an old career soldier with ruddy face

58

and pock-marked neck, the bristles on his upper lip stained from years of smoking.

'Where's the usual man? I haven't seen you before.'

Genia responded in a cheery, helpful manner. 'The poor man's got problems with his kid. You should meet that wife of his. She's worse than useless. I was called out at short notice.' He slapped his arms around his body, hoping that it would induce a feeling of chill in the guard, and remind him of the warmth in the building. It didn't work. The guard walked around the vehicle with Genia in tow and pointed at the luggage compartment.

'What have you got in here?' his voice a deep rumble.

'There are some engine parts for a trawler that's broken down in Kirkenes and the passengers' baggage.'

'Open it!'

The two words that he had dreaded. His pulse drummed in his temple, he strained to appear calm and somehow managed to smile at the guard before turning away.

'Sure. I'll get the key.' A few moments later he found himself in the cabin, pulling the keys from the ignition and tucking them into his rucksack pocket as he pulled it from under the seat. He walked back to the guard. He slung the rucksack from his shoulder and started to look inside it.

He stood up after a few seconds to stretch his back. 'They're in here somewhere. You can never be too careful with these Norwegians.' He made fleeting eye contact with the guard and it provided him with an opportunity to slow things down. He chattered on as he bent down to the bag again.

'I've had enough of them. You should have seen the state they were in when I picked them up. One of them has been puking all the way from Murmansk. I've had to stop three times. God knows what they were up to last night.' He laughed and stood straight again. The guard was nodding his head now.

'Tell me, do they always make this much trouble? If I'd known I wouldn't have accepted the few roubles I'm paid to drive this bone-shaker. You wouldn't believe the way the driver left it after the last trip...'

He kept talking as he looked for the key, all the while he was working out which way he would run when the guard found the skins. There was no one else on this side of the vehicle and if he rammed the guard's head against the locker door, he might buy sufficient time to run the fifty yards to the cover of the woods. There was a fair chance that he would make it before the alarm was called and bullets tore into his back. Once in the wood it was going to be hard to make good his escape. He would leave a track in the snow which a boy scout could follow. He could only hope that there was a path nearby that he could run along. He hadn't seen or heard any dogs at the checkpoint and his country's soldiers were not renowned for their initiative. The young conscripts wouldn't hesitate to empty their magazines at him, but wouldn't dare follow him without an order. There would certainly be a few minutes of confusion before a squad was sent out. It was worth the risk.

Genia had the keys in his hand now and once he had pulled the drawstring on his rucksack tight, he looped it over his shoulder and stood up. The guard was telling him about his forthcoming retirement and Genia was debating whether he would grab him by the neck or hair when slamming his head against the metal bulkhead, when a voice from the building diverted their attention.

'Come on driver! Your girlfriend can't be up to much or we'd be out of here by now.' There was laughter from inside the waiting room. The guard was annoyed at being interrupted and walked over to the man. He hadn't understood what the Norwegian had said, but didn't like his tone of voice.

Genia followed the guard and asked, 'Shall I tell him to shut up? They don't speak any Russian and I've had enough of him.'

The guard turned to Genia. 'No, just get him out of my sight. It wouldn't have been like this in the old days. I'd have made him sweat it out. You're welcome to him.' He turned and walked towards a battered BMW with tinted windows that had pulled up behind Genia's bus. It was a more obvious target for a search. Genia masked his relief through a public display of anger at the man. He hastily loaded up the vehicle and drove off waving at the guard. Sweating profusely, his mind was a cocktail of relief and receding fear as he drove the vehicle to the Norwegian checkpoint.

There was an air of expectancy in his passengers now. The men would, in a few hours, be back with their families and they began to behave more like businessmen; the girls were eager to see Kirkenes, their first foreign town. Tomorrow they would fly to

Trömso to meet the families with whom they would be staying for the duration of their course. Genia felt relaxed in comparison to the anxiety and tension of the Russian border. He knew that there was a chance that the Norwegians would find the furs, but if they did, he would claim ignorance, truthfully saying that he hadn't loaded the vehicle and knew nothing about them. He would lose a lot of money, Volodia would suffer and he might be held for a few weeks in a Norwegian detention centre, but that would be a holiday compared to three years in Murmashy Prison. He would have done his best.

They encountered no delays at the Norwegian side and Genia shuffled in his seat as they set out on the few remaining miles to Kirkenes. He had found a classical music station on the radio and his spirits lifted. He dropped the girls off at the library where a welcoming party awaited them. Their bags were exchanged for flowers, and Norwegian women, sensing the girls' insecurity, gave them maternal hugs. He drove on to the airport, a collection of buildings on a bleak plateau overlooking the main fjord, the landing lights glinting against the snow-cleared tarmac of the runway, awaiting the aircraft that would carry the four men to Oslo. His final passengers having disembarked, and now alone, he sang a boisterous accompaniment to the drinking song from *La Traviata*, his hoarse baritone torturing every note. He was hungry, but decided he would drop off the furs, collect his money and visit the hospital, before taking a break.

The garage was in a small industrial estate on the outskirts of Kirkenes. Little had changed since his last visit seven years ago except that the fir trees that surrounded the site had now formed an impenetrable barrier. He swung past the entrance to his garage and then reversed the vehicle up against the large rolling doors. He pushed the bell on the intercom and returned to the driver's seat. He heard the door's mechanism clatter into life. In his wing mirror he could see one man next to the opening. Another, larger, was hunched over a bench in the background. He switched off the radio but continued to hum as he reversed the vehicle into the garage. He turned off the engine and the doors closed in front of him. He got down and shook hands with the nearest man, a Russian, who did not meet Genia's eye.

'Did you have any trouble?'

'No, it all went just fine. Shall we get this lot unloaded?'

The man at the bench still had his back to him. He was Norwegian. 'Yeah, might as well. Get it out and put it over there.' He turned and gestured to the far wall.

'Aren't you going to help?'

'Don't be daft.'

Genia opened the locker and pulled the trawler parts out first. He then removed the flattened cardboard that covered the tarpaulin at the bottom of the locker. One by one he removed the skins, each of which had been tightly rolled into a ball the size of a beer keg. The men appeared unmoved by these rolls of once-living bear. Four large kilner jars beside them contained various organs destined for some oriental pharmacy; the skins were for bachelors' bedrooms. Genia was glad the products of his labours were being exposed in such anonymous surrounds; in public his embarrassment would have been visible. He closed the locker and walked back to the man at the rear of the garage.

'Well there they are: four adult furs. Have you got my money? I've got to get going.'

The Norwegian still had his back to Genia, his shoulders fitting uneasily into the mechanic's overall, his hair lying in greasy tresses over his collar. His legs were too long for the trousers, whose hems stopped a full three inches short of his boots. His stomach stretched the elasticated waist, once designed to give the overalls shape and form.

'Not until we've seen the merchandise,' he replied flatly.

'Look, I arranged it with Kim and Sergei. $2,000 in cash, upon delivery. Come on, don't mess me about.' He was struggling to remain calm. Why hadn't he anticipated this? It might be a try on but it appeared to be working. He had blindly driven into a locked garage, unloaded his cargo, leaving his only weapon in the vehicle. One of the pair looked menacing, even without the benefit of seeing him standing upright and head on. How could he have let it happen? He could still hear himself humming as he had reversed the bus into this trap of his own making.

'I used to do the run for Kim's father in the old days. I know he wouldn't want any problems. Just give me my money and then I'll be on my way.'

'And I told you – not until we've got the merchandise! So get

62

on with it and give it to us, or go away.' He pointed at the furs as he spoke.

Genia was about to reply but suddenly realised he had been betrayed. He returned to the furs and pulled the binding from them. It was in the third fur that he found what they were waiting for. He was at first relieved by what he saw, for the fur did not contain the cellophane-wrapped brown powder that he feared, but instead a large thermos flask. His curiosity showed clearly on his face.

'You haven't got a clue what this is all about, have you?'

'Look, all I know is I'm selling these furs to you. I don't know about the rest of it.'

The man laughed. 'Well, put it this way, I wouldn't go near a Geiger counter or you may get a nasty shock.'

'He'll find out anyway. He'll be glowing in the dark for a few weeks!' the other man sniggered.

Their scorn was as nothing compared to the anger that Genia was directing at himself. The container would have radioactive materials in it, stolen from the naval yards. Had he been caught at the border he would now be facing a life sentence. He and his passengers had been exposed to the radiation for over four hours; the flask hardly looked designed for the purpose. He pictured Kim's porcelain face and wanted to pulverise it. A darker thought emerged: had Sergei known? That question would have to wait; the money was his priority now.

'Just give me the dollars and I'll go.'

'If you think I'm picking that thing up, you're mad. Go to the back office – you'll find a metal box there. Bring it through and seal the flask in it.'

Genia did as he was told, his face flushed with anger: anger at himself, anger at Kim, anger at this man for his mockery. His position was helpless: he had to get the money. He found the metal trunk and dragged it across the floor to the skins. Opening the outer clasps revealed heavy lining material and an inner casket, which he opened to find more packing and a compartment for the flask. He picked up the flask and locked the compartment behind it, securing the main catches.

'Now give me my $2,000,' he said wearily.

'I wouldn't do that trip for ten times that sort of money. Do you know how much that stuff's worth? You've been plucked like a chicken,' he pointed at the trunk, 'a half-cooked chicken at that.' The smaller man added, 'Now piss off back to Murmansk. Kim can give you money if he wants, that's up to him.'

Genia knew that they would have the money somewhere in the garage and that he had to act quickly. He smiled as he approached the big Norwegian and when he was close enough, spat at his face. The man roared like a bull and swung a fist at Genia, who parried the blow with his arm and threw the man to the floor, landing heavily upon him. They both grunted. He fought desperately to grab hold of the Norwegian's arm and received several blows to the ribs. Genia now had him on his knees and with one arm around his neck, the other hand searched for his real target. The Russian had picked up a crowbar and approached Genia, but he was stopped in his tracks by a muffled crack and a feral shriek, the cry of an animal in a snare. Genia had broken the Norwegian's thumb and was grinding the bone upward into the wrist with all his might.

'You tell him to put that down or I'll tear this off!' He twisted the bone inwards again and the man cried out to the Russian who obeyed. 'Now tell him to get my money.' The Norwegian was sobbing now, his body limp with shock. Genia was incensed and close to tears himself. He found himself saying 'Why are you doing this? Why are you doing this? It wasn't necessary. Why are you doing this...?' He repeated it like a mantra, his lungs heaving with the effort of wrestling the man to the ground, his heart slowly recovering from its second adrenaline rush of the day. The money was produced and put on the floor in front of them. Genia looked at the untidy pile of notes that lay at the edge of a pool of oil.

Genia knelt behind the man one arm still tight around his throat, his hand still holding the thumb. Sweat dripped from his face on to Norwegian's neck, who was whimpering through clenched teeth. In front of him was the money and the Russian who looked increasingly confident. They would know that he had to return to Russia and that he would have to cross at the border. They would be sure to come after him if they were able. His only solution was to tie them up and hope that they didn't escape before he crossed. They also didn't know that he had to visit the hospital first. They had more time than they knew. His first priority was to keep the big man immobilised.

'Get that chain and bring it over here,' he said to the Russian and nodded his head at a tow chain in the corner. 'Right, unravel it, lay it out in front of me.' Addressing the Norwegian, he instructed 'You swing your legs forward slowly.' Genia kept applying the pressure and the movement hurt the Norwegian, so that the resultant groans kept the other at bay. Genia could sense the relief in the man once he was finally sitting on the floor, his legs in front of him.

'Wrap the chain, all of it, around his ankles and legs.' It was working.

The next five minutes were a blur as he choreographed the counting of the money and the tying up and gagging of the Norwegian by the other man, the anguish in his face silently pleading for no more pain. He bundled the Russian into the back room where he tied him to a chair before dragging the injured Norwegian in to join him. He made one final check to ensure that they were both securely bound and gagged, ripped the phone from its socket and locked the office door from the outside before opening the garage doors and driving out. He closed the doors behind him, and was still swearing to himself for his stupidity as he drove away. He thought of Sergei, Kim and of the betrayal of trust.

He drove in the direction of the hospital. He pulled over beside a snow-covered bench, got out and sat down. With his elbows on his knees he stared at his boots – a desolate figure in a children's playground. The full enormity of his predicament hit home. He thought of the creeping wound that had been inflicted by the cask and moaned to the empty park. Where was the radioactive material going to and who would use it? He debated whether to go back to the garage to get the trunk and hand it over to the police, but the men may have broken free and be on his trail. He had to get the medicine back across the border to Volodia. He must calm down and think straight. He screwed up his eyes and breathed deeply.

After a few moments he sat bolt upright, his eyes still closed as he breathed slowly through his nostrils, six seconds in, six seconds out. He thought of his hut, the whiteness, and the silence. Nearing composure, he grabbed a handful of snow and wiped it over his face and hands. He noticed for the first time a gash on the back of his left hand where the man's nails had dug deep, lifting a flap of flesh. The warm blood melted the snow into a pink trickle that ran into his cuff. Eventually he stood up, the pain of bruised ribs and the ache in his forearm had replaced the one in the small of his back. He knew how lucky he had been to have not been caught by the Customs and to have escaped with the money. If fate was on his side, he was surely being put to the test. 'Come on old man,' he said as he walked back to the bus.

The radio was playing Stravinsky and Genia vainly searched for a melody as he drove along the tree-lined sweep to the hospital, where leafless branches stood like skeletons against the noonday sun.

Chapter Seven

Genia sat counting the dollar notes into the sum that he needed for the medicines. He noticed blood had trickled from his wound, down his hand and across the well-fingered face of Benjamin Franklin. He reached for an oil-stained rag beside his seat; he wrapped it around his hand to staunch the flow and wiped the blood from the note with the back of his bandaged hand.

He walked into the hospital. The medicines had arrived from Oslo but additional drugs were needed from the pharmacy to complete the order. Although he tried his best to convince her that he just wanted to collect the prescription and go, the nurse who greeted him noticed his wound and insisted on treating it while they waited.

'I should really put a couple of stitches in this for you. It won't take a moment and it's going to take a while to get your package together,' she said as she examined his hand. She was wearing surgical gloves and her eyes were sympathetic above the mask. 'We can pop a bit of local anaesthetic in, it won't hurt.'

'No ... no ... just a bandage please,' he answered uneasily.

'You're not scared of needles are you? You'd be amazed how many men are.'

Genia had come to distrust needles. Military medicine had involved mainly the well-used variety and the pain and infection that went with them. 'We're all babies at heart,' he said. 'I was just thinking that I would have to be undergoing heart surgery to warrant all this attention back home. You really don't have to put yourself out – there must be other patients to see to.'

The nurse pointed to the car park that was empty except for Genia's bus, which was parked across several parking spaces. 'We aren't exactly rushed off our feet here and it would give me some practice. I haven't stitched anyone for quite a while.' A hidden grin and signs of laughter-lines made her eyes even more attractive.

'Thanks, but I really am in a hurry. Could we just patch it up? I'll collect the medicine and be on my way.'

He looked around the room. The cleanliness and sanitised brightness gave it serenity. The surfaces had not been cleaned of dirt; they were surfaces that had never known dirt. It was quiet. No rattling trolleys, shuffling of feet or crying children. A benign peace enveloped the building. He imagined a bed in a room, clean linen sheets, a hot shower to wash away the fear and brutality of the last few hours, warm laundered pyjamas against his bruised and aching flesh, dimmed lights and sleep.

'Are you all right?' The nurse's question brought him back to reality.

'Yes I'm fine. I was just thinking.' He turned his mind to the next half-hour. Would they be waiting for him, what would they do to him if they caught him?

'Tell me about your nephew.' She was swabbing the gash now, the antiseptic stinging as she worked oil and grime out of the wound.

The answer came in short sentences that flowed unevenly from him. 'He's a good boy. Bright but not precocious. He has my sister's kindness, but he's not too sensitive. He's been really hammered by the treatment though. There's hardly anything left of him. It's just as well they don't have mirrors in those wards. It's heartbreaking to see him. And he's one of the success stories...' He paused, and as he looked out of the window, a hooded crow fluttered into the branches of a tree, perched for a few seconds and then flew away again. He shivered. 'What else is there to say? I am really grateful, but I do have to get going.'

She finished dressing the wound and bandaged it tightly. His hand looked like a boxer's before the gloves went on. He wriggled his fingers and looked at his nails. The nurse lightly patted the back of his hand.

'There you are. Now don't go dropping any more toolboxes on it! You should be more careful. Come on, let's see if your parcel is ready.'

They went to the dispensary where two cardboard boxes awaited him. Genia handed over the dollars and was turning to leave when the nurse produced another box with a silver helium balloon attached to it.

'It says get well soon.' She had taken her mask off and was as pretty as Genia had imagined. 'We have a small charity budget and we have put in some more needles, some painkillers and things that should make life easier for him. The balloon was left by a patient.'

'Thank you! We don't have these in Murmansk.' He tugged at the string and it bounced off his head. He smiled and held her arm. 'Thank you, you've been truly kind.' He lifted his injured hand. 'I can't thank you enough.'

'I still think you're a baby. Good luck to your nephew.'

'Thank you.' He turned and pushed at the doors and stumbled as they parted automatically. He could still hear her laughter as the outside doors slid shut behind him. He turned and waved his bandaged hand and smiled with embarrassment.

He decided that it was too dangerous to drive the vehicle to the border. He had to consider the probability that one of the men would have freed himself by now. If that was the case, they could have reached the crossing and found out whether his vehicle had passed. He drove towards the centre of town and abandoned it in a side street. He unloaded the contents of his rucksack and replaced them with the boxes from the hospital. They just fitted. He stuffed some food into his pockets and chewed on some chocolate as he packed. He had initially decided to leave the balloon, but at the last moment he knew that, although it made him look ridiculously conspicuous, he would take it for Volodia. He made for the dock where lorries unloaded their freight before returning to Murmansk. He would try and hitch a ride, using the few remaining dollars to help his cause.

There were two likely trucks. One was being unloaded, while the driver of the other dozed in his cab. He tapped lightly on the window and the man shook his head as if irritated by an insect. He looked down at Genia who gestured for him to open the window. Reluctantly the driver wound the window down a few inches and said, 'Yeah, what?'

'I need help my friend. I need a lift to Murmansk. I've come here to buy medicine for my nephew who is in hospital.' He tugged at the balloon. 'I've had problems with my vehicle. My papers are in order and I can offer you a few dollars if it helps.'

69

'I can't take passengers. I'll lose my job for it if I'm caught.'

'Yes, I should have thought of that. I'll explain everything to the border guards. This kid's near to death with leukaemia. I've got to do the best I can for him.' Genia noticed a faded photograph of a woman and two children in a frame on the dashboard. The driver's job would mean a lot to him. 'I'm sorry to have troubled you, but I wouldn't have done it unless it was serious. I've got fifty dollars I can give you and I promise I'll take the can if anything goes wrong. I've got no other option. I really do need your help my friend.'

The driver yawned and looked at his watch. 'It's about time I got going anyway.' He paused. 'All right. Get in.'

Genia climbed into the cab. He placed the balloon and rucksack in the sleeping compartment and waited for the lorry to reach the outskirts of town before adding his final request.

'I need to hide in your bunk until we get to the border.'

The driver applied the brakes and the truck came to a hissing standstill. 'What are you playing at? Go on get out of here – this smells of trouble. I should have known.'

'Please listen to me. My vehicle broke down when I got here. I had it taken to a garage and they mended it but gave me a bill. I couldn't afford to pay it and for the medicine as well. $500 they wanted. It's a year's wages. They kept the vehicle but still wanted the cash and threatened they would wait for me at the border. I don't think they will, but I can't take any risks. Once I'm in the buildings they won't dare touch me. You've got to help me... Please?' Genia had had enough for one day – there was real emotion in his voice.

The driver sat, scratched his ear and said, 'Get in the back then. But if there are any more surprises you're out and if there's any trouble you're on your own.'

Genia didn't offend the man with platitudes. He had deceived him and they both knew it.

He moved as gingerly as he could into the tight confines of the bunk and closed the curtains behind him, his left flank throbbing from the bruising as he stretched out. After ten minutes the hiss of brakes told him that they had arrived at the border. The driver got out ahead of him leaving Genia to make his own way. He walked with his collar up and his head down, his eyes straining upwards to see if his assailants were waiting for him. His

70

frayed nerves made the pain disappear and his knees weak. The men were nowhere to be seen and he passed with great relief in through the control into no man's land. Once on the other side the driver offered him a cigarette.

'Thanks, I need one,' said Genia, as he took one out of the packet. 'I'm meant to have given up. Look, I'm sorry about back there...'

The driver smiled. 'I've had worse. Some joker put a whole family in the back once. I could have gone down for that if they'd been found by our lot.' He pointed at Genia's hand. 'Do you want to tell me what really happened back there? I didn't believe your story for a moment.'

'Why did you give me a lift?' Genia was almost relieved.

'You looked an honest sort. I've driven this old wagon all over the place, you get to be a fair judge of character in my job.'

'I told you the truth about my nephew and the hospital. I was owed some money in Kirkenes and had a problem collecting it. I'm glad it's all over now and we'll soon be on the way back into Russia. It feels like a long day already.' He looked at his watch. It was three o'clock and the stresses of the day began to take effect. 'Do you mind if I sleep when we cross into Russia? I could do with a rest.'

'No, that's OK. Don't mind if you hear me chuntering on though! I talk to myself all the time,' he laughed. 'It keeps me sane.' Genia knew what he meant, for he too had recently found himself speaking half-finished sentences to the walls of his cabin.

He lay in the cocoon snugness of the bunk, his body wedged against the sides, his eyes closed as the sway of the suspension sent him into a deep sleep. The aches in his body had become strange friends, diminishing with his slumber. Ignorant of the miles he was transported towards his family and Murmansk.

The clear skies that had attended his departure had been replaced by swirling, sleety rain propelled by a south-westerly gale, the first sign of an Arctic spring, although it would be several months before trees budded. Genia had been awake for the last two hours and the driver had been glad of the company. The windscreen wipers worked valiantly to keep the screen clear but were not equal to the challenge; each clean sweep swiftly filled with water, filtering the street lights into an eerie light that illuminated the faces in the cab. They talked about families and travel, the latent humour that was present in everyone. They talked of the unusual, often mystical things, which happened to travellers and of how they restored faith in human nature. Fate or coincidence, the driver said, it didn't matter – the effect was much the same.

The sleep had partially restored Genia but as they neared the outskirts of Murmansk he fell silent. His achievement in buying the drugs had lifted one shadow, but another far darker had replaced it. The truck passed one of the counters that displayed the daily levels of background radiation to the citizens of Murmansk. It occurred to him that the electronic counter would register an increase with his return to the city. He mouthed a curse. The driver, half-hearing him, asked him if he was all right, but Genia stared blankly out of the window.

The driver drove Genia to the foot of the zigzag of steps leading to Nadia's block. It was as close as the lorry could get to the building and it was still a long uphill haul. Genia offered to pay the man the last of his dollars but the driver refused to accept them. They shook hands and said their farewells, wishing each other good fortune. Genia swung his knapsack over one shoulder, pulled up his collar and pulled the hood of his anorak tight over his face. The balloon swung crazily in the wind as he started the long climb.

He was drenched by the time he reached the door of the apartment block and shook himself like a dog once he was in the shelter of the entrance. His face shiny with rain, he peeled back the hood and did his best to tidy his matted hair. He walked up the three flights of stairs to the flat and tapped on the door with his usual staccato knocks. His father opened the door. Over his father's shoulder he could see Nadia seated at the corner of the table, her face in her hands. Viktor was stroking her hair, staring blankly out of the window. Genia dropped his knapsack and sighed, 'Volodia...'

His father, ashen-faced, kept his eyes to the floor, and closed the door behind Genia who shrugged his coat from his shoulders onto the ground as he walked into the room; one sleeve remained in place, the coat dragging halfway across the floor. Viktor failed to acknowledge him but continued his gaze at the darkened window. Nadia stood up and cried, her arms by her side, her body shaking with emotion. Genia stretched out his arms and held her to him.

'He didn't deserve it... he didn't deserve it, Genia. They told us he would be all right. We saw him yesterday morning. They said he would be all right. What happened Genia, what happened?' She cried a deep, heaving, maternal cry. Her eyes were red and swollen. All that he could say in reply was, 'I know... I know...'

He wrapped his arms around her, held her face to his chest and rocked her gently from side to side. The trials of the last twelve hours disappeared into insignificance. He tried to find words of comfort and faith but had none. He closed his eyes and hoped that his physical presence provided some solace, for he knew he had nothing else to offer. His own sorrow was dwarfed by the grief that only a mother could know.

It was two in the morning when peace finally came to the flat. Their father in Volodia's room was lost in his own world. He had cried alone for his wife and wanted more than ever to join her before he fell asleep on a mattress on the floor. The hospital had given Nadia and Viktor strong sedatives. Viktor had swallowed some with vodka before going to bed. Nadia had refused them, insisting on experiencing her grief. She didn't want to blot out a single image of their precious son. 'It's a mother's right to grieve. I won't take pills to help me, Genia,' she had said angrily as he asked her to take them. She was close to breakdown. He finally warmed some milk and sugared it heavily before dropping two sedatives into the steaming mug. As they took effect he guided her to the bedroom where Viktor was asleep. He tucked her under a blanket beside him and kissed her forehead, holding her hand until her breathing became deep and regular.

He returned to the hall to phone Irina.

'I need to see you.'

'I know. I heard at the hospital when I went to see how he was. He was such a cheerful child. I'm so sorry Genia...'

He scribbled a note leaving Irina's number, before picking up his coat from the middle of the room and collecting his knapsack. As he closed the front door his face brushed the string of the balloon that was floating against the ceiling of the corridor. He

took it in his bandaged hand and slowly made his way downstairs into the wind and the rain. Once outside he lifted his face
to the sky and let the large heavy drops splash against his face.
He opened his eyes and lifting his arm, let the balloon fly. He
followed its progress upwards as it caught the reflection from a
street light before disappearing into the darkness beyond. He
dropped his hand to his side and stood with his face set against
the driving rain. Cold drops mingled with the warm tears from
his eyes.

Irina lay awake, nestling under his arm as he slept. From time
to time she kissed his chest and traced a finger over the bruises
on his ribs. They had talked late into the night and had slept,
not making love. She thought of the times in the past when they
had longed to spend the night together. Slowly she lifted the blanket and looked down along his naked body. The hairs on his chest
were showing their first signs of grey. His legs were long and
lean against the fullness of her thighs, her head buoyed on his
chest as he breathed. She wanted to go to the bathroom but did-
n't want to break the moment. She looked at his hand as it lay
on the sheet, its ragged palm upturned. Silently she asked,
'Where have you been Genia?' Outside Murmansk was awake.
She was already late for the hospital but for once she would
phone in saying that she was unwell.

He awoke with a start, and opening his eyes sighed as the
events of yesterday flooded in. She raised her hand and stroked
the side of his face.

'Tell me it didn't happen, Irina. Tell me it hasn't happened.'
Gingerly, she hugged him to her and kissed his cheek. She had
no words to offer. 'I still can't believe it.'

'It's all right, it's all right...'

'I'd better phone Nadia.'

'You can stay as long as you want, you know.'

'And I've got to track down Sergei. I need to know what I've
been exposed to.' He was about to focus on revenge, but the grief
of Volodia's death intervened. He shook his head. 'What a waste
of a life, what a horrible tortuous death for a child. What is the
point of it ... what is the point?' She stroked his face.

'You know, I truly believed he would heal. Not just the drugs
from Norway – no ... no. I saw Volodia's face, those eyes, and I

believed that I knew that he would live. That's what hurts the most. I thought I knew he would live. I told Viktor.' He shook his head. 'What is the point?'

She brushed some strands of hair across his forehead with her hand.

'How do you live with that in the hospital every day? How can you watch it? What do I say to Nadia?' He raised his bandaged hand. 'What's the answer? I thought I knew. "Everything has a reason", they say. Well, what reason can there be in making a child suffer a lingering death? When I was in Afghanistan, I was saved by an Afghan goatherd. That's what he said – everything has a reason. I'd have a word or two to say to him now.' He slapped his hand onto the bed and pushed Irina away. 'I've got to get going.'

Irina recoiled. 'Sure? Don't you want some breakfast?'

'How can I eat?' he snapped at her, as he found his trousers and the rest of his clothes, grimacing as he slipped his shirt over his head.

'Take it gently, there's no hurry...'

'I'll be fine. I've just got to get going, that's all.'

She knew it was pointless. 'Yes. I'm late for the hospital. I'd better get going as well.'

She walked over to him and tried to hug him. 'Do you want to stay with me tonight?' He brushed her aside without answering.

'Don't treat me like this Genia Sukov!'

'You don't understand...'

'I understand. I understand that you phoned me last night and I welcomed you into my house and into my bed. Now act like a man. I've said I will help you. If you want to wallow there's a bottle of vodka on the shelf. Go and drink it all and then cry like a baby, but be gone when I get back.'

He stood, his eyes blinking slowly as he stared at the floor. He ran his hand through his hair in embarrassment. He stood for some time before looking up to her. 'I am truly sorry, Irina. I don't know what I'm thinking. You are right, I know. But it's more than Volodia. Everything is changing around me. I don't know which way I'm pointing, let alone know where I'm going... Pathetic!'

'It's the same for all of us. You think too much instead of just getting on with life.'

He stood round-shouldered. 'I know, I know...'

She took his hand and placed it on her breast and standing on her tiptoes kissed his lips. 'Here, take my comfort – I give it freely to you.' He pulled her to him.

'Irina, I don't deserve this.' They hugged for a while, each enjoying reassurance in each other's arms. He smiled as he raised his fingers to her earlobe and gently tugged it. 'Thank you but, I just...'

She smiled sadly. 'Maybe it's best if you stay with your family. I don't want you here just because you feel you ought to be.'

Genia didn't reply. He was in his own world and he didn't need her.

Genia leant against the wall in the station staring angrily at the handset. Sergei's phone had been engaged for over an hour. Normally he would have been patient and read the newspaper but the phone's refusal to answer only fuelled his frustration. A woman was waiting to use the phone, but he turned his back on her seemingly unaware of her presence. Finally the line cleared, and Sergei answered.

Genia's tone was unequivocal. 'I'm at the station. Be here in half an hour... No I don't want to go to the Arctic Hotel... Don't tell me to calm down, I'm at the end of my tether... What do I want? I want the truth... Yes, in the café. I'm the fool with a bandaged hand, bruised ribs and a poisoned body... Bring who you like but I suggest it isn't Kim because I'll fucking kill him... I don't give a damn!'

He slammed the handset back into the cradle. He had never lost his temper like this before and certainly not with Sergei. He then realised that he was in the café with other people. It was as if he was watching himself from the other side of the room. He turned to the woman and was about to apologise for his behaviour, but she had gone out into the cold to find another phone.

He sat at a table and drank a Pepsi, drumming his fingers on the table as he prepared for the confrontation. He was about to buy some cigarettes when Sergei swept in through the doors. He was alone and furious. Anger was the only emotion that Genia hadn't bargained for. He stood up to meet him, and the two men stood frighteningly close to each other. A couple of lovers were

76

disturbed from their farewells, the barman stopped emptying ashtrays. A policeman, enjoying a quiet smoke, took one look at the two men as they squared up to each other and decided it was best to leave. The hem of Sergei's black leather coat skimmed the floor as he folded his arms across his chest and spoke to Genia.

'Well?'

'Oh no!' Genia waved his hand dismissively, 'Oh no, not like that. You tell me Sergei. You bloody well tell me what's going on.'

'What do you mean? You got your money.'

'I mean, getting me to smuggle an extra package in the skins. I mean, not getting paid when I got there. I mean, taking a beating. I mean – I want to know why you would do this to me.'

'I swear on my mother's life, I didn't know about the extra cargo.'

'You look me in the eye and tell me that again.' No one spoke to Sergei like this, but Genia was beyond caring.

'Kim told me about it when he phoned last night to find out where the bus is. All hell's broken loose. There were five passengers meant to be returning with you. They want to know where it is. I tried to contact you last night but no one was at your father's apartment.'

Genia was beside himself with anger. 'Sergei, I don't give a damn about the bus and some passengers. I'm talking about my health. What was in the flask? There were six of us in that bus for over five hours. Do you know what that means? I wasn't at my father's flat because little Volodia died yesterday and I'm trying to hold my family together at the moment.' His hands curled into fists, they seemed to shake the air in front of him. 'Had I been caught it wouldn't just be a couple of years in prison. They'd have thrown away the key. I've been betrayed by you and I'm more angry than you can imagine. Don't talk to me about buses!'

Sergei wiped the spittle from his face that had sprayed from Genia's mouth as he had finished his sentence. He raised his hand to Genia's cheek and hissed through gritted teeth. 'I swear to you I did not know about the flask. That's the last time I'm saying it.' The indentations on Genia's cheek blanched as Sergei squeezed hard to make his point. 'Come on, this isn't the place to be talking about this. We've both been deceived, Genia. I'm as angry as you are. Let's go across the road, we can talk more easily there.'

Genia brushed Sergei's hand aside, leaving a reddening mark on his cheek. 'What was in the flask, Sergei? I must know.'

Sergei shrugged. 'The stupid thing is that the flask had depleted uranium it. Bits of used fuel rods stolen from Andreeva. You couldn't start a car with it let alone a war. They thought they were buying weapons grade material. Kim had double-crossed the Norwegians as well. It was a one-off deal – the boy thinks it's amusing. He's asked me to tell you not to overreact, but he wants to know where the bus is.' Genia was about to launch into another tirade, but Sergei put his hand up to stop him. 'Look, you got your money and you're here to tell the tale. Genia, you took a risk and it paid off. How many people in this town can get that type of money?'

'Sergei, you are not going to tell me I should be grateful?'

'Genia, I'm telling you that you got what you wanted, not necessarily how you wanted it, but that's not my fault. And that's why I object to being dragged down here to justify myself. Think about it.'

The café was beginning to fill with people and the policeman had returned to his seat, relieved that his services would not be called upon.

Sergei continued, 'Look, I'm very sorry about your nephew, it's happening too much nowadays. Come, on let's go. We should stick to fishing and hunting, those are things we understand.'

'I suppose it's too much to expect an apology?'

Sergei patted him on the back. 'I wouldn't insult you with one.'

Chapter Eight

Jody sat cross-legged on the floor, her back leaning against the sofa where Meg was stretched out. Around them lay the remains of a TV supper and a near-empty bottle of burgundy, plundered from Greg's cellar. They had already watched the video of *Shakespeare in Love* once and were now replaying the early scenes between Shakespeare and Viola. The remote control lay in Jody's lap as both women gazed at the screen.

'That voice ... mmh!' Meg squirmed on the sofa. 'Turn it up and then go back to the beginning again.'

'Shhhh! They haven't finished yet.' A few moments passed and Jody reached for the controller and pressed the pause button. 'When did Tommy last say "You are my sickness and my cure" to you?'

'Round about the same time that Greg told you that you were his "hunger and his sustenance". Where did we go wrong, Jody?'

'We just lifted up the wrong rocks, I guess. I knew you'd like it.'

'Paltrow made such a fool of herself at the Oscars, I couldn't believe she would be any good in the movie. I didn't realise. You most probably get more out of it though; we didn't have much Shakespeare in my business degree.'

'I wasn't much better. We pretty much crammed him and I found it dull. It was only when we went to the New York premiere of the movie it all opened up for me. Greg loathed it. "pretentious English mush" was one of his more flattering remarks. I got the video as soon as it was released. I must have worn it thin by now.' She switched the television off and the screen crackled with static. With another remote control she started her CD player; Bonny Raitt's craggy voice filled the room.

Jody cupped the glass in her hands. 'You know, with the men

I loved before Greg, there was always one moment that I remember more than any other. It was that moment when I knew that I could trust a man enough to tell him just how I really felt.'

'What, you mean in bed?'

'Sure, that would be part of it. But it was much more. You suddenly had the confidence in him and, more importantly, in yourself. You knew who you were, and you almost didn't care if he responded badly, because you knew it was how you felt. It was a weird mixture. Relief, power and submission all rolled into one. See what I mean?'

Meg made an encouraging, but unconvincing. 'Uh ... uh.'

'Until then, it's like a game of cards. How much of your hand do you reveal? How much do you give away? How much do you allow him to take? You'd hide it all inside. Bottle it up. Then there's that moment when you know he's serious, for real, not full of crap, not just sticking around for the sex. And you tell him.' She took a sip from her glass. '"Keep them guessing." I never felt good with all that. I was never really happy in love until I had reached that stage.'

Meg understood her now. 'I've always been too frightened of scaring 'em off to try that. Besides, half the time I was all over the place – I never knew what I really felt.' She reached over and laid a slab of cheese onto some bread.

Jody continued. 'I suppose that's what I was trying to say. That for once I actually did know myself and what I was thinking. If it scared the guy off, well, so be it. I could either let him go or fight for him, but the choice was mine.'

'So, when did you reach this great milestone with Greg?'

'That was what I was thinking as we were watching the film. And the sad, lousy truth is that I never got there... I never felt it.' There was a pause. 'It all happened so quickly after Dad's death. We were all in such a state of shock. Still are in some ways.' Jody felt a lump in her throat.

'He was such a grand character your father. We all miss him.' Meg tried to comfort her. 'With you and Greg it all seemed to happen so quickly. Tommy and I could never figure it out.'

'I know. The boys say that.' Jody thought of her three brothers. 'I was in such a mess. When Mom died, I pretty much gave up work to look after him. You know – the whole fishing thing, and helping out with the Foundation. I threw myself into it. We became closer than we'd ever been before. Until then he had spent most of his time and energies on the boys. I was always a "nice to have", an add-on. It was Mom who was responsible for my upbringing. He was always there – sure – but in the distance. When she died it all changed. He was lonely. Of course he spoke to the boys, each and every day. But they talked in the way they always had – he couldn't admit his grief. He couldn't, or wouldn't, tell them the truth. I'd just split up with Phil and I didn't have anyone else on the scene. I suppose I was happy to just lie dormant for a while.' She prodded the cheese with her finger, was about to tear off a piece, but continued, 'Dad was my life for nearly two years. When we used to go to parties together, he would take my arm and say, 'What a fine couple we make – if only your mother could see us now!'

Meg smiled. 'I remember you both opening that Impressionist exhibition at the Met. Do you remember that journalist asking about you being his new wife?'

'Of course. Dad exploded, but I think, secretly he was rather flattered. It was there that I met Greg. We dated a few times; he was keen, but nothing came of it. He was flying backwards and forwards from LA and I was with Dad.' Jody picked up a slither of pickle and chewed on it as she continued. 'Then Dad died...'

She paused. She hadn't spoken about Greg to anyone before. She hadn't truly analysed her thoughts herself. She was wary of what she might say and, in a strange way, curious.

'You see, Meg, I know what you all think of Greg. I don't need to be told what the boys and their wives say behind my back. I realise what goes on. I'm not a fool.' Meg tried to interrupt her. 'No, hear me out. You see, Greg was there for me when Dad died. The boys weren't. It's as simple as that. For that, I will always, always ... be grateful.' She hesitated over the choice of the last word. She had been going to say love, but couldn't.

Jody smiled a cheerless smile. '"The king is dead – long live the king." Bobby took over the Foundation. The Harrison fortune was distributed amongst us siblings. Do you remember the memorial service at St Bart's? Hundreds in the congregation, everyone taking it in their stride; it was a cocktail party without the canapés. What *did* we celebrate that day? Time passes, an old man dies, the world keeps on spinning? I nearly believed it myself. But, the day after the funeral I realised that I would never see him again. I would never hear his laughter, take his arm. I would never smell his cologne or brush flecks from his shoulders. I realised that I was alone.' She swivelled her wedding ring backwards and forwards around her finger as she spoke. 'I had committed so much to him and he had left me. It almost felt like he had deserted me. I didn't know who I was anymore.' She gulped the last drops from her glass, reached for the bottle and then filled the glass to the top of the milled pattern.

'So Greg. Well, Greg wrote to me. He sent me flowers. He took me out; he was attentive. He showed interest in me, he listened to me and above all he sympathised and gave me comfort. When I introduced him to the boys it was clear that they didn't like him. What is it they say in England? "Damning with faint praise". They tolerated him, and it only served to throw me closer to him. He was attractive, we travelled a lot, the sex was good, we drank and we laughed a lot. He proposed, I said yes – we married. What more can I tell you?' Her voice faltered. 'Look, I'll go make us some coffee. Are you still on decaff?'

'Jody...' Meg made an effort to stand up, but Jody waved her back. 'Do you want some help?'

'No, I'll be fine, you stay here.' She lifted a few plates and piled them on a table but left them as she felt the tears well up. She went through to a bathroom nearby and washed her face with cold water, telling herself to 'get a grip' before going to the kitchen. She caught a reflection of herself in the glass of the window, and was readjusting her ponytail when the phone rang.

'Jody my dear.' It was Michael Cummings. He lifted her mood immediately. She tucked the handset under her chin, as she filled the kettle with water. 'How is my favourite American this evening?'

'Michael, I'm well and how are you?'

'I'm very well indeed, and I just can't wait! It's only ten days now and I'm counting. Ginny's all excited too. God, what's that noise in the background? Are you in the bathroom? Are you about to go out?'

'No it's fine.'

'Now look. What has young Tigger been up to?' His ambiguous

82

nickname for Greg always amused Jody. She reached into a cupboard, pulled out two mugs and put them by the kettle. 'You really must keep him under control.'

'Why what's happened?' Jody wasn't too concerned as Michael always exaggerated.

'Well, he's been onto poor old Steve Newman, who now thinks he's organising a re-run of Desert Storm. A proud military career I may have had, but Norman Schwartzkopf I most certainly am not!' Michael always hammed it up for his American friends.

Jody glanced at her watch. Michael was probably enjoying his nightcap before going to bed.

'Jody, I love your husband dearly, but you've got to get him to wind his neck in.'

Jody was sixteen when she had first met Michael with her father on a fishing holiday in Scotland. Michael had at first been reluctant to, as he put it, 'waste a rod' on a girl. But he should have trusted his friend better, for when he saw Jody cast, any doubts he had disappeared immediately. 'She's a natural – a bloody natural!' he had told his friend.

'I'll speak to Greg in the morning. What's the problem?'

'He's got his boy, Tracey or some such, crawling all over the travel arrangements asking for extra security. There *is* a serious side to visiting Russia, but I'm afraid I can't do much about that. All I can say is that I've been going there for years now and if I thought the risks were unacceptable I wouldn't go.'

'I'm not going to let you get away with that Michael. It's partly your fault. You've filled him full of tales of military helicopters and poachers. After all, it was you who said, "I'd flaming well shoot my way in there if I had to!" You know how paranoid we Americans are!'

'I've always treated you as an exception to the rule.' Michael was rarely caught out. 'See what you can do, will you?

'Now I've got this new line I want you to get for me. I can't get it in London yet and the New York office always balls up the simplest fishing order.'

'Have you tried ordering it from the net?'

'Don't be ridiculous!'

'Well, you're in luck. Tomorrow's my big day – I'm going into New York. Is there anything else I can get you?'

'A new elbow would help! Mine nearly seized up during my spring week. But no, bless you. I'm all equipped. Have you got a pen and paper handy?'

Jody wrote down the details and, after a short argument over the weight of line, they said their goodbyes.

She had put Greg to the back of her mind and she took the coffee into the sitting room. Meg was leafing through a magazine.

'Jody, are you OK?'

'Yeah, I'm fine. A few glasses of wine and that god-damned movie; they get me every time!'

The light from the shutters filtered across the floor to the bed where Greg lay. The room was quiet apart from the muffled sound of the air conditioning unit and the gentle breathing from the mop of sun-bleached hair resting on the pillow beside him. Greg was awake, gazing at the tanned body that lay in a semi-foetal position and he congratulated himself as he marvelled at the part-illuminated shoulder and back. He took stock of his own well-being. There was the gentle throb of a hangover and the first signs of paranoia. He looked around the room and found the causes. What he saw was a scene of debauchery – a bottle of champagne, vodka miniatures, silk underwear, a bottle of massage oil and a wrap of cocaine. All empty. There was other paraphernalia lying around but his eyes closed as his headache took hold.

He opened them again slowly and looked at his watch. It was still early but he would have to get up. He had several meetings scheduled during the morning. He turned on his side and tucked in against the bronzed rump; with one hand he held her against him, with other he gently ran his hand up and down the clearly defined vertebrae. Eventually there was a sign of life and the body stretched against him, rolling over to kiss him fully on the lips. Greg responded, holding her head in his hands. He smiled into the sleepy eyes and kissed the girl again.

'You'd better get going soon,' he said softly, stroking her face.

'What time is it?'

'Six fifteen.'

'We've only just gotten off to sleep.'

84

'Are you working today?' His hand stroked the girl's thigh.

'Just hangin' out. I'll crash out when I get back to my apartment. Have you got any Nurofen or something? My head's killing me. We really went for it last night.' She wrinkled her eyes closed and reached down to pull the sheet over her. 'Can you turn the aircon down? It's freezing in here.'

Greg smiled, wrapped a towel around him and walked across the room to the control and switched it off. He found a bottle of water and rummaged in his sponge bag for some painkillers. He swallowed two and gulped them down with water from the neck of the bottle. He filled a glass and put two more on the table next to the girl.

'There you go. Now, keep your eyes closed.' He found his sunglasses and perched them on his nose before opening the shutters. A bright shaft of light poured into the room and the girl groaned. He opened the door and walked out onto the balcony. Below him lay Santa Monica beach. The early morning roller-bladers were heading back to their cars as solitary figures sweated their way up the beach path that ran between the hotel and the Pacific Ocean. The sounds of the city mingled with those of the sea, but in another hour he would be able to hear the surf for the constant throb of traffic on the Pacific Coastal Highway. He wandered to the sunlit end of the balcony and stretched as the warmth of the morning rays bathed his shoulders. He scratched the black hairs that that curled across his flat stomach and smiled contentedly to himself as his mind turned bedwards. He was feeling better already.

Jody was fast asleep. At four o'clock in the morning she had given in to the temptation of Greg's medicine cupboard and had taken a sleeping pill. Earlier, she had tried all her normal remedies for sleeplessness. She had read a chapter from a Henry James novel. She lay in the darkness counting sheep, fishing her favourite pools, listing her classmates at Princeton, all to no avail. Later, in a darkened bathroom she had taken a warm lavender bath, in it she had brought herself to an unsatisfactory climax. It had only made her feel more restless. At four o'clock she feared that sleep was going to elude her completely. She reached for a little brown bottle, one of many in Greg's bathroom cupboard. The one marked 'Sleepers – Strong' in his tidy handwriting over the typed label seemed to offer the best solution.

She awoke with a start and looked at her watch. It was nearly ten o'clock. She normally awoke at seven. 'Oh no...' She willed herself out of bed, slipped on a long, white, cotton T-shirt, shuffled her feet into a pair of battered lambskin slippers and padded downstairs into the kitchen. The pills had made her feel pleasantly drowsy but she was due in New York for a meeting with her trustees. Finding a mellow jazz station on the radio she set about breakfast. Jody could not function without a proper breakfast. She decided on a bacon, tomato and Swiss cheese melt on toasted rye to be washed down with a jug of dark coffee. A few slices of her favourite pickled gherkin gave the finishing touch to her ultimate breakfast.

She pushed the cheese-laden pile under the grill and reached for her address book, fingering her sticky way to the hotel section. Keeping an eye on her sandwich, she dialled Greg's hotel. He would have been up for some time now.

She was put through to his room where the phone rang a few times before being picked up.

'Hello?'

'It's seven fifteen Pacific Standard Time. My name's Cindy and I'll be your alarm call this morning. Cock a doodle doo! Hi hun! How'ya doing?'

'Hey, how are you?' Greg gave an authentic impression of waking up. 'Jeez! I better get going. Are you OK? You haven't just got up have you?' The noise of trickle and splash from the shower seeped through the gap in the bathroom door. He put his hand over the mouthpiece to muffle the sound. Jody hardly ever called him while he was away. 'You haven't been foolin' around have you?'

'Nah, the bastard did a no show!' She eased a spatula under the toast and slid the steaming mound onto a plate. She felt juices of anticipation in her mouth and licked some of the melted cheese from the blade. 'We've got to talk about Russia. I had Michael on the phone last night and he said that Tracey had been on to him. Is this a good time?' She sensed something, but didn't know what.

'I'm running a bit late.' The shower turned off and the girl started to sing tunelessly in the bathroom. He leapt across the

86

bed and switched on the radio. 'Let me grab a shower and I'll call you back in ten.'

'Yeah sure, it won't take long though.'

The girl came out of the room wearing only her small triangle of hair. Greg creased his face and put a finger to his lips. She shrugged and walked over to the breakfast trays and, scooping up some scrambled egg with her finger, licked it slowly, smiling all the while at Greg. 'Its no matter. I'd just like to get some breakfast ordered. I'll call you straight back.'

Jody picked up the plate and took it over to the coffee pot. She was about to tuck in but she was troubled. She thought for a few seconds, then picked up the phone and dialled the hotel again.

'Palisades Plaza, how may I help you?'

'My name's Mrs Lucas, we are staying in the Welles Suite.'

'Yes, Mrs Lucas how can I help you?'

'I'm driving in from LAX at the moment and I want to order some breakfast. Could you put me through to room service.'

'Why, certainly.' Jody had never done anything like this before. Maybe it was her talk with Meg, but whatever it was she knew Greg was lying about something. The phone rang twice.

'Room service, how may I help you?'

'Hi, I'm Mrs Lucas, the Welles Suite. I would just like to confirm our breakfast order.'

'Let me see here... Mrs Lucas, it looks like we delivered your breakfasts over half an hour ago. Do you want me to check?'

'No it must be my mistake, thank you.'

Jody pushed her plate to one side and slumped into the back of the chair. She felt ill. Her mind raced and she fought to slow it down. Could it be a mistake? Why would he lie? Did the girl say breakfasts plural or was it singular? As she was going through it in her mind the phone rang.

'Hi Hun. You still awake?' Greg's voice sounded normal. 'What's Mike so uptight about?'

She explained it all to him, as though nothing had happened. By the end of the conversation she had almost forgotten the incident, but just as they were about to say goodbye she asked, 'So what's for breakfast this morning?' There was something in her voice; he sensed a trap and looking at the two trays he replied, 'You know, I was so hungry I went through the whole card. They'll need at least three of those "wetbacks" to deliver it. It's late though. I'd better chase them. I'll do an extra workout this evening. I'll back off a bit and give Mike a call later. I'll see you tomorrow. Love you.' He breathed a sigh of relief.

'Love you,' she heard herself say, then she threw the handset across the kitchen.

Chapter Nine

Genia bent down to scoop soil from the small pile that lay beside the grave. He was the last to throw his three handfuls. The earth, still part frozen, rattled like marbles on the coffin. The grave-digger stood a short distance away talking to the taxi driver who had delivered the small family group to the cemetery. Two hunched figures, they both secreted cigarettes in curled hands behind their backs, more to protect the glowing ash from the elements than out of respect for the dead. The digger's engine puttered diesel fumes into the air, the noise from the engine merging with the sounds of seagulls as they circled overhead. Beside the grave, Viktor held Nadia while their father looked longingly to the other side of the cemetery where his wife was buried. Genia stood stony-faced and erect, dropping the earth into the hole. He held his hat in one hand and wiped the remnants of soil from the other on his coat. His hair curled across his face in the breeze, which carried with it the sound of a hooter from a ship newly-arrived at the docks. Genia looked over to his sister. She held a handkerchief to her cheek, more for comfort than anything else, as she had no more tears to shed. In the distance behind her he could see the row of garages. It had only been a few days since his arrival at Number 422, but it seemed like a year. He looked at his family, his eyes emotionless.

'We should go now. Let the man get on with his work.' Viktor kissed Nadia's cheek as he spoke. She didn't reply but remained staring at the coffin. 'Come on, my love. We will come back tomorrow and make this a special place for him. There's nothing more we can do now. It's time to go home.'

She turned her face to his and nodded in agreement. 'Home...' fell sadly from her lips. The word had lost its meaning; it was now as empty as her son's bedroom.

Genia and Viktor sat at the table with the remnants of supper lying around them. In their midst stood a half-empty bottle of Scotch whisky that Viktor had brought back from Amsterdam. Nadia came from the kitchen to collect the plates.

'Leave these. We'll tidy up later. Why don't you go to bed now?' Viktor said as she came over and held his hand.

'Yes, I'll leave you both to it. Genia if you want to lay your head here for the evening, there's Volodia's room.'

'I know, but I'd best go home to be with Dad.'

She wrapped her arms around Viktor's neck and kissed the balding patch on the crown of his head. 'And don't you be too long old man.'

Viktor held her hands. 'Ah ... the love of a good woman. Kindness and understanding as you travel down the dusty road of life, warmth and tenderness at the end of the long day!' The words he had used so often brought the wisp of a smile to Nadia's face. Viktor opened her palms and kissed them. 'Goodnight, my love. I won't be long.'

Viktor reached for the bottle and filled their glasses. Genia looked at his friend's face as he poured the whisky. The stubbornness, which was its main characteristic, was still apparent although softened by the years. Viktor often complained about the effect that his face had on people. 'I'm really not as angry as I look,' he would say. 'Mind you, they soon know if I am.' He was a loving and attentive husband and father, who was able to see the importance of the family amidst the chaos that was his contemporary Russia. Now the bulb from the overhead light made his face appear as if it had been covered in a film of wax. His eyes had lost their intensity. Genia knew that his friend had not yet come to accept his son's death. He was still too involved in supporting his wife.

'What about you? Don't you want to call it a day?' Genia asked.

'No. I'm fine. If I go to sleep now I'll only be awake at four. I'll take some more anaesthetic with you before I retire.' Viktor pointed at the bottle, sighed and then continued. 'Now where was I? Ah yes, there I am in the lobby of the hotel. It's two in the morning and I'm ready for bed. I have given my speech to the plenary session earlier that day – which of course was a triumph – when this British couple comes up to me and says, "Viktor, we just didn't realise what was going on up there. We are concerned for you and your family. You are sitting on the doorstep of the next Chernobyl." I must have been rather drunk and lost my English because instead of saying, "In Russia it's hard to choose your neighbours", it came out as "I'd prefer that to having you as my neighbours"! Anyway, I've definitely lost two votes when the council elections come in the spring. It was only when I got into bed that I realised what I had said.'

Genia, too, was relieved to find humour. 'They'll have forgotten all about it by now – or put it down to some dark Russian philosophy.' Viktor offered him a cigarette, which Genia declined with a shake of his head.

'These foreign delegates trouble me. When they look at me, its almost like I'm some sort of victim. There's pity in their eyes, in the tone of their voices – it's like I've just arrived from Nigeria with a begging bowl. Most of them have never visited our country but they have all the statistics at their fingertips: fifty years to clean up the nuclear waste; one third of the world's spent nuclear fuel; central government funding of $1.5 million against a requirement of $3 billion. The trouble is you get the feeling that although they talk about "action now", they really enjoy the bureaucracy and the politics of it all. There wasn't one proposal discussed in the whole week that would create pressure to speed up the process and release more funds – to make something happen.'

He knocked his cigarette against the side of the ashtray and then drew on it heavily. He noticed a crust of bread that had fallen from the table as he had piled up the plates and bent over to pick it up. Smoke drifted into his face and he screwed up his eyes.

He took a bite out of the crust and laughed. 'I hate waste! Do you remember when Medina was formed, just after the first radiation leaks started? There I was chained to the railings at Andreeva, pleading for the world to join us in clearing the fjord from the nuclear menace. Me and fifteen other activists.'

Genia laughed. 'I remember the Navy creating a ten-kilometre cordon around you and your ragbag of headcases by announcing a radiation alert. That kept people away. And you obliged them by providing your own lock and key. How long did they leave you there to cool off? Two days? You were lucky it was the summer. Mind you Nadia still recoils at the mention of your trousers.'

'You have a cruelly selective memory, my brother-in-law. The main trouble now is that the environment isn't the issue that it used to be. It used to have an excitement about it: rubber dinghies being run over by whaling ships, pop stars saving rain forests and – yes – people like me chaining themselves to nuclear installations. We've become victims of our own success. The world has seen enough of the same tired images, and governments have swallowed the issues up and made them their own. The result? Atrophy!'

'Oh no! I sense a visit to the ironmongers? Make sure you buy a set of boltcutters this time.'

'I'm serious, Genia.' Viktor was becoming light-headed with emotional release.

'You were then, but you can't rely on Nadia to clean you up a second time.' He gestured at the bottle and Viktor poured some more. 'Give in gracefully to middle age and enjoy your position. You travel the world supporting the process. However slow it may be, you seem trusted and respected and, whatever I might say to the contrary, you do make a real contribution.'

'But the fact that they let me travel means I've effectively sold out – a sad neutered activist.' He stubbed out his cigarette and reached for another. 'I'd find it impossible to find fifteen people in this town to chain themselves to anything, unless it had a Mercedes logo on it.'

'Viktor, there is nothing sensible you can do to change it and besides, you are far too old for any swashbuckling stuff. Even if you did do something no one would see it – they are too busy watching *The Simpsons*. No one does anything in this country now unless it's for money. Idealism is out of the window.'

'Genia – always so defeatist!'

'I have never been against trying to change things for the better, but all you lot do is buzz around like wasps at a bad picnic. Fools created the problem that lies ten kilometres up the bay. Just because you are on the other side of the argument doesn't prevent you from being a fool yourself. You used to work for the Maritime Institute. The people who work there now are good people doing what they can with limited resources and with growing international support. Why rock the boat?'

'Because nothing is happening, Genia, that's why. Nothing is happening. Where were you this afternoon, for God's sake? How many more children do you want to see die?' He picked up the bottle. 'Do you know, the only thing that has changed is that I now have these conversations with you fuelled by Scotch whisky instead of vodka? That, and the fact that I have lost my only son...' His voice faltered as he fumbled for the bottle cap and screwed it firmly into place. He levered himself out of his chair and went to the corner cupboard replacing the near-empty whisky bottle with one of vodka. 'Now let's drink as Russians, let's dare to rock the boat! Nadia bring me the padlocks!' he boomed as he dropped back into his chair, his face newly animated.

'Here's another expression for you: "the cult of the celebrity". The whole world is obsessed by celebrity. We see it here in Russia. Do you know, in the USA when teenagers were shown pictures of their president and a movie star ninety-five per cent recognised the movie star but only sixty-five per cent could identify the President? I won't trouble you with the star's name.'

'Tom Cruise. I've seen him on the video in the camp.'

'These people are more famous than the President. Then of course there's money. The rich are famous for being rich. There are people in the USA worth more than countries. I bet some of them visit that camp of yours – you see them, you know what they are like. It's the mega-rich who could shape opinion but they do nothing about the real issues. Instead they feed their public with a daily diet of trivia and feed themselves on the coverage they receive in the media.'

'It's a harmless transaction.'

'No, it's not. Think what could be achieved. Look, the point is the world has become obsessed with the immediate. How many TV channels do we have here? Six. In my hotel in Amsterdam there were forty-seven. Eleven of those were news channels, but the news was all the same. An issue becomes an issue only if the news editors decide it is an issue. Then they all flock to it with their special correspondents and sit there covering the issue until something bigger comes along.'

Genia stifled a yawn.

'No, listen to me! No one has the patience for long-term policies any more, everything has to be quick fix. We see it here. We have almost given up on the idea of involvement in government. "Leave it to them at the top; they should know." What we need to bring our cause to the top of the agenda is a new policy or action that responds to these changes. Otherwise we might as well give up.'

Genia raised his hand in the air, spilling vodka from his glass as he did so.

'Chain Tom Cruise to the railings!'

'Well, now that you mention it,' Victor rubbed his chin, 'could you imagine the stir that would cause?'

'Look, I'll get a pen and paper, we can write to him this evening. He's bound to have a few days free later in the year. We'd better tell him to bring a few spare pairs of trousers. Here, pass me the bottle.' He splashed more into each glass. 'You stick to your committees, Viktor. True progress is slow – you know that better than anyone.'

The word committee touched a nerve with Viktor. He gulped from his glass and stared at Genia, the whites of his eyes traced with fine veins and bulging slightly.

'You always know best, don't you? Is there nothing you would put your head on the block for? A man must have principles or beliefs that he would fight for – die for, if necessary.'

Genia nearly asked Viktor why he'd smuggled the skins into Norway, but thought better of it. Instead he stood up and walked over to the window, drew the curtains and wiped a patch of condensation from the large pane of glass. Through the smear, the sodium lights of Murmansk lit up the hill. On the other side of the fjord car lights wound their way down the road and steam billowed out of the heating chimneys nearby. 'Come and look at this.' Genia put his hands in his pockets and shivered, the alcohol was getting to him. He wiped away some more condensation with his handkerchief as both men stared out of the window. 'We had an American who came to the camp a few years ago. He loved poker. He used to say, "You can only play the hand you're dealt". You can only do a limited amount. It doesn't mean that you don't try, you just have to manage your aspirations. This isn't a place for grand gestures and high principles. It's a place for survival and seeking solace in the simple pleasures that life sometimes provides.' He put his arm round Viktor's shoulder. 'Come on now. You've had a hellish time but you have good things too. You must hold onto them. "The love of a good woman", remember? Your work is of importance.' He turned him round, pinched his cheek and smiled. 'Don't throw it all away. Come on, its time for bed.'

Viktor was about to reply but his grief resurfaced. He wiped his eyes with the back of his hand and smiled bravely. 'Are you going to stay?'

'No, I'll walk home. The air will do me good.'

'Are you sure?'

'I'm a big boy Viktor. Besides you should go and look after my sister. You don't need me getting in your way.'

Genia went to the chair near the front door and fumbled with the laces of his boots. He rose to his feet and layered his clothing around his frame. Finally, he pulled his hat onto his head and untied the flaps. One dropped over an ear, the other stuck comically upright. Viktor found laughter again and folded down the offending flap.

'Come on, Bugs Bunny! Let's get you home.'

'You sleep well, my friend, and keep those padlocks in the cupboard.' The two men hugged.

Greg walked along the pontoon to the picnic launch that lay moored alongside. The Tuxedo Committee had long since banned petrol motors from the lake. The only boats that were allowed now were sailing dinghies, canoes and flat bottomed launches that were powered by electric engines. They made their way silently around the lake and were a popular weekend recreation for families and friends. Jody had arranged for an evening supper cruise with Tommy and Meg upon Greg's return from LA. She was loading a wicker basket onto the boat when her mobile phone rang. It was Meg.

'Oh Meg, I'm really sorry to hear that.'

Greg was listening keenly. 'They're not jacking out are they?' he said, pointing at the piles of supplies.

Jody motioned for him to keep quiet. 'Look of course we understand, it's really nice of Tommy to look after you. Let us know if there's anything we can do. I'll give you a call in the morning to see how you are. Are you in bed now? Well you just stay there. I'll catch you tomorrow.'

'Don't tell me they're not coming. What are we meant to do with all this stuff?'

'Meg's got one of her migraines. Tommy's got her in a dark room and is looking after her.'

'We might as well get all this back into the car.'

'Hey, it's a lovely evening why don't we go out anyway? We're loaded up; all we've got to do is cast off. We don't have to stay out for long.'

Greg shrugged and stepped onto the boat leaving Jody to fold the boat cover and stow it.

'Leave it there. No one's going to steal it.'

'You know the rules Greg. "Pontoons to be kept tidy at all times",' she said to taunt him.

'The people who came up with that kinda' crap should be dying a lingering death.'

'I don't remember that being your attitude when you were up before the Committee, but maybe then there's a lot I don't remember about you.'

Greg let the remark pass. He switched the battery power on and put the motor into reverse. Jody barely had time to untie the last mooring rope and jump onto the boat before it left the pontoon.

'Why don't we go to the narrows and see how those duckling are getting on?'

'Suits me.' He turned the wheel and they set off down the middle of the lake. It was a still evening. The fractured rays of the sun shone through trees leaving long shadows across the lake. Here and there, trout rising to emerging fly broke the flat surface. Silvery mallards flew in untidy formation around the lake before landing in shoots of spray near the water's edge. Two children paddled a dinghy back to the boathouse, their limp sail powerless in the still air.

She uncorked a bottle of wine and offered Greg a glass, which he accepted without comment. His mind was elsewhere. He pulled a handkerchief from his pocket and blew his nose.

'Have you picked up a cold or something?' she asked, for he had been sniffling since his return a few hours ago.

'It's just my sinuses. They always play up in that place. Smog and air-conditioning – it always gets them going. How about here?' Greg asked, turning off the motor. The craft drifted to a standstill and the remnants of its wake washed away, leaving them becalmed in the peace of the evening. He reached to turn on the CD player.

'Let's just leave it quiet for a few moments.' There was a time when they used to come out at twilight on this boat to make love, returning only when darkness had fallen. She looked around the lake, took comfort from its familiarity and strength from her own sense of calm.

'Greg, let me ask you a question.'

'Hell, this sounds serious!' He gave her his warmest smile. 'Go ahead, shoot!'

'Did you have someone in the room when I phoned you yesterday morning?'

'Hey, what is this?' His mind raced. He had been his usual cautious self, and she couldn't have heard the girl singing. It must be a shot in the dark. 'Honey, of course not!'

'Are you sure?' She looked into his eyes.

'Why, honey of course I'm sure. What's all this about?' He looked back at her, but too earnestly.

'You see Greg, I think you did.'

'Well, that's the truth. If you want me to lie I can say yes, if that will make you feel better.'

'This is not about making me feel better. I just want an honest answer to a simple question.' She was amazed at her calmness.

Greg leant back with both hands against the guard-rail. They were the only people on the lake now. It all became clear to him. 'Did you arrange all of this? The boat trip, Meg's migraine, just so you that you could ask me a question. How much does she know?'

'She knows nothing. I just said I wanted a quiet evening with you on the lake and I needed their help in arranging it. There's even a bottle of Krug from them to help us celebrate your home-coming.' He was hating this and she almost felt sorry for him. 'I wanted you alone, no place you could run to, no den to lock yourself into. Just you, me and the truth. We've got two of those passengers, so why don't we welcome the third on board?' She paused, surprised at her own rhetoric. 'Well?'

'That's just pathetic Jody.' He was cornered and getting angry.

He had never seen her look so determined before. 'OK, you ask your questions – but you had better make sure you can handle the answers. Are you sure you can handle the answers? There's a lot at stake here you know.' He tried to gain the initiative but she was having none of it.

'I've given a lot of time to this recently. Time that I should have spent long ago. I wouldn't be asking the question if I didn't think I could handle the answer. So don't patronise me, wipe that tired expression off your face and get your brain round the fact that this is serious. OK, let's try another one. Are you doing coke again? And how about the booze? I know I've had a drink or two,' she pointed to her glass.

He looked away and over to the club house where the lights had just been switched on in the dining room. The two children had lifted the dinghy onto its trailer and were wearily towing it up the slipway. He wished he was back in Los Angeles.

'What's that got to do with anything? This is crazy.'

'What it's got to do with is that I'm here trying everything known to man to have children. We're both meant to be cleaned out, and I don't think you're committed. Greg, I don't like all the crap I've got to go through to have kids, and if you're not being straight on this, then I'd rather stop and think it over.'

'What do you mean "think it over" for Chrissakes? We're both committed. It will make our marriage, Jody. We've discussed this. I want nothing more than to see you pregnant. Lots of children. How many times have we said that? Come on now, this isn't right.'

'I suppose while you've been away I've been thinking, and I'm not sure that I trust you and if I don't trust you, then I don't want to have children with you. A child doesn't make a bad relationship good – it just seals over the cracks, and I'm too old to live my life that way.' The words came naturally to her. An hour before Greg arrived she had tried to rehearse what she would say and had panicked. She had gone for a run to clear her head – the strategy had worked. She knew she was right to address this now and almost felt detached.

'Honey, I can see that you feel bad about this.'

'I don't feel bad, Greg. If I just felt bad, I would take a drink and I'd feel better. I don't know how I feel and, trust me, that's far harder.'

'So what do you want then?'

98

'I want you to tell me the truth.'

Greg said dismissively, 'When it comes to relationships, the truth is what people want to believe, Jody. You know that as well as I do. You've decided what you want so why keep asking me? Just quit it. This isn't getting us anywhere.'

'That's not a great answer, Greg. I don't want to argue or fight with you.'

'You've got a strange way of showing it, lady!'

'I just want to know want to know the truth.' She was still sitting with her arms wrapped around her knees. 'OK. Let's move you out of this for a moment. Let's talk about me. I'm not going to have your child until I feel sure I want to spend the rest of my life with you, and right now I'm not sure.'

'Well, you could have thought about all this just a little bit sooner. We've been married for – how long now? What's gotten into you? This is plain crazy. No marriage is perfect, Jody. It's a compromise – always has been, always will be. Your folks, my folks, for everyone in this goddamn park – it's a compromise. As for trust, if you didn't trust me you shouldn't have married me.'

'I know it, Greg. Darlin' how I know it.'

They both fell silent, Greg leaning against the rail, Jody on the bench. The shadows covered the lake now and the last rays of the sun lit the top of the hill overlooking the park.

He tried to coax her. 'We're all under stress. We've got a week away. Let's enjoy it. This will work itself out.'

'I've been thinking about that. I don't think *we* should go.' She looked at him and added, 'I'm going to go by myself. I need time to work all this out, and I know you aren't that keen. It'll be good for you, too, to spend some time here at home.'

'Look, I'll decide what's good for me. Either we both go or no one goes. Is that clear? You're not going to Russia without me.'

'It's already arranged. I spoke to Michael on the phone this afternoon and told him that you were up to your neck in it and really sorry. He understands, Greg. He's cool about it.'

'You did what?' He sprang forward from the rail, rocking the boat and causing ripples to circle out from the hull. He loomed over her. 'I just can't believe that you would do that! I tell you Jody... How could you do that? I do work with Mike. This is important.'

'Greg, I know. But he also happens to be an old friend and,

99

not to put too fine a point on it, it was my invitation anyway.' She knew this was the wrong approach and before he could respond she added, 'Greg, I really need to do this trip by myself. I know that you're pissed off about it but, please, try and see beyond that. Please try and understand.'

'Well I ain't in the understanding mood, Jody. First of all you hijack me, accuse me of lying to you. You tell me you don't trust me, then you say you're not sure you want to be married to me, so having children is on ice and – Oh, by the way – I'm not allowed on holiday with you. You give me one good reason why I should understand? Oh yeah, I forgot to mention that you phone up a man who I do most of my UK business with and tell him I can't handle the pace.' He was furious, but it was fury laced with guile, not the outrage that the words warranted. She had seen this performance acted out a hundred times on the phone when he wanted to get his way in a deal. It was Jody who found outrage but managed to keep her tone just below anger.

'What's that phrase you use? "Whatever they say, find a lie and just keep repeating it. Grab the moral high ground even if you're crawling in the mire." Is that what this is about Greg? How many times have you told me that? It was a big mistake to try and appeal to your non-existent sense of reason. You haven't even answered my questions. All I've had from you is hot air and that won't wash. I told you not to play games with me. I've told you my solution, so think long and hard before you start hard-balling me on this. It isn't some deal. This is our lives here.'

He thought for a while, his eyes focused on the flagstaff at the end of the lake, although he saw nothing. His mind was churning. He knew she had decided, and although it was difficult, he had to give in. Besides, she hadn't found out about the girl. He could always fly her to New York. Some imported tan for a week would be far better than some Arctic fishing hole. He put his hand to her face, stroked her cheek and laughed. 'Hot air never washes, you dumb bitch!'

'Did I say that?' She looked at him amused and irritated. 'It does too – if you're in a car wash!'

'No, that's steam.' The tension was easing, and both of them were relieved. 'Hey, I'm sorry if I over reacted, but Jeez you came at me! You know what I'm like. You're right. Some time apart won't do any harm. You'll only catch more fish than me anyway. You go and I'll be here when you get back.'

'Thank you. It's got to be the right thing.' She was relieved. The doubt that she had been carrying had grown into a burden over the years; now she felt half way to freeing herself of it. 'Hell, open that Krug! We shouldn't waste it.'

He went to the icebox and she went to the wheel, turned on the motor and headed the boat to the far end of the lake, where the last of the evening rise was showing.

Chapter Ten

Viktor's face had become blotched and puffy, his eyes darkly ringed, a legacy of becoming a solitary drinker since Volodia's death. Nadia and he were living in separate worlds. His was alcohol-fuelled and the induced moodswings took him from the dark into the abyss. The previous night he had failed to attend the Medina dinner. He had spent an hour at the reception and then left. He was in no mood for, nor capable of, coherent discussion. Seeking isolation, he spent the remains of his meagre expenses on a bottle of vodka, which he downed morosely in his Oslo hotel room. The photograph of Nadia and his son remained in his case. He did not want them to witness him in this state. The minibar in his room had contained peanuts, crisps and pretzels, which he washed down with the vodka as he watched Eurosport on the television. Still hungry, he found at the back of the refrigerated cupboard a small bar of Toblerone. The bar that he had given to Volodia remained untouched on the boy's bed in Murmansk. Viktor's head lolled to one side. He moaned and poured the remains of the bottle into his glass.

He was awoken by a knock on the door. It was his breakfast delivery, for which he had managed to pin the order to the door before sinking into bed. The only light in the room came from a muted television showing a motorcycle race. It wasn't until the third bout of knocking that he lifted his body from the bed and ambled to the door. He took with him a dark depression and a blinding headache. He fumbled with the chain on the door, finally opening it to the beaming smile of a black African waiter.

'Good morning sir. Where would you like your breakfast this morning?'

The words made no sense to Viktor. He walked into the bathroom leaving the waiter to put his tray down wherever he found

102

space. Viktor was too embarrassed at the turmoil in his room to want to witness the waiter's reaction. He drank some water, looked at his watch and went back to bed; he would miss the morning's meetings.

A few hours later he was woken again by more knocking on the door. The blue light of a badminton court now fell from the screen.

He shouted, 'Who is it? Leave me alone!'

'Housekeeping, sir. We've come to make up your room. There was no sign saying not to.'

'Go away. I'm asleep,' which he was, the moment his head made renewed contact with the pillow.

It was not until two o'clock that he finally awoke. He knew for the first time the true meaning of the word despair. He had lost his son and with him his self-control. Next would be Nadia.

For a while he lay motionless huddled in the bedclothes. He pushed the sheets back and opened the curtains, turning to look at his face in the mirror. He saw the weary, dishevelled character that he had recently become. He inspected his eyes and the flesh around them and saw something new: a once decent man had become weak and furtive. He continued the examination for some time, seeing himself as Nadia, Genia and Volodia would have done. The reflection became pitiable, as silent tears formed in his eyes and pooled before trickling away. He remained transfixed. Some time passed before he used the back of his hand to wipe his eyes and face.

'You are better than this, Viktor,' he said to his reflection as he resolved to fight back.

The wind blew in from the sea and rattled the branches of the trees that surrounded Storgata. The first flourishes of green were emerging on the matted grass, and occasional gusts lifted spray from the lips of the fountains forming pools on the granite pavement. By the fountain in front of the National Theatre, brightly coloured figures lined up to promote the annual *Ruskenaksjonen*, a holiday when the people of Oslo cleared the cigarette ends, chewing gum and litter which had accumulated in the city's covering of snow during the previous four months. Children in yellow and red boiler suits had been brought in for a photo call, and the resulting images would feature on the front page of tomorrow's *Dagbladet* urging the citizens of Norway to put this public holiday to good use and clean the area near their homes.

Viktor watched the young children as they posed for the photographers, and his mind went to Murmansk and his apartment block. He pictured himself handing out leaflets to the residents urging them to assist in the common good. 'One good day's work from each of us and our city will be clean.' He would be a local hero at a stroke: features in *Pravda*, pictures on billboards, radio interviews, a celebratory dinner with the Governor. He developed the plan as he walked up Karl Johans Gate. An honest, simple act fostered neither by the State nor by greed. One day's work: such an easy gesture. This year Murmansk, next year the rest of the country.

Enjoying the vision of potential greatness, and with a new sense of esteem, Viktor made his way amidst the straggle of tourists up the gentle incline. To his left, he noticed a bronze statue. Its magisterial severity was sullied by the presence of pigeon droppings which drizzled like icing over head and beard. *Christian Krohg* was etched boldly on the plinth and proclaimed the identity of one of Oslo's radical thinkers. Viktor stepped backwards, pondering whether, when it came to it, he would be sculpted standing or seated, when he was hit hard on the leg and tumbled to the granite pavement.

'You stupid old man!' shrieked a voice.

The ball of vitriol picked herself up from the pavement, glaring at Viktor as she lifted up her stainless steel push-scooter. Viktor rose to his feet, also struggling to remove his gaze from this exquisite creature. Dressed from head to toe in purple, her exposed midriff revealed fine blond hairs and a navel pierced with three gold rings.

'I'm truly sorry. Are you all right?' His thigh throbbed from the impact.

'Are you blind or something? Or is it just too much booze? You old fart! They shouldn't let people like you out.'

She pushed a purple wedged boot against the slope and wove the chrome scooter and herself out of his life, leaving Viktor bruised and reflective. How could a girl so beautiful spit out those words? It was like phlegm from a fishwife. He was hurt and felt

104

vulnerable – an ungainly, middle-aged Russian adrift in the real world. The reflection in the hotel mirror beckoned.

It was six o'clock and he had at least two hours before his meeting. He had already been walking for four hours; he was hungry and now increasingly maudlin. The tourists were thinning out as they returned to their hotels for a bath and supper. He saw a father lift his young son onto his shoulders while the mother was window-shopping. He gazed at the bouncing blond hair and the delight on the face of the boy. He thought of Volodia, clenched his fists and wished he could be spirited home.

He pulled his mind away and caught the strains of a guitar and a mouth organ, their clarity distorted by the buildings that lined the street. He looked ahead and saw a cluster of people around a pile of empty plastic beer crates. As he approached, he could hear a man, singing now, his voice lyrical and gentle. Viktor didn't know the song. It didn't sound American and he couldn't hear the words, but the warmth of the man's voice revived his spirits as he nudged himself into the middle of the small audience.

A guitar case lay open in front of the singer, silver coins studding the faded velour. To his foot was attached a tambourine with which he tapped out the beat. Leaning against the amplifier was a white stick.

'And now here's a little song about the men who go a'fishing. It's called *The Shoals of Herring*. It's got no chorus to it and it goes on a bit, but it's one of me favourites. So youse just have to put up with it.' Nimble fingers picked metal strings; a honeyed voice held the tune.

Viktor looked around and saw people swaying to the rhythm. The singer's face gently creased as he leant towards the battered microphone. He wished Nadia was beside him. The song was sweet but too long, and the audience drifted away. 'Does he know?' he thought, 'does he care?' The song finished, and Viktor walked forward to drop a coin into the case.

'Why thank you. Now here's one of me own. I'm a bit of the romantic don't you know?' The musician checked the tuning and applied a capo to the neck of his guitar. Viktor was now one of five listening. The song was about love and being far away. Simple, tender words filled the street and echoed off the build-

ings. It took him a while to distinguish the chorus but he eventually made it out.

> *Your love will carry me to you,*
> *As your love will carry me through life.*
> *My love will hold you close to me,*
> *Sleep soft, my darling wife.*

Viktor looked around the emptying street and thought of Nadia
and Volodia. He wanted to hold them, hug them, be with them.
He had never been this homesick before, so completely alone and
despondent.

The song came to an end. Now Viktor was the only person
listening and his hands clapped light approval.

'Well, I might as well call it a day.' The singer unplugged the
lead from the soundbox, coiled it up and fumbled for his guitar
case.

'Can I help you?' Viktor offered shyly.

'Why sir, that would a truly Christian act, so it would! You
sound like you're a long way from home yourself. Is that a bit of
the Russian I can hear in your voice? I always forget where I
leave everything. The Missus usually helps me pack up, but I've
finished early this evening. She'll be along soon. So is it Russia?'

'Yes, Murmansk. I'm here for a few days.'

'I've never been to your great country, but you've got some of
our Celtic sadness to you; that and the booze of course. They're
a fatal combination.'

Viktor looked at his eyes. They didn't seem milky or deformed,
yet clearly he was struggling to see things. The singer smiled.
'Poor Blind Pete, that's what they call me round here. Three
names and none of them right. My wife's got some money, me
real name's Padraig, and I'm only partially sighted. That stick
over there lets people know I'm coming,' he added, waving a
nicotine-stained finger at a dustbin. 'Can I buy you a beer while
we wait for the Missus?'

'That would be kind, but I'm afraid I don't have money to buy
you a drink.'

'Ah, don't worry about that. Let's get this lot bundled up and
we'll go for a wee libation. It's not often I've had a Russian roadie!'
He chuckled and Viktor laughed too, hardly understanding him.

Viktor helped him tie his equipment to a trolley, formerly the property of the Norwegian Post Office. Lengths of elastic cord were stretched around the guitar case, the car battery and the amplifier, and when Pete was satisfied, he tucked his stick under his arm and grabbed hold of Viktor.

'Right, we're off to Murphy's – without doubt the worst drinking hole in Oslo.'

Viktor looked at the pile of equipment. 'What about this?'

'It's as safe as houses. Besides the Missus will pick it up and catch us at the bar. Now I have to warn you – what's your name? Jeez! I should have asked earlier.'

'Viktor. My name is Viktor.'

'Viktor. A pleasure to meet you. Vik the Roadie!' He laughed again. 'Now, about Murphy's, it's the biggest pile of fake wood, sheleilahs and toucans you'll see this side of the Atlantic. I'll be the only authentic Irish thing in the place – and I'm half Scot. I sing there out of desperation when it rains. But me credit's good and they charge me Kerry prices. All they want to hear is *Wac Fol Me Daddio* and *Galway Races*.' Viktor could hardly understand a word he was saying but was happy to have found a friend.

They strode down the pavement, Pete talking and Viktor tilting his head as he strained to hear the Irishman. They walked off the kerb and stumbled. Bone met bone and Viktor shuffled to support Pete, who strode on unperturbed. Viktor took renewed confidence from his half-blind, wholly crazed mentor and realised just how miserable he must have been.

'Now will you just listen to that?'

Viktor strained but could hear nothing above the noise of the traffic.

'That bastard's murdering that song! Mind you, it's the best thing that could happen to it. Keep close,' exhorted Pete as he pushed Viktor through the swing doors and into a wall of people. 'Keep walking – I'll do the talking.' Viktor tapped a few shoulders and smiled meekly but the wall of people remained intact.

'Now you've got to push and shove a bit or we'll have to be applying for planning permission. Make way! Make way! Blind man and Russian guide dog coming through!' A large Norwegian sporting a Notre Dame jacket approached and took Pete's hand.

'Hey Pete, what's up?'

'Why, the sky as always! Per, will you clear us some seats now?' Per obliged and the two men squeezed into a booth. 'Keep your money in your pockets. Per will bring us the drinks.' Viktor looked around the bar. It was only seven o'clock but the party was in full swing.

'So tell me Rick, what are you doing here?'

'No, my name's Viktor. I'm here with Medina...' The words were left hanging in the air as Pete gazed into the middle distance.

'Well, wherever she is you shouldn't leave her for too long. Women stray you know.' Two foaming glasses of Guinness with vodka chasers were brought on a green tray. 'At last. *Na zdorovye* as we say in Kerry!'

'*Na zdorovye*, Pete,' said Viktor, warming to his new-found friend.

As they drank *I'm a Rover Seldom Sober* boomed out of the speakers above their booth. Pete made a passable imitation of having been hit over the head by a baseball bat. Raising his head off the table he asked, 'So where's your lady then?'

Viktor persevered. 'Medina is an organisation that tries to prevent pollution in the Arctic Circle. I'm its Russian delegate.'

'What a bit like the Greens? I thought that they knew what they were up to that lot. But there's no substance – they're all balls and bang your arse!' The man in the Notre Dame jacket came over and spoke into Pete's ear. 'No, I won't play in this miserable hovel. I'm an artist. I'm enjoying the company of one of Russia's leading environmentalists. How dare you disturb me?' Viktor was spellbound.

'I'm a man of peace myself. But you've heard of the IRA?'

The acronym was unintelligible to Viktor who felt he could risk a straight 'no'.

'You must have. The Troubles – the bombing. Can you believe that two dozen drug-crazed idiots, a few hundred Kalashnikovs and fifty kilos of Semtex brought Clinton and Blair scuttling to peace talks?'

Viktor understood him now. 'But they had the television and the Irish vote in the USA. It's not so easy in Murmansk.'

'Guilt and sentiment – they work every time.' Pete raised his arm. 'More drinks for my roadie – he's in danger of talking sense.' A few people came over urging Pete to sing. One man grasped his shoulder but Pete swatted the hand away. 'Get back! I'm no fucking racehorse. It's a crazy old world, Rick. There I was, a happy man living a simple life. Me brothers and I ran a pub in Sneem. A singing pub it was, and we had some good boys come and play. Then one morning I woke up, looked at the door and instead of seeing one, I saw three. I closed my eyes, opened them again and saw five. Jesus! I thought – but it was no hangover. The doc said it would go away but it didn't. So a month later ups we goes to Dublin and the man tells me I've got Papillitis. I'm basically as blind as a bat – but at least I've got points of reference. I can remember things: colours, shapes, vivid images.' He laughed. 'I bet you're one ugly son of a bitch!' He laughed again, and raised his glass. 'Here's to you, my brute of a Russian!' Without pause, he continued, 'And do you know the stupidest thing? I didn't care. I had my friends, my living and,' he held Viktor's shoulder and said conspiratorially, 'listen carefully to me now – you don't need your eyes!'

Viktor, who with the alcohol was newly confident retorted, 'That's crazy! Of course you need your eyes.'

'Viktor, you're a bright man. Think again.' The Notre Dame coat was hovering with a guitar. 'Ah, give me the bloody thing. But I'm not getting on the platform. You can set me up here.' He worked on the tuning. 'This is a cudgel, not an instrument. Well, have you worked it out?'

Viktor was becoming agitated; it was all too frenetic. 'No, you speak too quickly I...'

'Look, there I was as smug as hell. I could play this thing a bit. I could sing a bit, had me fun with the odd American lady and, for Christ's sake, owned a third of the best boozer in Kerry. I had me bum in the butter. Then kaboom! The forty-foot lorry of life knocks me sideways. And look! I still have my friends. I hear better, play better, sing better and – not a word of a lie – I actually see better. Now back to you.' His eyes locked without focusing onto Viktor's face. 'There has to be great things for you, my man. I can sense it. Don't pussy around! It's grand actions that win the day. Some bastard American claimed to have come up with the term, "When you've got them by the balls their hearts and minds will follow." Well, it wasn't an American – it was Eamonn De Valera – and he got rid of the Brits. You show 'em what Rick the Roadie's made of.'

A microphone was thrust in front of Pete's face. 'Three, four –

three, four!' he winked sightlessly at Viktor to test that it was working. 'Original as ever. Now let's empty this place!' He laughed, downed his vodka and started singing *La Marseillaise*.

Viktor saw an elfin-faced blonde girl making her way to the table. She was smiling as she squeezed her way through the crowd to stand beside them. When Pete had finished singing, he sniffed the smoky air and turned to Viktor. 'Meet Ilsa the broad-beamed slapper who masquerades as a wife. I'll just sing a few more my dear, then we'll be off for a frolic!'

'I suppose Pete's told you about seeing better? Well that's as maybe, but he's completely forgotten the gift for listening.' She was enchanting. 'Will you stay for another drink?'

Viktor looked at his watch. He was going to be late. 'No, no – he's been so kind. But I must go. Please say goodbye to him for me.'

He pushed his way through the crowd and onto the street. His long walk around the city had made his feet sore, his one pair of smart shoes being ill-suited to the task. Now, though, he strode with new confidence. He felt that after the despondency of the last day his meeting with the mad Irish singer was in fact part of his destiny, the first rung of the ladder out of despair. He hummed his way from the bar to the Hotel Opera. His time in the Irish bar had left him in the foothills of inebriation. He made no connection with his present condition and his feelings this morning, for this drunkenness was of the friendly variety, the warm empowering ally that would help him in his hour of need. The singer had renewed his confidence; there was a future, he was a somebody in this foreign town, he was capable of much. 'Grand actions win the day' he remembered, and it was in this mood that he entered the meeting of World Environmental Action 2000, Medina's radical splinter group.

Chapter Eleven

Spring came slowly to the Kola Peninsula. The days lengthened and the noonday shadows shortened across the tundra, as the earth revolved ever closer to the sun. The white highway that once was a solid thoroughfare now showed dark boiling pools. Large angular slabs of ice had been squeezed outwards and piled high along the banks, where they shimmered as they melted in the sun's rays. The Volna had become a river once again.

The rise in temperature caused the snow that had blanketed the vast acres to melt, filling the streams that fed the river, and soon a powerful torrent swirled and drove its way south to the sea. The crack and groan of ice replaced the wintry silence of the tundra as the river forced its way downstream. It swept away everything in its path, carrying with it trunks and branches which had broken under the pressure. Fast flowing, it created foaming swirls around boulders as they emerged in the lowering water. The latter days of May witnessed the last remnants of ice and the first signs of green amongst the battered browns of the previous year's dead foliage. It was at this time, when the river dropped back to a steady height and the water temperature rose, that the first salmon started to run upstream from the sea.

On the knoll that overlooked the river as it twisted through the narrow valley, sat the fishing camp. The sun shone on the log cabins that lined the bank in a tidy row. Blankets and bedding swung as they aired in the breeze, windows were propped open and dust was swept through doors, as workers busied themselves in preparation for the fishermen. The staff were young and willing, the work was steady and the food plentiful. Genia watched with detached amusement the comings and goings of the young men and women as they settled into camp life. Pecking orders were established, friendships made and attractions developed as they applied themselves to their tasks. Some had worked at the camp for several years and had stories to tell and pranks to play on the uninitiated. In the main they were open honest types selected by Sergei from the Collective, mostly students or sons and daughters of favoured friends. Pana, Genia's dog, followed him wherever he went, his old battle scar white against his fur. He barked at the newcomers and ignored the camp cats. His mate was in litter again and she lay content under the main hut awaiting the arrival of her pups.

Genia had supervised the work assisted by Valery as the aluminium-hulled fishing boats were hauled from beneath their winter covers. Their outboard engines, which had been packed with grease and oil to prevent rust over winter, were stripped and prepared for service. The helicopter pad was cleared of debris and sheets of corrugated iron were re-bolted to the wooden frame to prevent wheels from sinking into the spongy surface. The windsock was retrieved from the store and the frayed edges, a legacy of several years of battering, were once again repaired. When finally erected, it looked more like a quilt than an aeronautical aid. The drainage pipes were sluiced through and the generator sprang into life at the first push of the starter-motor's button. Darkened bulbs flickered into light, water pumped throughout the camp and the sounds of pop videos were heard from the kitchen windows. In a few days the Camp Manager and Cook would arrive from England, but until then it was Genia's domain.

While the camp staff busied themselves on the bank the reason for their labours were equally active below the surface of the ice that was gradually melting over the White Sea. Under the blue light of the frozen canopy, hundreds of thousands of salmon prepared to return to the river of their creation and so maintain their life cycle. The ice had kept the trawlers away and the salmon had been left over winter to grow in a sea rich with krill and crustacea. As a result these shoals of Arctic salmon were the largest in the world. There was no other feeding ground like it, and this unique harvest provided fishermen with the most prolific run of its kind.

Some unseen signal told the shoals when it was time to leave their saltwater environment and return to the freshwater river of their nascence, and they made their way from the frozen ice cap to the mouth of the river. The *zakroika*, the summer run, was about to start. As the salmon reached the mouth of the river their bodies sensed the presence of fresh water. They ceased eating and focused their energy on migrating their way against the current to the spawning grounds of their birth.

At the end of the first week of preparations Genia decided to take one of the boats and travel upstream to his cabin to see how it had fared in his absence. He needed a night to himself away from the chatter and noise of the camp. He loaded up his box of supplies with kerosene for the lamps and some basic food. He'd catch some grayling for supper, which would taste even better if the wild garlic had started to show. He looked at the cases of vodka in the sealed stores but decided not to succumb. Finally, he left instructions with Valery on how he wanted to find the camp upon his return. He knew well that when the sound of his outboard had faded in the distance the staff would stop work and have a party. There would be pandemonium in the morning as they worked through the job list restoring the camp to an orderly state before his return.

The river was still high and flowing fast. Genia stood with one knee resting on the thwart, his hand on the tiller, as he wove the boat up the slacker water beside the bank avoiding the occasional block of ice. Although he was out of the main flow, the jet outboard often had to be at full throttle to cope with the current. Pana stood in the prow of the boat like a figurehead, mouth open with pleasure, ears flapping, barking at the spray, which from time to time, washed over the bows. Occasionally the hull banged against a submerged obstacle, and Genia scolded himself for forgetting the rocky features of the riverbed. Pana would lurch forward, barely managing to maintain his balance, looking back questioningly at the helmsman, who smiled in reply.

It took them nearly two hours to travel the ten miles to the small log cabin which was Genia's true home. It sat on the junction of the main river with a smaller tributary. Patches of snow still clung to the roof, reluctant to give in to the demands of the season. As he eased the pressure on the throttle, he noticed that the rocky steps that he had created down to the waterside had resisted the corrosive effects of the winter's ice and he edged the boat slowly and gently alongside the small jetty. A cuckoo flew in alarm in a low straight trajectory away across the river from the rowan tree that sheltered the hut. It would have to find some other home to invade. Pana leapt to the shore before the boat reached the jetty and bounded up the steps to sniff out any intruders which might have set up home beneath the hut. Genia dragged the boat up the gravel bank and tied the painter to a tree. He carried his possessions to the steps that led to the door, turning to look downstream, savouring the splendour of what he saw. A few minutes passed before he noticed the vapour in his breath and he decided to light the stove without delay. There was no cloud; it would be a cold night.

Genia and Pana busied themselves in their familiar routine of introducing comfort into their home. Genia collected water while Pana chased away the newly established colony of shrews that had set up home beneath the floorboards. Genia used dried tree moss and wood shavings from the last carving he had made for Volodia for kindling. He wiped dust from the frame that held the boy's photograph as the stove crackled into life. He smiled sadly at the concentration on the boy's face, pictured as he struggled to return his first salmon to the river. 'My darling boy,' he muttered, and picked a rod from the shelf. The grayling would be lying in the slack water under the bank. Pana at first sat beside him, but then found keener interests in the scents that adorned the river's path, leaving his master to fish alone.

The light dimmed and Pana returned to find Genia enjoying once again his natural environment, oblivious to his lack of success. He had moved some way from the hut as he cast the sunken lure downstream, close to the bank. The line tightened and he lifted the rod tip hard to strike the hook home. The rod bent. This was no grayling. His quarry bored deep and lunged back towards the bank. It was a good-sized pike.

'Food for us all Pana! You should have brought your family with you, you selfish hound.' The dog tilted his head to one side, trying to understand the babble from his master's mouth.

The pike weighed over eight pounds and once on the bank Genia had quite a tussle trying to hold on to it, wary of the rows of inverted teeth. Pana ran around him, barking at the fish as it slapped and struggled. At last it was dispatched with several blows from a rock. The pair made their way back to the jetty, the pike dangling from Genia's hand, Pana licking the fish's

114

scales as they walked. Genia squatted by the river to gut the fish with his knife. His hands felt warm in the water, and he noticed for the first time how much the air temperature had dropped. He looked downstream where mist swirled like steam from a cup. His task finished, he walked up the steps to the hut and opened the door where the warmth brought life to his numb cheeks. Pana lay down near the stove.

Genia carved long fillets from the fish keeping the head to take back to the camp. The staff would nail the mask to the trophy wall. He simmered the flesh with wild herbs and dried spices from his larder, while potatoes boiled in another pot. Later, sharing the meal with Pana, he remarked, 'Too much salt in the fish, Pana. What do you think?' The dog bolted his food in happy ignorance.

Genia decided to take one last look outside and was rewarded with a clear star-laced sky. The mist had vanished and the moon was rising behind the hut. A heavy frost crunched under his boots, and ice crystals sparkled on Pana's coat as he returned from his last forage in the undergrowth.

'Come on, time for bed.' The dog was already inside by the time the words were spoken.

Genia stared at the heavens and breathed the cold, clear air deep into his lungs. He breathed ever deeper and, light-headed with the oxygen, felt that he could almost hear the stars above the sound of the running water. Murmansk was another world.

He was in his shirtsleeves, and he waited until the cold became uncomfortable before returning inside to read. The cassette recorder played a well-worn tape of highlights from *Cosi fan Tutti*, the opera's mellifluous sounds seeming to coat the rough-hewn timber walls. Genia stretched out on his bed, his head propped up against several pillows as he read. Memories of the events of the last few weeks tried in vain to disturb him, but his determination warded them off. He had resolved to address them in the morning, but for now he experienced the simple comforts that brought him peace and happiness. Half an hour later the lamp flickered and the tape came to an end. He hardly noticed the metallic click from the machine as he settled with Pana, who had crept onto the broad bed and tucked up beside him. The book lay half-open, half-read on his lap as he slept a tranquil sleep. He was happy to be home.

He awoke before dawn, aware of the warmth of another body beside him. Realising that it was Pana, Genia pushed him off the bed and the dog tumbled to the floor. Genia groaned with the effort of sitting upright, his back letting him know that he had slept awkwardly. His mild irritation was greeted by the submissive wag of a tail, and he responded by patting the furry head. They were friends once again. 'If only all relationships were this easy,' he muttered.

The last embers had died in the stove and frost lined the windows. He reached for his boots, which were stiff with cold and made fire-lighting his first priority. He placed some logs into the stove, sprinkling some kerosene from the lamp over them. He threw in a match, which ignited the vapour and sent a whoosh of flame up the chimney, and out of the stove door. He leapt back – but not quickly enough. He could smell singed hair as he sat laughing on the floor. He reminded himself of how many times he'd instructed the camp staff never to light fires this way. Pana crouched in a corner growling.

'You've seen me do this before. There, it's warmer already. Breakfast is going to be a feast this morning. I've brought some duck eggs and we have some dried mushrooms from last year. Now, how many of your relatives have omelette for breakfast you ungrateful mongrel? None, I can tell you. If it weren't for me you would have been drowned at birth.' He talked to the dog as he busied himself collecting water. The dawn had just broken and he went to wash in the river. Stripping off his shirt and kneeling on the bank, he plunged his head and shoulders into the water. He swung his head back and a cockscomb of spray flew from his head. He let out a shuddering roar as he splashed cold water into his armpits and over his chest. He cleaned his teeth with his fingers. Pana sniffed a nearby tree oblivious to his master's display of virility. Returning to the hut they found that the frost had thawed on the windows and had been replaced with condensation from the water simmering on the stove. He poured some of the steaming water into a plastic bowl, shaved and put on a clean shirt from his bag. Music filled the room from the cassette player. 'You see Pana, it's all about the simple pleasures. Why do we always make life so difficult?' The canine brow wrinkled again as Genia cracked duck eggs into a bowl.

Breakfast finished, and his home's simple contents returned to their orderly state, he walked upstream with Pana, his hands thrust deep into his pockets, his lightheartedness replaced by brooding.

He had first come here several years ago, and it was here that he had finally found contentment after the trauma he had suffered in Afghanistan. But now in Murmansk, Volodia's spent body lay buried, Nadia had locked herself into her own world of grief, their father was teetering on the edge of depression and Viktor was in the throes of a bitter drunken denial. Why was he here in the Kola now when he could help his family? Sergei would have understood, and would probably have insisted that he stay at home.

He tripped on a birch branch that lay flattened across the path, stumbling awkwardly, his hands still in his pockets. He grunted as his shoulder took the brunt of the fall against a rotten stump. Picking himself up, he swore and strode on. Normally he would have pushed the timber to one side but on this morning, he left the obstruction alone.

Genia had done all he could to help Nadia and Viktor, but he was incapable of delivering the one thing that would make any difference. In Afghanistan he had been taught to accept that life was characterised by suffering, that to wish that someone had not died was also to wish that they had not been born. Genia had ranted at the apparent injustice of Volodia's death, but he ultimately found comfort through faith. His sober approach to Volodia's dying had eventually brought resentment from Nadia and alienated him from his family. His way was viewed as alien. He strode on, muttering to himself while Pana walked obediently a few feet behind, his nose and tail down – he knew his mood.

Genia crossed the strip of land that divided the two rivers and walked back to his cabin. He was more composed, and reluctantly set about preparing for his return to the camp. He wished he could have spent another night at the cabin but there was work to be done. He would not sleep again under this roof for at least a month, although he would pass tantalisingly close with fishermen who wanted to fish the upper reaches. He brought some kindling and logs inside to dry, wiped the windows and closed the door behind him. Pana was already in the boat as he untied the painter and pushed the boat back over the shingle towards the water. He climbed aboard and pulled the engine into life.

When the engine was idling he pushed the bows out into the main stream. Dog and master assumed their habitual positions as the craft picked up the current that swept them away. It would take them just over an hour to reach the camp.

Travelling downstream, Genia noticed a wisp of smoke rising from a clump of firs beside the tail of Governor's Pool. He steered the craft into the bank and Pana leapt onto the bank barking. Genia knew that the poachers would have scattered at the sound of his engine. It was a still day and they would have had plenty of time to scramble up the bank. They would be well into the wasteland beyond by now. He decided not to chase them, but to see whether they had left anything in their panic. He called Pana back to him and found the poachers' fire. It was obvious that at least three people had spent the night there. Empty tins, and the inevitable vodka bottles littered the area. They were recreational poachers. They had grabbed most of their belongings, but Genia took what was left to the boat. He walked along the bank to the slack water looking for the string that would reveal the keep net. The poachers may not have had time to grab it before his arrival. If they had, they would not be able to run far carrying a heavy load of fish.

He found the cord and pulled the net towards him. There were twelve salmon, which he returned to the river. One that was bleeding from the gills had to be killed – it wouldn't have survived. He put the keep net and the dead fish into the boat and made a final inspection of the bank, noticing where the purple sheen of fish scales silvered the rocks. Ready to leave, the pike's head in the bows of the boat caught his eye. He returned to the poachers' camp and placed the angry jaw over the neck of a half-full vodka bottle. They would be planning to return for that.

'Skulka!' he barked into the woods. He used the Russian word for the river's fiercest predator, the pike, as he set the head firmly on the glass bottle. 'Come on Pana, the new season has begun.'

Genia was in good spirits as he rounded the bend in the river that led to the home waters. Slowing down as he navigated his way through the shoal of rocks at the top of the camp pool, he smiled as Pana started barking for his mate, who would normally be on the bank greeting any arrival.

'She's having your pups. She'll be under the hut and won't want you disturbing her.'

He nosed the boat into the mooring as a man appeared from one of the huts, strode across the grass to the bank and stood with his hands on his hips as Genia tied the boat to the post.

'Where the hell have you been?' It was a tone and manner of voice Genia had come across several times before, more brittle and demanding than its American counterpart. Genia put his hand to his ear and pointed to the river, miming incomprehension, although he had received the Camp Manager's message only too well. He guessed this would be Tim, the representative sent by *Touch the Wild* to look after their customers. Genia found himself asking why he hadn't accepted Sergei's offer, when the man spoke again.

'It's Genvia, isn't it? Where have you been? This place looks like a gypsy encampment.' Pana was now ashore and barking around the man. Genia carried his load up the bank holding the salmon through the gills.

'Well, are you Genvia?'

'My name is Genia.' He looked at the wiry, strutting figure in front of him and wondered how the British ever got their reputation for natural leadership.

Tim was beyond listening. 'We arrived here this morning to find the place looking as if a bomb had hit it. You're meant to be the man in charge. What *is* going on?'

Genia decided that he wasn't going to let the man's insecurities wash away the peace of the last two days.

'I am happy to meet you. I didn't expect you until tomorrow. I am sorry I was not here but I was up-river last night and found poachers on my way back.' He pointed to the salmon and the keep net. Tim eyed the fish suspiciously and, although mollified by Genia's smile and apology, had already decided that he was going have to take control.

'All right. Get yourself sorted out and then we'll have a walk around the camp. I want to have a look at the Home Beat before dinner so that I can get the lie of the land. Ah!' his tone softened, 'Here's Bumble.' A tidy, bubbly figure wearing jeans and an apron bounced over to them. 'Bumble – meet Genvia. He's the head man here.'

'Hello. Isn't this place just magic? It's just like home!' An open,

119

amicable, freckly greeting revived Genia's beliefs in the British. She offered her warm, flour-covered hand, which he shook. 'Oops – sorry!' She wiped her hand on her apron. 'I'm getting to grips with bread-making. It's a pleasure to meet you. My brother, Fergus Maclean, has told me a lot about you. He fished here with Mr Cummings a few years ago.'

The relationship made sense. Her brother was equally affable and had taught Genia how to tie salmon flies. One happy evening they created a fly they christened the *Volna Allsorts* – a garish mixture of a bit of everything in Fergus's box. Genia still kept his in a tobacco tin. They had become good friends. 'Do you fish, Bumble?' Genia asked, but before she could answer, Tim interjected.

'We all do, but we haven't got time for that now. Come on, there's work to be done.' Genia and Bumble exchanged glances.

'Tim, what time do you want to eat?' Bumble asked.

'Let's make it nine. We'll all eat together tonight, Genvia, don't you think? Get all the guides and camp staff together.' He had a good face that was spoiled by a weak mouth and bad teeth. It was hard to age him, but Genia thought that he was probably between thirty-five and forty; his hair was fine and already receding.

'Sure,' he replied, just as Kim had done to Sergei in the Arctic Hotel so many weeks ago. Genia was surprised to find that he could ever have learnt anything useful from Kim.

Bumble returned to the kitchen and Genia noticed one of the younger guides skulking behind one of the huts.

Tim continued, 'I was going to suggest that we all have a drink, but it looks as if your merry men did enough of that last night. There was one of them honking as our chopper landed. Not a good start, I can tell you.'

'Sure, no problem.' He tuned away. The Englishman had still not told him his name and Genia was damned if he was going to ask him. He decided to use his well-tried method for dealing with foreign people who treated him impolitely. Receive the request, smile, nod the head affirmatively, say 'No problem' – and then go on doing what you were going to do anyway. Kim had given him an extra word to stretch out the response. This without doubt was going to be his last year. Tim would ensure that.

Genia called the young guide over to him and handed him the fish. He asked him to find Valery. He needed to talk to him before he had another confrontation with Tim. Genia walked back to the cluster of huts where the camp staff were quartered and dropped the poachers' equipment outside his hut. In the winter he had the hut to himself but during the fishing season he had to share it with Valery. Inside it was unrecognisable and he felt some empathy with Tim.

'Genia it wasn't too bad, I promise you,' the words had started before Valery entered the hut. 'How were we to know he would turn up when he did?'

Genia dropped his knapsack on his bunk, looked around at the mess in the hut and spread his palms towards Valery. The silent criticism was sufficient for the Valery to give a gesture that meant 'I know, I know,' in return.

'How bad was it?' Genia looked at Valery's guilt ridden face. 'That bad, mmhh?' He paused, then asked. 'Did anyone touch the sealed stores?' If the stores had been breached, Valery would be out of the camp.

'No, I made sure they didn't. A boatload of guides came from the lower camp and they had more than enough. They only just got away as the helicopter landed. There was a bit of a scuffle – that cleaner from last year came with them and tempers ran high.'

'Are any of our lot hurt?'

'Nothing visible, but it was just as well it took place outside or we might have had some windows to replace.'

Genia eased the tension. 'Tim caught me unawares too, but you get this mob cleaned up and let them know I'm after them. We're all eating together tonight, and not until nine. Make sure everyone feels hungry. If he offers vodka I don't want anyone touching it. Just a beer each.' They were interrupted by the sound of a voice.

'Genvia, where are you?' It was Tim, still fifty yards from the hut and still with an edge to his voice.

'Genvia?' laughed Valery.

'At least he's trying. I'll see you later.'

He walked out to Tim, who was by the river trying unsuccessfully to move two cats from their favourite bench. 'Ah, there you are. Can we do something about these? I hate cats.'

'Sure, no problem.'

'And it looks like you've got a sick dog under the camp hut. We can't have that flea-ridden thing lurking around under where

121

we eat. It's some way under – I tried to prod it with a broom handle; all it did was growl at me.'

'Sure.'

Having tried both responses, he decided that the shorter version was actually better. It sounded more positive but actually committed less. The additional 'no problem' could carry an implied interpretation of an actual intention to perform the task. He would use Kim's method for a day or two and see how it went.

The doors and windows were all newly painted. A row of duckboards joined each hut to the main camp hut where they ate and drank. Most of the time this wooden pathway wasn't needed, but after a few days of consistent rain the spongy ground turned to mud. Tim carried out a full inspection of the camp. Genia was pleased to find that he had a better understanding of the generator and pumps than most of his predecessors.

Tim told Genia that he had been brought up on a farm and had always enjoyed tinkering with things. Genia thought back to the days when he first met these British farmers. He had been amazed that they could afford to travel. It was only when Bumble's brother had explained the significant difference in the meaning of the words that he understood. 'Genia,' Fergus had begun, 'a person who farms usually owns half the county. A farmer is the poor sod who works for him.' He had continued, 'In the case of my family, to make it more confusing, my father used to farm, but now – because of the way things are – I'm a farmer who farms government grants. Work that out if you can, it's beyond me!' Dropping the momentary solemnity, he had resumed his light-hearted manner. 'Come on, let's see if we can catch another one.' Genia smiled as he remembered the words and pictured the face that would rather smile than do anything else. He could still see the bulk of Fergus's shoulders and the wake his thighs created, as he ploughed through the water in his waders, smoke swirling from his cigarette.

Tim broke into Genia's reverie. 'Right, let's go and have a look down river shall we?'

'Sure.'

They walked back to the bank. Tim jumped into the boat and gave a rudimentary inspection of the high-powered outboard.

'These are jet, not prop, but they work just the same don't they?'

Genia nodded.

'Right, you push her off and I'll start her up.'

Genia was presented with an interesting dilemma. If he pushed them out into the current, they would be swept at least fifty yards downstream before the boat started. The river was flowing hard and the engine was still warm. Tim might just get it started before the next line of rocks. As he untied the mooring line he decided to offer assistance.

'Do you want me to start the engine?'

'No, I've used one of these in Cornwall. We'll be fine. Push us off will you?'

Genia leapt on board, pushing the bank away and sat in the bows. Pana leapt in at the last second, his hind legs scrabbling for a hold. A small gallery of camp staff emerged from their various duties and lined the bank. Amongst them he could see the stripes of Bumble's apron. Tim opened the choke, applied full throttle and pulled hard on the cord, an act that was greeted by a spluttering cloud of white fumes. Above the mechanical noise could be heard a wholly human 'Bugger!'

Tim looked at Genia in the bows who gave a Sergei-like shrug; his evening at the Arctic Hotel was paying off handsomely. The forces of nature were not to be denied, and the boat started to circle its way down the fast stream, leaving the camp at one moment on the left, the next on the right. Three more pulls on the engine's starter and enough was enough; they were getting ever closer to the rocks.

'Tim, you should let me help you. The mixture is too rich and the engine is still warm. She can be very temperamental. She's an old engine – you weren't to know.' Tim thought for a moment, his face set with a stubbornness that showed his mouth at its worst. He looked up and saw the line of people on the bank, most of them laughing. 'You sod!' The words were audible for some distance.

Has he calmed down a bit?' Valery asked. Genia was surprised to smell the mixed scents of shampoo and soap, and realised that the guide must have his eyes on Bumble. He wouldn't make that effort for the local staff.

'He's fine. He knows more than most – it was just a bad start. Is there something you want to tell me?' he asked, audibly sniffing the air.

'I just thought I would set an example to the others, that's all.' Genia didn't need light to know that there were blushes on his cheeks. Valery would still look a mess though, his hair wild, the rest of him dishevelled – but he always had a girlfriend.

'Is your English good enough do you think?'

Valery pretended not to hear, busying himself with the outboard.

'Bumble may work for the camp but her brother was a guest, and is a friend of our top customer. Do you want me to say more?'

In the darkness Genia could just make out Valery's 'I know, I know' gesture for the second time that day.

The guides stood silently in a group holding tins of Heineken, leaving the glasses that Bumble had laid out on the table untouched. The five domestic staff sat transfixed by the television screen, watching a recording of last year's pop music awards. As Genia entered, Bumble was busy working at the stove and Tim was trying to coax conversation out of Valery. Tim had a glass of whisky in his hand and was clearly more relaxed.

'Ah, it's himself! Would you like some of this? I managed to get it here without breaking it, but it doesn't seem too popular with the others.'

'Thank you, that would be good.' The guides all noticed his acceptance and took exaggerated sips from their cans, as Tim poured a large measure of single malt into a glass, which he handed to Genia.

Tim took him aside. 'They don't say much do they?'

'They're fine. Not many speak good English, except for Valery. They aren't happy about this morning. They didn't know you were coming.'

'I know. It hasn't been a great start has it? Well never mind. How's it coming, Bumble? Are we about there?'

'We are indeed.' Her hair was piled on her head and her face gleamed above a T-shirt printed with the legend *The White Stuff*. 'Come on, it's ready to go. Valery, will you help me with one of these?'

Valery had tried to do something with his hair, but it wasn't doing him any favours. Whatever he had found to plaster the curls down, it made he look more like an apprentice undertaker than a hunter-guide. The girls in the corner found it amusing. One of them said something that made them all laugh. Two large steaming bowls of salmon mixed with rice and sliced hard-boiled eggs were placed on the table. Bumble picked a flake of fish from one of the bowls and slipped it into her mouth.

'This salmon is so delicious, it's almost a shame to cook it!'

She returned to the oven and produced a large loaf of bread, which she asked Valery to cut into slices. This brought more laughter from the girls, who had never seen him do anything in the kitchen before. He set about the loaf with a surgeon's concentration.

'Right, it's TV off then, and who sits where?' Tim ventured.

'Tim, what we normally do is turn the volume down and let everyone sit where they want. We're happier that way.'

'Yes. Quite right, I see,' and then, struggling to have one successful notion added, 'I've put some of these in the deep freeze.' He went to the big chest freezer and pulled out three half-pint bottles of vodka. Ice formed immediately on the glass, obliterating the labels. Genia could feel numerous pairs of eyes trained on him.

'Tim that's very kind. We would all like some.'

'It's called Rasputin or something.' He rubbed the ice from the label and tried to decipher the contents. 'Whatever it's called, I'm sure it's a good honest drop.'

Tim unscrewed the cap and started pouring. His actions were greeted with the first warm response he had received since his arrival. Cans of beer that had been nursed were emptied in seconds, and glasses pushed forward. The steam in the kitchen was having a curious effect on Valery's hair, which was now springing free from its chemical confines, causing more laughter from his friends. He was unaware as his eyes focused on the cook.

A newly coy Bumble said to Genia, 'Fergus will be so pleased when I tell him that you are still here. He sent you a message, but I don't think I know you well enough to pass it on.'

Genia laughed. 'I imagine he said, "Give Boris a kick up the arse from me!" although it was probably less polite.' He did a fair imitation of Fergus' booming voice.

Bumble beamed. 'It was just that – with a few added suggestions if you didn't help me get my first Russian fish. He's shameless my brother! Why do we let him get away with it? He said he sent you some photographs of his visit. Have you got them in the camp?'

'They are at my hut higher up the river. I will pick them up next time I'm there – maybe tomorrow. Do you know, when Fergus first arrived he upset me?'

'Why, what happened?'

'He refused to call me by my name. He kept calling me Boris. On the second day I told him that I was upset, and that I was too old to be called names. He looked really hurt and said, "But I'm only rude to people I like. Don't you see?" That evening he had one of the cleaners put a bottle of whisky on my bed. We never spoke about it again, but he still called me Boris. He's the only person who I would ever let do that.'

'He's a big softy at heart.'

The kitchen filled with the clatter of steel, china and glass, all being put to their best domestic uses. The bowls of kedgeree disappeared swiftly, and crumbs were all that remained of the loaf. The guides sat back in their chairs, drank and rolled cigarettes. Some of the girls chatted, the others looked at the television screen tapping their fingers and mouthing the words to last year's hits. Tim sat at the top of the table, his face flushed with heat, alcohol and the first signs of friendship. He smiled contentedly in a way that he imagined some ancestor would have done, many years ago in a foreign land, in service of the empire.

'Genvia, have one of these.' He offered a cigar. 'They're small but delicious. I'm afraid I don't stretch to the thigh-rubbed variety.'

Genia declined. One of the guides asked Genia a question, which caused amusement around the table. 'What are they saying?'

'They are asking me why you call me a brand of light bulb and not my normal name.'

'What do they mean?'

'My name is Genia. What you call me is something different.'

'Oh God. I'm sorry – Ge-n-ia.'

There was laughter from the guides as they pointed at Tim who asked, 'What's all that about now?'

'The boat this afternoon. They want to know if you can swim?'

There was an uneasy pause. He replied by laughing and picking up a bottle of vodka. 'You tell them that there's a bottle of this for anyone who rescues me.'

Genia translated. A reply came back with more laughter. 'What did they say? What did they say?'

'Well, politely translated, they said, "we'll be drunk all the time."'

Tim made all the outward signs of finding humour in the remark.

Chapter Twelve

The evening on the boat had brought about a change in Jody and Greg's relationship. There had been a re-balancing which tilted the scales in Jody's favour; she was less willing to go along with Greg's authority – less compliant. It was in the small issues that it was most noticeable, whether to go into New York, whether to play tennis or what they were going to eat. The daily proposals that Greg would make and to which Jody would normally acquiesce she now found herself suggesting alternatives. Greg saw this as a power struggle and one that he had to win. He tried to retain the status quo by using his old tactics of petulance and tantrums, but Jody was newly immune to them.

He knew that the trip to Russia was pivotal in his future and did all he could to obstruct her plans. His office temporarily mislaid her visa. He exaggerated stories of kidnap threats, and finally he suggested that they went to Mexico instead. The transparency of his efforts made her more resolute. She patiently counted the hours until the car would arrive and take her and her fishing equipment to JFK Airport.

One morning, she got out the photo albums of her childhood and college, and on each page she saw her face full of laughter, her natural exuberance clear in every image. She then took out the photographs of her time with Greg, and saw in each carefully staged scene, whether it had been Thanksgiving, Christmas, Hallowe'en or the Fourth of July, that there lay a shadow of disquiet under each forced smile. Each picture contained issues. They came alive to her as she looked. Greg upset with so and so. Greg delayed in Los Angeles. There was always an undercurrent. Even their honeymoon had been shadowed by his arguments with the hotel management. She rued the wasted years and determined that her life going forward would not be lived under this man's shadow. As each hour passed she felt her burden lighten.

The limousine arrived early and the driver loaded the boot. Jody knew in her heart that this was the end of their relationship and felt tears well up. It was the end of a chapter in her life. She had no plans for the future. She looked at the Lincoln's open door and thought of the adventure ahead. 'Go girl,' she said. 'Go while you can. Go girl!' She had made her decision, she was in control. She had found a determination that she had not felt in years.

The car swept out of the drive and she didn't look back.

She was welcomed like a daughter by Michael who hugged her to him when she arrived at the Cummings' house in Knightsbridge.

'Ah, Jody! If only your old father could be here it would complete the picture.' She, Michael and Ginny had a quiet supper together, talking about their early days.

Greg had only occasionally entered the conversation, and it was clear by the lukewarm interest that his presence was not going to be missed by Michael. Ginny had asked all the usual polite questions and offered her regrets that he was unable to be with them, but Jody knew that Ginny could tell that the story about his work commitments wasn't true.

It was a happy evening and she went to bed feeling a sense of excitement that she hadn't had for a long time. She hadn't had to worry about Greg, what he was saying or how he was going to act. This was just her and her friends going to a river that her father would have loved. She was tired and soon fell asleep, waking at five, when a breakfast tray was brought to her room. She was packed and ready before anyone else in the house.

The black cab splashed to a halt in front of the Northolt passenger building. Jody watched the frantic activity of the two passengers as they tried to organise themselves. Michael had been simmering for the last fifteen minutes as the pilot had informed him that the departure slot was in jeopardy. Fergus and Simon had closed a night club only two hours earlier and had not left enough time to collect their bags, change and reach the airfield by the appointed six-fifteen.

Michael was struggling to contain his irritation at seeing

the state of the pair as they tumbled out of the taxi, but Gary couldn't resist a remark. 'If this is the heir to the Cummings dynasty, I think I'll put my money elsewhere. Sandra, pass me the phone. I'm sure that Soros fella will take my call.'

Steve was just relieved to see them and immediately contacted the pilot to tell him that they would make their slot. Fergus kept his head down, fumbling with his luggage, whilst Simon took the brunt of his father's criticism. Michael's voice echoed through the departure hall. '...and don't give me any of that "I don't do mornings" nonsense, you bugger.' He turned round and found Fergus peeling off an old label. 'And as for you Fergus sodding Maclean. Remember you're here under sufferance. A short notice invitation, a stop gap, a convenience, a glorified ghillie – have it as you will, but you are bottom of the food chain here, and don't forget it. God, what was I thinking of? I must have some other friends who'd take a week in Russia at short notice. I swore never again after your last visit. It was obviously too much to hope that you would have grown up by now.'

'Yes, sir. Good morning, sir. We encountered a few problems leaving London but we're here now – all ship-shape and correct. These cabbies – you can't trust them, can you?' He turned and addressed the rest of the party with a flourish of his hand. 'Good morning, one and all. I suggest we leave the formalities until we've got our bums on the leather, as we seem to be running a tad late.'

'Stop blathering and get yourself organised, you arse!'

'Yes sir. Right away sir.'

By way of diversion, Ginny explained to Jody that this was the airport where the Prince of Wales had flown from to collect the body of his Princess, but Jody was far too amused by Fergus and Michael to listen. She couldn't help but be entertained by the antics of the thirty-five year old as he charmed Michael out of his anger.

Learjet G-TEDD applied full throttles and accelerated down the south-west runway at Northolt towards the suburban sprawl that surrounded the airport, banking hard to avoid Heathrow only a few miles beyond. On board the eight passengers were in various states of preparedness and excitement. Michael sat next to Ginny holding her hand, as he always did on take-off and landing. Her head nestled onto his shoulder. Sandra and her husband, Gary, peered through the small window catching the few last glimpses of the bungalows and semi-detached houses as they were lost in the cloud base – a poorer, blander replica of their Sydney home. Jody sat next to Steve on a bench seat. She had already unfastened her seat belt and scrunched her legs under her and was flicking through the latest copy of *Field and Stream*. At the back Simon Cummings was already half asleep and next to him was the seemingly comatose figure of Fergus Maclean, his head lolling against the headrest with his mouth wide open. His snores were audible above the straining engines.

The aircraft bumped and bounced as it climbed through the cloud turbulence. Ginny squeezed Michael's hand and he responded by patting her shoulder and leaning over to kiss her head. She smiled, as she had a hundred times before, comforted by his tender consideration. He eased further into the seat, enjoying the firmness of the leather and in anticipation of the breakfast that would shortly be delivered. The stewardess had already started work in the galley and the smell of coffee and bacon soon wafted into the cabin. Fergus awoke from his slumbers, for his nostrils had received messages causing happy expectancy in his brain that could not be disregarded. A sideways glance at Simon confirmed that there would be all the more for him.

The aircraft reached its cruising altitude and breakfast was served to light-hearted chatter and laughter, most of it directed at Simon and Fergus. Soon the Lear pierced the cloud layer and they were greeted by a bright blue sky. Simon reached for his sunglasses and Fergus felt he could look the world in the face again.

'Why don't you ease the cork on a bottle of fizz to liven up the orange juice?' Fergus asked the stewardess as she served him. 'I'm sure our leader won't mind. God, those sausages look good. Si, do you want yours?' Simon groaned, and Fergus gestured for the girl to put some more on his plate. 'And mustard please, English mustard.' She smiled and returned to the galley where the gentle hiss of escaping gas could just be heard. She reappeared with a napkin-wrapped bottle. Gary saw the bottle and pushed his glass towards her.

'Don't mind if I do. Cheers, Mikey!' Gary's leathery hand cradled the glass. Years of outback sun had taken their toll on flesh that had become as rough as mottled bark. 'How about you San, would you like a drop?' His wife shook her head sleepily.

Michael smiled. 'My pleasure Gary.' He turned to Ginny. 'My darling, would you like a glass?'

'No. I'll have some later. We've got a long day – or should I say week – ahead of us.' She gestured at Simon and Fergus before her head nestled into his shoulder again.

The bottle made its way to Fergus, who had poured the remains of his orange juice into the sleeping Simon's coffee cup. 'Ah, bless you nurse! Fill her up. I could never see the point of fruit juice for breakfast. It's almost as bad as cereal.' He lightly touched her hand and whispered, 'Why don't you leave the bottle here? We don't want that old Aussie overdoing it. They can be a bit thirsty, that lot.' He gave a conspiratorial wink as he spoke. She laughed as she turned away, holding firmly on to the bottle.

Jody made an attempt to read her magazine but was too excited to concentrate. She flicked through the pages, idly looking at the pictures. In no time at all, they were crossing the Norwegian coastline, well on their way to Murmansk.

The pilot throttled back the engines and the Learjet started its descent, penetrating the cloud layer and leaving the blue sky behind. It was early June, but sleet and rain would greet them as they disembarked.

Steve returned from the cockpit. 'It's a cold day in Murmansk. If you've got an extra pullover put it on.' He crouched down next to Michael. 'I've spoken to the ground staff. Our helicopter only landed a few minutes ago. We'll be on the ground for approximately fifteen minutes as long as we aren't delayed by Immigration.'

'What about the weather to Volna?'

'It's a low cloud base, but we should get over the mountains without too many detours. They know you want to get there ASAP. When we land, I'll disembark first and meet the local cover. I've already spoken to them on the radio and they sound pretty clued up. They tried to get Immigration to clear us on board, but the Russians weren't going for it. It was a smart idea though. I'll hand the passports and visas in, and then come back when I'm happy with everything. If I'm not happy I'll stay in the terminal and you'll taxi back to a holding point some way away from main buildings, until we agree what to do.' He showed Michael his walkie-talkie. 'The pilot has got the other half of this and is briefed. Is that OK?'

'Received loud and clear.'

'Is there a problem darling?' Ginny touched his arm.

'No, just the usual security.'

Jody looked out of the window to catch her first glimpse of Russia, enjoying the anticipation that every fisherman feels at nearing the river. Michael had told her that the previous year their party had caught over four hundred salmon in one week. He had added quickly, '...but of course it's not about numbers.' Her swift reply, 'Oh yeah?' had made him laugh. She was trying to remember the last trip that she had made without Greg. She had forgotten the enjoyment of travelling alone, even within a group. Michael and Ginny were good hosts and put everyone at their ease. She was going to enjoy the week, she knew it.

The tyres gave a high-pitched squeal of complaint as they touched down on the main runway. Much to the pilot's embarrassment they bounced their way along the concrete to a halt. It was not his fault, for the once pristine surface was suffering from years of neglect; the ice-riven strip treated all aircraft with the same indifference.

'Have you seen those things?' Gary pointed to the ageing helicopters and biplanes that were strewn around the airfield. Flapping tarpaulins failed to protect the cannibalised engines from the elements. 'We're not flying to this river in one of those bastards, are we?'

'That's nothing, Gary. Ours will have just been recovered from a ditch somewhere,' came from Fergus from the rear of the plane.

The windows smeared with sleety rain as the passengers busied themselves with preparing for arrival. Fergus elbowed Simon into life.

'Come on, Lightning. It's time for ordeal by helicopter.'

Simon wiped his sunglasses from his nose and stretched his legs. Yawning, he blinked and peered out of the window.

'My God! It's a hell hole!'

'Right now, listen up everybody!' Michael stood up. 'We've arrived. Steve will go off ahead of us to sort out the formalities.

We will wait until he comes back before checking through Customs. It won't take long, and then we will board the helicopter that will take us to the river. If there are any local problems with officials, or anyone else for that matter, Steve is in control, is that clear? Fergus wake up! Is that clear?'

'Yes, sir.'

'Thank you.'

Steve returned to the aircraft. The lenses in his glasses had misted up, and he wiped them with a handkerchief as he addressed everyone.

'Right, we're all ready to go. If you could bring all your hand luggage we've got a short walk into the building. The main luggage will go through separately and you'll be asked to identify it before we board the helicopter. If there are any problems, please let me sort them out.'

'He's not exactly James Bond, is he?' Fergus joked to Jody.

'He's a nice guy. He seems to know what he's doing.' Jody still hadn't got the measure of Fergus.

'Yes, I'll give you that. "He's not much, but he's our horse." I've always rather fancied myself doing the cloak and dagger bit. Fergus Maclean – it would look pretty good on the MI5 register. Ah well, another missed opportunity! I always saw myself as a born leader, but the Army declined my offer to join them.'

'I can't blame them. I wouldn't follow you – even out of curiosity!' Gary laughed as he made his way down the stairs.

'I'll have you know that I've served my time down under, Gary, working on a property in the middle of nowhere. I think they were rather fond of me by the time I left.'

'It's strange what emotions an imminent departure can induce.'

Fergus pouted. 'I know you don't mean that Michael, but it still hurts.'

The four blades of the transport helicopter hung like lines in a Dali painting. The battered blue paintwork and streams of dirt from the exhaust fans completed the image of a machine more comfortable on the ground than in the air. People milled around the hulking frame, some in a huddle having a last cigarette, the others watching the activities of the baggage handlers as they loaded the large blue trunks that contained the week's additional food and wine supplies. Gary walked some distance from the helicopter so that he could fit its bulk into the viewfinder of his camera. He returned shaking his head.

'I thought you were joking!' he said to Fergus. 'God, it's ugly!'

'It all comes back to me. I hate these things at the best of times. It's not exactly a Jet Ranger is it?'

'Steve, what's' the story on this thing?'

'Better than it looks. They're the Russian Army's workhorses. It's capable of carrying three times more than we've loaded on it without a murmur; it's just a bit agricultural that's all. The pilots are the best available. They can land it on a sixpence.'

'They sometimes have to,' added Fergus.

'Right, we're all loaded. We're ready to board when you are Michael.' Steve shepherded his charges up the battered metal staircase and handed each person a set of ear protectors as they passed. They each filtered to sit by a window except for Ginny, who sat next to Michael. Jody was glad to be off the exposed tarmac and shivered as she curled herself into the seat, strapping the belt loosely over her lap. There was no door to the cockpit and she caught odd words of Russian as the pilots chatted. Only one of the three-man crew seemed intent on pre-flight checks. All of them were smoking and in various styles of uniform. She enjoyed the strange smell of their tobacco and the obvious pleasure these men took in their work. She looked at her fellow travellers, and realised that she hadn't felt so happy for a long time. Here she was in Russia, in a Russian military helicopter north of the Arctic Circle. It was June and yet sleet was falling. And there was the small matter of the largest run of Atlantic salmon just over an hour away. 'Hell, this ain't no dude ranch,' her father would have said. She smiled.

The crew became more focused on their tasks and there was a co-ordinated flicking of switches and nodding of heads. The sound of engines starting and blades rotating had the passengers all reaching for their ear protectors. The helicopter lifted slowly, the mighty weight easing from the wheels. It hovered noisily as the last minute checks were completed. Then, to Jody's alarm, the hulk unexpectedly swept backwards, tilting its tail high behind. It hovered in this ungainly position for a few seconds, before swooping forward and accelerating along the runway, the blades blasting spray around them as they picked up speed, and climbed upwards and away from the airport. Silently mouthing an incredulous 'Wow!' Jody looked over to Fergus who dramatically bit his nails, wiped his brow and crossed himself, all in one extended movement. Simon was already asleep, his sunglasses propped uncomfortably against the glass of the window.

Jody tried to read but it seemed that every time she managed to pick up where she had left off, something happened to grab her attention. The cloud was low, and from time to time they seemed to fly perilously close to the rocky surface; at these times the helicopter would bank to avoid the high ground. At one stage she was aware that they were flying in a circle making a tight turn to her side. Out of her window she could see a small herd of elk, and looking forward she noticed that Steve had put himself in the co-pilot's seat and was smiling boyishly. They flew over half-frozen lakes, where snow still drifted over unmelted ice. Everywhere the wilderness was traced with tracks and paths. Trees had fallen, broken and battered, as if after a nuclear strike. It was a bleak unwelcoming place. She looked at her watch and noticed that they had been flying for over an hour. She was pleased to see a band of blue sky on the horizon, which grew ever broader. They would arrive in sunlight. A warm anticipation grew in the passengers as they neared the river. Nothing was said but, one by one, they stopped reading or dozing and looked out of their windows. Even Simon was now fully awake. It was as if the river had given them each a silent greeting.

Soon, a glittering silver ribbon appeared from behind a scrub-lined hill, and the helicopter dived downwards into the narrow valley. They wound their way through a gorge. Jody saw the trees above the blades through her window. Below she could see the river and looking across the cabin, could see nothing but green flashing past the window. Through the cockpit she saw the river and its valley snaking away ahead of them. They flew at thirty feet over the sparkling water, on past the junction of the two rivers, where leaves were thrown skywards by the downthrust, swirling around Genia's hut, and on to the camp. Suddenly the helicopter reared up, and they climbed in a circle around the line of huts. People were waving and dogs were running around excitedly. Jody enjoyed the sudden pull of G-force and caught a glimpse of the helicopter's shadow as it flew in to land. She caught the flash of red in the fur of a man's hat. In each

136

arm he held a puppy. He was smiling as he tried to settle them; their heavy-teated mother stood by scratching her ear with her hind leg. Her mate stood barking from a safe distance. The undercarriage once again took up the weight of the machine and the blades came to an uneven stop. The passengers enjoyed a few seconds of silence as their ears recovered from the battering they had just received.

Bumble hadn't been told that her brother had taken Greg's place. Michael had decided to make it a surprise. He told *Touch the Wild* that he was bringing an eligible landowner. Fergus persuaded him to add a further piece of information, to the effect that this man was a vegetarian. Jody stretched and laughed as Fergus ducked down so he could not be seen. She went forward and down the steps, eager to put her feet on Kola soil.

Jody watched the frenetic activity round the helicopter and decided to keep out of the way. The man with the puppies had disappeared, so she followed the path that led to the huts and caught sight of the river. In her excitement she half-walked, half-skipped to the bank. Standing on the grass with her hands thrust deep into her pockets, she looked down onto the water. The river was wider than she had expected, the water level higher. The sun shone brightly and she reached for her sunglasses to protect her eyes from the reflected glare. The polaroid in her lenses made the greens more verdant, the blues of the water darker. She could make out the rocks that had given the name *The Camel's Humps* to the pool. Michael had mentioned them to her, and she tried to work out the likely salmon lies, but with the river flowing fast and high, she found it hard to read the water. It was going to be a challenge. She was beginning to feel daunted by the prospect of wading and catching fish in these conditions.

'It's quite a sight, isn't it?' Michael stood next to her, already wearing his chest waders and with a rod in his hand. Over his shoulder was slung the cord of his stout wooden wading stick.

'Oh, Michael! It sure is. Is it always this big?'

'No, it's about two foot higher than we really want, but I've spoken to the Camp Manager who tells me it's falling back. We could have ideal conditions. The water temperature is rising, the river is dropping and fish have been caught above and below the camp. If it carries on like this we'll be fishing floating lines in a couple of days.'

'What have you got on now, an intermediate?'

'No, I'm using that newfangled line you sent me with a sink tip on the end. We'll see how it goes – it cost me an arm and a leg!'

'Well, don't stand here talking to me – go and catch a fish. I'll go and put my waders on and I'll ghillie for you.'

'Don't do that. Put your rod up and fish down in front of me. We've got an hour before dinner.'

'No, I'll be happy enough to watch you, and learn a bit more about the river. Where am I sleeping?'

'Oh God, I should have told you! I've managed to get you in a cabin by yourself. You're in the one furthest away from the main camp hut. Your bags should be outside it by now.'

'Thanks. I'll see you in a few minutes.'

Jody walked over the grass to her hut and saw a woman attacking Fergus.

'Jody, help me! Help me! Ouch! God that hurt! That's no way to treat your guests. Did you see that Jody? Did you see what she just did? I'll be complaining, I can tell you. And if you think you're getting a tip from me you can forget it. Ouch! Oh, by the way, this is my sister Bumble. She'll be poisoning us for the next few days.'

Bumble stopped and shook Jody's hand and straightened her hair. It had fallen into disarray whilst tussling with Fergus.

'Hello. How do you feel after your trip?'

'Just fine. Happy to be here.'

'This is Tim, our Camp Manager, he can take you to your hut and show you how it all works. I'd better get back to the kitchen. We're eating in about an hour if that's all right. It's cauliflower *gratin* for you, you oaf,' she said, taking a final kick at a retreating Fergus. 'I've been in a panic for the last few days trying to get vegetarian recipes from cooks in the other camps.'

'He seems quite a handful.'

'He's all right. Its great to see him, but don't tell him I told you will you?'

'I've got a brother a bit like that at home. Are you the youngest?'

'Does it show?'

'No, it just normally turns out like that.'

'When did you come over from the States?'

'Yesterday, but it seems a week ago.'

138

'You must be tired.'

'Strangely enough I'm not. Jet lag normally hits me flying west to east, but so far I feel fine. I'll most probably collapse after dinner.'

She set off with Tim to find her hut.

Jody waved at Michael but at first he didn't see her. He had waded only a few feet out from the bank and was concentrating on his line as it swung downstream with the current. She waited until the line was almost running parallel to the bank before whistling. Smiling, Michael looked round and gestured for her to stand next to him. She put her stick into the water and waded across to him. She could feel the comparative coolness of the water as her waders compressed against her legs. Her feet could sense a loose gravelly bottom through her felt soles.

'Any luck?' she asked, as Michael retrieved some line with his hand.

'Not yet. I've had a pull though. It shouldn't be long now.' Jody stood by his side. The current was pressing strongly against the backs of her legs, the water just over her knees, and she leant on her wading stick for support. Michael retrieved some more line with his hand before lifting his double-handed rod and flicking the tip backward in an arc over his head. The line lifted from the water like a long whip and, just before it was extended fully behind him, he propelled the rod forward again, casting the line downstream across the current. A yellow snake, it straightened out in front of him. Jody could just make out the glimmer of the salmon fly, before it dropped into the water. It had all been one effortless movement, and yet the line had planted the fly some thirty yards away in the middle of the stream.

'I'm still getting the hang of this line.'

'Looked all right from where I was standing.'

They both stood eyeing the water, looking at where they thought the fly would be as the flow carried it below the surface of the water. They might see the swirl of a fish as it came to the fly. The fly fished its way quite quickly round as the current was pushing the line hard. When it was pointing downstream again, Michael retrieved a few feet with one hand and walked a few short paces downstream, before casting again. Jody walked with him, remembering just how much she enjoyed watching other

139

people fish. She had first fished with her father when she was fifteen in America. She could still recall the day when he had hooked a salmon. 'It's like a trout just bigger I guess,' he had said as he handed her the rod, leaving her standing in the river whilst he walked back to the bank to watch and add encouragement. She did quite well, but the fish was lost after five minutes of frantic activity. She was distraught but her father had just laughed.

'It's quite easy wading here you'll find. It's mostly pretty gravelly, but you may encounter the odd rocky patch that needs care,' Michael advised, his eyes focused on his line.

'I didn't realise it was going to be this big.' There was a touch of apprehension in her voice.

'Yes, it is high, but you really don't have to wade too far out or too deep. With this height most of the fish work their way up the sides of the river. If you go out too far you'll only be walking through the lies. You'll have no problem covering the fish with your casting. The river doesn't tell you much at this height though. I've been here when it's been really low, and that does give one a better understanding of what's going on below. You'll work it out. It's just like any other river. Hello...'

Michael's line straightened and the grating sound of the cogs in his reel confirmed that he had hooked a fish. A silver form leapt, twisted and splashed near where the fly had been cast. The fish ran downstream, taking line with it and the spool sounded like a metallic Catherine wheel as it span wildly. No sooner had it started than it was over, the line went slack. The fish had escaped.

'If you weren't here I'd swear! Shall we just leave it at Oh dear?'

'You get it off your chest, Michael. We don't want you getting retentive on us.'

He needed little encouragement. 'Bugger! That's better. Well at least it was where it should have been. You should remember this stretch. There are a few rocks just where it took. There's usually the odd salmon lurking around them. It's very popular after dinner when you have an audience adding the usual kind words of encouragement.'

He tucked the rod under his arm and pulled the line towards him working it through his hands, until he got to the end where a length of fine nylon held the fly. He pulled the nylon through his hands, checking for wind-knots. He looked witheringly at the fly.

'You are a most unsatisfactory object! But I'm going to give you one more chance.'

Jody looked at the black fly with a flash of silver in it, tied to a single hook

'Still fishing *The Stoat*, Michael?'

'That's right,' he smiled at her as he dropped the fly back into the water.

They both said together, 'any colour as long as it's black!' and laughed.

'God, how many times have I heard you say that? I think you're just plain lazy Michael, you can't be bothered to try different flies.'

'This sport's complicated enough without bringing colour into it. It's a tactic that suits me. You fish with whatever confection you like, but I'll stick to what I know. My God, is that the time? Three more casts then we'd better head back.'

The sun was still high on the horizon and retained some warmth from the rays that cast lengthening shadows through the trees. They fished for another fifteen minutes before returning, unsuccessful, but happily to the camp.

Tim held a magnum of champagne and was walking from guest to guest refilling glasses as they stood by the fire in the main hut. Fergus had caught a fish and was quietly delighted at his singular triumph. Although neither of them would admit it, both he and Michael would be determined to catch more than the other during the course of the week. Michael sat in his usual chair with his fishing record book open on his lap.

'So, do we have any news from the river?'

'We went for a walk. We're saving our energies for tomorrow.' Gary took a gulp from his glass and nudged it towards the passing Tim for attention.

'Simon, I take it you didn't fish.' His son, standing by a table looking at a flybox, nodded his head in agreement.

'Steve, anything to report?'

'I've been playing with my box of tricks. Our satellite phones are working if anyone wants to make contact with the outside world.' Steve declined another glass of champagne.

'Yes of course, if anyone wants to phone that's fine. Just ask Steve and he'll set it up for you.

'So the only fish so far is Fergus's. We drew a blank.'

'Just the one. I'd say it was just over ten pounds and it was caught on an *Ally's Shrimp*.'

'Good. We've opened the scoring. Where did you catch it?'

'Below the camp. What is it called? *Igor*'s or something.'

'*Ivan*'s, Fergus. *Ivan*'s.'

Fergus shrugged and took a large handful of pistachio nuts. He shelled and ate with one hand, using his thumbnail to prise them open, before throwing the empty husks into the fire. Sandra stood beside him. It was her first time fishing and she was asking Fergus for advice.

'To be honest, I don't know what I do. I just know when it's on. The next thing is that it's either splashing around on the end of my line or I'm breaking the rod over my knee. The bit in the middle is a complete blur. I don't know how people ever know if they strike or not. You'd better ask Michael – he's the great techno-fisherman amongst us. He's read every book, gets every magazine, has got all the latest kit. Doesn't make any difference, mind you!'

Tim, who was hovering nearby, listening, couldn't resist the opportunity to offer advice.

'You should never strike. Just keep a short length of line in your hand and when the fish takes, let it pull that through to the reel and then lift your rod and it's on. It works every time.'

'Well there you are, our Camp Manager has spoken. Doubtless he will have informed the fish. Do you read many fishing books Tim?'

'Oh yes, I've got them all. Falkus, Oglesby, Waddington, Wulf – you name it.'

'I thought so. If you want to suck up to our leader ask him his opinion. He won't draw breath. Where's Genia? I haven't seen him.'

'Oh, I sent him out to make sure we had no poachers upstream, he'll be back later.'

'Who's Genia?' asked Sandra.

Fergus threw the last of the shells into the fire. 'He's a lovely fellow. He hunts and fishes up here. He knows the river better than anyone. He's also got the advantage of speaking English. We had several amusing evenings when I was last here.'

'Most of our guides are good. I've got them pretty well trained now.'

'I'm sure they feel the same about you, Tim,' Fergus laughed as he emptied his glass. 'You don't have a drop more do you?'

Tim poured the sparkling liquid into Fergus's glass. Bubbles formed at the stem and rose to the surface, sap in the wood crackled as the fire blazed and Jody stifled a yawn, for tiredness had caught up with her.

Ginny touched her arm. 'I'm weary too. It's been a long day. But you must be exhausted.'

'I've just started to feel scratchy eyeballed! I'll go to bed right after dinner.'

'You don't have to stay up if you don't want to. Michael will understand.'

'No, I'm fine. I'm hungry.'

'If you want to phone Greg feel free.'

'We don't normally call each other when he's away. I may call later in the week, to let him know how we're getting on.'

The decanter made its way around the table and met a large box of cigars coming the other way. The flimsy curtains behind Michael had been closed to shield his neighbours' eyes from the sun, which was setting on the horizon to the north. The door to the hut was open, and the light frame holding the mosquito screen banged softly in the breeze. Jody stood up to close it and stayed for a while, watching the puppies playing in front of the hut. The sound of an outboard could be heard above the laughter inside as a metal boat rounded the bend and headed towards the shore. In the bows a dog was barking, and at the wheel stood the man with the fur hat. The dog leapt ashore and the man picked up his knapsack as the sound of the engine petered out. He dragged the boat a few feet up the bank, stopped and looked towards the camp hut where Jody stood behind the fly-screen. She remained there for a few moments and then turned to the others.

'I'm going to call it a day. I'm done. Goodnight everybody.' Their goodnights could still be heard as the screen-door bumped to close behind her.

143

Jody looked at her watch as she walked across the grass to her hut; she was now nine hours ahead of East Coast time. It was nearly eleven o'clock at night, and yet it was still broad daylight and the birds were still singing. She closed the cabin door behind her and noticed that the curtains only served to take the gleam out of the light. Outside she could hear the muffled throb of the generator and above its sound, Fergus's laughter as he shouted out 'Boris' in greeting. She wondered if she would ever get to sleep. She fumbled in her bag, found a strip of pills and swallowed one. Her clothes dropped to the floor where she stood, and finding a T-shirt she slipped it over her head. The bed creaked as she stretched under the covers and perched her book on her chest. The bookmark had fallen out and she struggled to find her place.

The next thing she knew, there was a gentle knock on the door; it was morning.

Chapter Thirteen

Genia awoke to the sounds of Valery attending to his noisy ablutions. The room was filled with cigarette smoke. Genia growled at him from under his pillow.

'How can you smoke this early in the morning?'

Valery didn't reply. He was too busy inspecting himself in the mirror. He was stripped to the waist and plucking lint from his navel as he sang along to the music that rattled out of the cassette player. Genia's throat was dry and his head a reminder of his reunion with Fergus. They had stayed out until two in the morning, when they had all but drained the bottle of brandy that Simon had been sent to retrieve from his father's supplies.

Genia rolled his head to the other side of the pillow. 'What time is it?'

'Seven thirty. Tim's out there already. He's like a chicken with its head cut off. He's going through all the same old stuff again. Can't you talk to him?'

'Not this morning.'

'I thought you'd given up drinking.'

'I thought you'd given up smoking in the hut, leaving the place like a tip and playing that music. I just wish you felt as bad as I do.'

'Do you want any breakfast?'

'Yes, make sure you leave some for me.' Genia picked his head off the pillow and, resting on his elbows squinted at Valery. 'You know that was her brother I was with last night don't you? You hadn't bargained for that had you?' Valery's telltale wave of the arms answered the question. 'Does Tim know what you're up to? And don't just flap like a cormorant. Let me know, because at least with him I can help you.'

'He's blind to everything. Besides it's not his problem. I can do what I like.'

'It became his problem when Bumble's brother stepped off the helicopter. We're here for another four weeks. That's a lot of dollars in tips. He can have you sacked, so don't fool yourself.'

Valery pulled a sweatshirt over his head and Genia was left rubbing his eye with the back of his hand, barking 'Leave it open!' as the door slammed shut. 'This is definitely the last year,' he muttered.

He pulled himself out of bed and put his hand into the water. It would be warm enough for a shave. Grabbing a threadbare towel he ambled down to the river. The cold water brought him back to life. Pana emerged from the bushes to watch his master shake his head under the surface. They returned to the hut together to find Tim waiting by the door. Genia sighed.

Tim's shoulders were hunched and his jaw had set. It was their first meeting all over again. 'What time did you come back last night?'

Genia gestured to his state of undress and looked quizzically at him.

'Look, I asked you a question! This camp is my responsibility. I need to know if you are fishing with clients after dinner. You should have come and found me. There's an empty bottle of ancient brandy on the table. Is that anything to do with you? Do you know how much that stuff costs? Half a year's wages where you come from – and I could get the blame for it.'

Genia rubbed his hair with the towel, as Tim followed him into the hut. Genia reached for his soap and razor as the Camp Manager continued haranguing him.

'I thought you and I had sorted ourselves out, but since this new party has arrived things have started to go pear-shaped, and I don't know why. And another thing. What's Valery up to? I can never find him. So when did you get back?'

Genia had lathered his face and was shaving the soap from his chin.

'Well?'

'Tim, this is not a good morning for you to talk to me like this. I was with the clients and they were safe. Michael's son brought the drink. The staff are all doing their jobs and the camp is happy. So you should just relax. Now please, leave me to shave.

If you want, we can continue this conversation later, but after I've had my breakfast.'

'Well, that's not good enough!'

Genia dropped his razor into the bowl, picked up his towel to dry his face and turned his back on Tim. He picked a shirt off the shelf.

'And why don't you wear the clothes that *Touch the Wild* have provided? Everyone else does, even Valery.'

'Tim, please. After breakfast. *Pazhalysta?*' He put his hands together and smiled.

'All right after breakfast. But I want this week to run like clockwork, and it hasn't started well.'

Jody pulled her silk long johns up over her waist and tucked the matching vest into them. She looked at herself in the mirror and was not unhappy with her reflection. Her long legs and full bosom, when wrapped in the soft material, did her figure justice. The sleeping pill had made her feel drowsy, but she had washed her face and taken her usual handful of vitamins which had the effect, even as a placebo, of bringing her to life. She brushed and flossed her teeth and applied moisturiser to her skin. The fragrance seemed unusually strong in the un-polluted atmosphere.

Her hut looked as if she'd been living there for a week. Clothes were strewn everywhere. Her efforts at unpacking had been limited to opening her bags and selecting the items she wanted; she smiled as she thought of Greg complaining. She climbed down the steps and walked along the duckboards to the camp hut, enjoying the bounce and spring of the wood. The door to Michael and Ginny's hut was open. Michael greeted her and the morning.

'Ah, Jody, my dear! What a glorious way to start the day. You lift a man's spirits. Good morning.'

'Good morning, Michael. Wow, what are you wearing?'

Michael was sporting a T-shirt. Stretched across his chest were the words, written in large letters, *Women Love Me. Fish Fear Me*. Unabashed, he raised his eyebrows and replied in a vaude-ville accent, 'That's nothing, baby! Check this out,' reaching inside the hut to put a *Touch the Wild* baseball cap on his head.

'Now, I've seen it all. Ginny did you buy him all this? What's gotten in to him?'

'He spent a week bone fishing in the Bahamas. He's never been the same since.'

'Nonsense. I've been on the road to Damascus. I've seen the light. I'm a reconstituted fisherman.'

'If we're going to get biblical about this, wasn't it you who used the expression "And America so loved the world, that they gave it the baseball cap?" What happened to the good old tweed and Lockes? My dad spent a fortune there because of you; I'm wearing one of his caps this week. I've had it altered especially.'

'I'll have you know, that this...' (he lifted the baseball cap from his head to admire it more closely) '...is the ultimate fishing prerequisite. Water-resistant, airy, comfortable and, above all, the last word in style.' He put it on his head, back to front. 'What do you think?'

Fergus took one look at Michael, and then lurched past to the camp hut, muttering, 'Good grief! I can't take that before breakfast.'

'Philistine!' Michael shouted after him.

'Come on, stop showing off and get dressed.' Ginny pulled him back into the hut.

Breakfast was quiet in comparison to the clamour of the night before. The guests drifted in to the muted greeting that is the hallmark of a group at ease with itself. The gentle rattle of knifes and forks as they loaded guests with essential calories for their day on the river, mixed with occasional talk and gentle laughter. Simon entered last, but still in time for breakfast. Michael and Ginny exchanged mystified glances as he helped himself from the dishes.

'Michael, have you decided where you would like everyone to fish?' Tim asked as he finished his breakfast.

'Yes, I think so. What I propose is that Gary and Sandra fish the left bank downstream. They are both right-handed and they can fish all of that with an overhead cast, so it shouldn't be too problematical. Gary, would you like Tim to spend some time with you and Sandra?'

'We'll take all the help we can get, if that's all right with you Tim?'

'Absolutely'

'Simon and Fergus, right bank downstream. Ginny and Jody,

left bank upstream. That leaves Steve and me to fish right bank upstream.

'As far as guides are concerned I don't mind who goes with who, but I would like Genia to go with Ginny. We won't fish the upper river today. Let's see what we've got around the camp – unless anyone particularly wants to go up there.

'What's the river doing, Tim? Is it still dropping? It looks as if it is.'

'It's fallen about two inches overnight. The water temperature is 46°. I recommend an intermediate or a sink-tip.'

Fergus let out a mighty groan.

'Listen Fergus, and you may learn something. Some of us shape our day around these details.' Michael tapped his unused spoon on the table as he spoke.

Fergus prodded his fork into his sausage. 'Is our leader all right, Ginny? First I see him wearing a baseball cap, and now he's talking water temperatures. What's he on? It's not good for him. And what the hell is "Shaping a day" when it's at home? He'll be talking fly sizes next.'

'Damn right I will! I'll have you converted by the end of the week. Water a bit coloured and still highish. Sixes or eights – something like that?' Tim nodded with enthusiasm.

Sandra was looking bemused. 'I hope someone's going to explain all this to me. I'm lost already and we haven't started.'

'Don't listen to that gobbledegook, Sandra,' said Fergus reassuringly, 'listen to the sermon according to Saint Fergus, patron saint of duffers. Chuck it in, let it swing round and if it hits the salmon on the hooter, he'll take a bite at it.' He demonstrated the process with his sausage-laden fork, taking a large bite as it swung past his mouth. 'That's all there is to it, always has been and always will be, forever and ever, Amen! Don't let them confuse you.'

'There is something in that, I have to confess. But our Fergus takes an amazingly old-fashioned approach for one so young. He should bend to the winds of progress, be a bit more ecumenical.'

'If that means wearing a baseball cap and wandering around with a water thermometer stuffed up my backside, you can forget it. That's my equivalent of the Wailing Wall. Instead of talking about fishing, is there any chance of us actually going out there and getting on with it?' He washed the remains

149

of his breakfast down his throat with a gulp from his cup, before announcing, 'Si, I'm returning to our hut to do that which only I can do. I suggest you leave me until I sound the All Clear.'

Sandra grimaced. 'Too much information Fergus, too much information.'

Simon nodded in agreement. 'Not only that. It was like sleeping with a badger last night. Can't I change huts Dad?'

'It was your suggestion he came. You made your bed so you'll have to lie in it, I'm afraid. Besides no one else will have him.'

The line of small white clouds that drifted across the sun were the only features in an otherwise blue sky. A soft, cool breeze greeted Jody as she came out of her hut and sat on the steps to wriggle into her waders. It was still quite cold in spite of the sun as the wind came straight from the Arctic icecap. She was wearing a high polo neck sweater under a fleece and a beige cashmere scarf was wrapped loosely around her neck. She picked up her short wading jacket and zipped it closed. Finally, she plonked her father's baggy tweed cap on her head. She was now fully waterproof and protected against the elements.

She found Ginny trying to help Sandra with all her new equipment.

'Hi, Jody! I'm not so sure that this is a good idea, I'd prefer the beach anyday. There's a bit too much chest hair around here for my liking.'

'You're Australian – surely you're used to it by now?'

'I know, but Gary and I tend to go our separate ways. He plays golf or goes sailing with his mates and I flop out. We've got all day with that guy Tim. He's not going to last long with Gary unless he loosens up a bit.'

'You'll be fine,' Ginny said encouragingly. 'Ah, here's Genia.' The three women turned to greet him.

'I can see you've got yourself sorted out all right, Ginny!' whispered Sandra.

'He is a bit of a dish isn't he?' Ginny replied. 'Genia, how nice to see you! It seems like the year has flown. This is Jody who will be coming with us today, and this is Sandra.'

Genia took off his hat and shook their hands. He carried the rods and equipment to the boat and helped Ginny and Jody aboard. Around his neck hung a walkie-talkie in a waterproof case. Pana climbed aboard as Genia pushed the boat stern-first into the water. Just as they were about to leave, Michael came over to say goodbye.

'How far up will you go, Genia? Above *The Ford*?'

'I think it's too high. Maybe we'll fish *The Honeypots* down to *Red Rocks*.'

'That seems to make sense. What do you think about the right bank?'

'Start at the top of the *Long Stream*. You can fish it from the bank almost all the way down now.'

'Right-oh.' Michael doffed his new acquisition from his head and flourished it at the women. 'Tight lines one and all!'

Jody sat in the bows of the boat and put an arm round Pana as the boat sped up river. She had to grab her hat several times as the wind lifted the brim. She was glad she had put on so many layers of clothing. As the spray misted her face she was reminded of how cold the water would be. Soon the sound of the engine stopped and they were ashore. Genia left the women to organise themselves, while he tied up the boat and lifted the knapsack and large landing net to the shore. Pana set off into the woods barking. They would not see him again until lunchtime.

'Would you like salmon for lunch today?' Ginny asked. 'Genia cooks it to perfection.'

'If that's not too much trouble, I can't think of anything better.' Jody smiled at Genia.

'Sure, it would be my pleasure.'

'Whoever catches the first fish will knock it on the head. Do you want Genia to ghillie for you?'

'I prefer to be alone if that's OK. But I could do with a bit of help landing. I always get in a muddle. Where should I start?'

Genia pointed to the path. 'You can start anywhere here and work your way down. It stops fishing by that fallen trunk about 150 metres away.'

'I've got it – by the white water. OK you two, get going and no peeking. I'm always a bit rusty when I start. If I catch any-thing, I'll whistle.'

Genia picked up the knapsack and net, and escorted Ginny to a pool further downstream. He waded a few paces into the current with her, holding her arm as they negotiated an underwater rock. They both waved as the boat carrying Michael and Steve passed by, slowing down so as not to flood them with its wake.

Jody was happy. She had been travelling for over forty-eight hours and had only just started fishing. She watched with un-alloyed pleasure as her line swung round with the current, the product of her first cast on Russian waters. She started by fishing a short line and stood close to the bank. Gradually with each cast she lengthened her line until she was fishing a comfortable distance, not using too much effort, letting the rod do the work. Her fishing fell into a natural rhythm: cast, retrieve, a few paces downstream then cast again. From time to time, when her fly went through the faster water, she would flick an upstream mend into the line to slow it down. The conditions were ideal. A slight downstream breeze, the sun high in the sky behind the fish, and, although she needed no further encouragement, she was excited to see a fish that tailed a few yards downstream of her fly.

Two more casts and she felt her line tighten. The fish seemed to pluck at her fly in a succession of small tugs. She held her breath, kept her rod-tip down and let the fly swing further round. As it did so the salmon turned to follow it and took the fly. The hook caught in the scissors of its jaw and the fight was on. The reel whooshed out line and she slowly raised her rod-tip. This had the dual impact of driving the barbless hook home, as the bent rod allowed the cogs in the reel to take effect and slow the fish down. She waded slowly to the shore as she played the fish, reeling in when the line went slack, letting line out as the fish ran for freedom. Several times the fish leapt out of the water, seeming to stand vertically, propelling itself across the ripples with its tail. Jody found herself standing on the bank with most of the contents of her reel stretched out across the current.

With one hand she held the line against the butt of her rod and she whistled for Genia as she would have done for one of her brothers. Ginny turned and waved, as Genia waded to the shore and the path that would take him to Jody. Seconds seemed like minutes as she fought the fish. Sometimes her sixteen-foot rod was bent in an arc, at others it was almost straight. The salmon pulled its way into the main current and with its assis-tance, tugged the remains of the line from the reel leaving Jody to handle the fine backing, over 150 metres of strong but fine line. It felt weaker and less responsive than the fishing line. She became aware of the sound of footsteps pounding up the path. She greeted Genia as a long lost friend.

'Boy, am I glad to see you!'

Genia grinned from ear to ear and patted her shoulder, his eyes alive under the fur of his hat. 'Your first Russian fish.'

'I've got to land it yet.'

'You will. No problem.' He laughed, sharing her excitement.

'How big do you think it is? It's pulling hard in that current.'

'Maybe eleven or twelve pounds, but very fresh.'

Gradually the battle went her way, the fish weakened and Jody was able to reel the backing back onto her spool and was now again playing the line. The fish then surprised her by seeming to swim directly towards her. The line went slack and she muttered 'Holy shit!' as she wound the small reel at a hectic pace to keep up with the approaching fish. She walked away further up the bank to help tighten the line.

The fish soon gave its first sign of tiring by turning on its side in the water, it's bright silver flank a purple flash in the water.

'Nearly there, nearly there.'

Genia picked up the long wooden handle of his net and walked a few paces upstream. He picked up a stone the size of a fist and dropped it into the webbing before lowering it into the water. Jody steered the fish to the mouth of the net and Genia scooped it out of the water, raising the net in a shower of spray over them both. He placed the net well up the bank before removing the fish. He held it flapping by its tail and reached for the rock at the bottom of the net. With a look he asked Jody the question, and she replied, 'It's my first Russian salmon. Let's put it back.'

Genia nodded and carefully lowered the fish back into the water. He removed the hook from its mouth with his fingers, signalling for Jody to take the fish so that she could release it herself. She wetted her hands as she stood next to him in the river. She could feel the hardness of his palms as he slipped the fish into her hands. The fur of his hat brushed across her face. She gazed happily at the salmon, its white mouth opening and closing rhythmically, its nose to the current.

'My God, it's beautiful! What's the word for that in Russian?' she beamed at him.

'*Krasivaya.*' His voice trailed away as he looked at her, '*krasi-vaya…*'

He stood back and watched as Jody moved the fish from side to side, before finally releasing it. At first it seemed to sink nose first to the bottom and then with one twitch of its tail it was gone. Jody stood with water dripping from her sleeves, looked at Genia and impulsively hugged him, laughing and whooping with excitement. Genia patted her back and gently squeezed her in return. She enjoyed the strength in his arms before softly withdrawing. Downstream the sun glinted off Ginny's rod and in the stream the remnants of a salmon's splash could be seen. Genia let her go.

'Look, Ginny's got one. It will have to be lunch or we'll starve!'

'You'd better get down there. You've got your work cut out today boy!'

As he strode down the bank, he could hear her whistle and, once again, he turned to her.

'Thank you!' He waved to her, the net swinging behind him.

She sat on the bank for a while to relive the experience. Fumbling in her waders, she found a packet of cigarettes, the remnants of another trip, but just about smokeable. Half of her wanted to get back in the water and catch another fish, the other half wanted to sit and savour the moment. She lit the cigarette and stretched out on the bank. She rested her head on her cap and removed her sunglasses. She squinted as the rays warmed the freckles on her face. It had all happened so quickly, but she knew that she had 'done it right', as her father would have said. She touched her face where the fur of Genia's hat had brushed her skin and smiled.

'Tick, tock, tick, tock! There can you see – forwards, backwards – two o'clock, ten o'clock. Tick, tock! It's easy Sandra!' Tim's casting lessons were proving less than successful.

They were standing together on the bank and Gary was further downstream with Valery, happily ignorant of the tension that was building between master and pupil.

'Don't keep saying it's easy, Tim, because I'm finding it bloody impossible. I've pretended I'm cracking a whip, flicking a towel, spinning a top and now I'm supposed to be a frigging clock – but I'm no closer to catching a salmon!'

'Sandra you are close, honestly! You know how to play golf. Casting is much easier than a golf swing – or even hitting a tennis ball. Now once again, watch me.' He took the rod from her. 'Lift the rod-tip until it's at ten o'clock. Raise it back to two o'clock, and stop. A short wait – and then punch it forward to ten o'clock. And there, the line shoots forward and now it's fishing. Tick, tock. What could be simpler?'

'I'll tell you what could be simpler. Saying no to Gary when he comes up with his hair-brained schemes.' She took his arm and looked earnestly at him. 'Let me explain. Lying by the pool and shopping, darling, those are simple things. What you are teaching me is unnecessary and complicated, and not giving me one iota of pleasure.'

'Look, I tell you what. Why don't you come and stand with me further down. I'll see if I can catch a fish and then you can play it. It might get you in the mood.'

Sandra somehow resisted the temptation to tell Tim what sort of things got her in the mood. Instead she replied, 'Sweetheart, you go and fish. Let me know when you've caught something and, unless you can direct me to the nearest shopping mall, I'm going to read my book and get some rays.'

To compound her displeasure, Gary had caught his second fish of the morning and had turned to make sure that Sandra was watching him play it. She could picture the irritating grin on his face, full of false modesty. He usually wore it when he had just sunk a long putt.

Tim was delighted to have the opportunity to fish and walked some distance from her, hoping she wouldn't bother to join him if he caught anything. As he went, he muttered to himself, 'Pearls before swine, pearls before swine!'

The moss crackled into flames and Genia added some twigs. The wood had been under the snow for the last six months, and it was a slow and gradual process getting it to light. He blew at the base of the fire to encourage the ashes that would cook the fish. He worked at it until he had a strong blaze, then left the fire and walked down to the river, where Ginny's salmon was lying in some slack water. At five pounds it was an ideal lunch fish and he pulled his knife from his pocket and cleaned and filleted the fish in the water.

He cut the fillets in half and then returned to the fire where he found some tinfoil in his bag. He began to make parcels of each fillet; anything that was left over would be eaten by the guides for their supper. His culinary duties were interrupted by the piercing whistle that he had come to enjoy. Smiling, he reached for his net and walked up the path to help Jody, watching her as he went. This would be the fifth fish that she had hooked; two had got off and two she had landed. Three on a first morning was good start by anyone's standards.

He watched her wade backwards against the current to the bank, concentrating all the while as she played the fish. She had let her first fish run too much, treating it too softly. She had been used to fishing with double barbed hooks. Here her single, barbless fly, whilst far more humane when it came to releasing the fish, could dislodge if the line slackened for a moment. He had advised her to keep the line tighter, more in contact with the salmon. They had chatted and enjoyed each other's company on each occasion that he had helped her. He had found himself attracted to the warmth of her smile and her easy laughter.

'Where have you been? I've got a fish on, and you're playing housewife in the kitchen. Shame on you!' she teased.

Genia ran his hand across the surface of the river and shot a spray of water in her direction as he waded across to her. The spray fell short but made her laugh.

'It's been all over the place – upstream, downstream – it almost leapt onto the bank at one stage!' He stood by her with his net as she played the fish out. Slowly she brought it to the surface and into the waiting net. Genia returned the fish to the water while she reeled in her line and unzipped her jacket. Looking at her watch, she declared, 'I don't know about you, but I could do with a drink. Come on, let's go get a beer.'

She led the way back to the fire. As she walked, the heat haze was visible against the brightness of the sky, the smell of woodsmoke greeting them as they approached. Once Jody had dropped her rod and equipment, Genia handed her a bottle-opener and pointed to a ring of stones in the shallow water. She collected two bottles from where they were cooling in the river. He returned to his cooking, producing a piece of rolled up newspaper from his bag which he unravelled to expose his special

156

mixture of dried herbs, bunches of which he laid artistically across the fillets before sealing the foil envelopes. Jody returned to find him brushing the bulk of the fire to one side so that he could lay the fish in the ashes. He nodded gratefully as she handed him a beer. Ginny was wading out of the water downstream. She, too, had had enough for one morning.

'What a morning! Thank you. Genia, let's drink to my first Russian fish.' Jody raised her bottle to his.

'To Jody's first Kola fish.'

'It was everything I thought it was going to be, but better. I've never fished in such a remote place before. You really feel like you are at the top of the world. No cars, no nothing – just the sound of the water – and as for the fishing?' She shook her head and smiled. 'Something else, as we say back home.'

'You did well, the river's still high.'

'I wasn't sure if I was casting far enough. It looked like I was less than a quarter of the way across.'

'You don't need to reach too far. Too many people spend their time trying to land their fly on the other bank, instead of fishing where the fish are. If the river drops a little more they will start holding in the pools; then you will see something.'

She reached into her waders and found the packet of cigarettes and offered him one.

'Do you smoke?'

'No, thank you.'

'You must be the only Russian who doesn't!'

'I try not to. It's a throwback from medical school. I live in Murmansk, eat Russian vegetables, drink Murmansk water, I could send a Geiger counter off the scale and I drink vodka – but I try not to smoke.'

'A man of principle?'

'Something like that.'

He felt suddenly awkward, shy even. She treated him like a brother, but he sensed she felt more. Perhaps she was like this with everyone. He watched her as she applied some sun cream to her face.

'You've got a slight American accent. Where did that come from?' She offered the tube to him as she asked.

'I learnt English at school and later it was part of my university course, but that was standard English. It's only since I've been a guide and been exposed to your fellow countrymen that it's happened. I also spent two weeks in Montana with some guests who fished here. Is it that strong? I can't tell.'

'Don't worry, I didn't think you came from the Bronx.' He laughed with her but the Bronx meant nothing to him. Normally, he would have asked but today he felt almost tongue-tied. He felt a sense of relief to see Ginny approach.

'Ginny, how'd it go? Here have one of these. Genia's being the perfect host. I tell you, those old turkeys on the Spey had better watch out.'

'I know what you mean. They can be a touch doom-laden. But it's a different type of fishing isn't it? Genia, is that contraption of yours working? Why don't you see if you can raise Michael and see how he's getting on.'

Genia spoke into the walkie-talkie and after opening the conversation in Russian for a few moments with the guide, he gave the handset to Ginny.

'He wants to speak to you.'

'Hello darling. Yes, we've had a lovely morning. We've landed five and lost quite a few more. How about you?' There was a pause while Michael responded. 'Oh really? Shall I send Jody over? You are obviously in need of help. We've caught all ours on *Varzy-Warzy*'s. Have you thought of using something with a bit of a colour in it?' She winked at Jody. 'It seems to be working for us.' There was another pause and Ginny laughed, 'Balls! All right, we'll speak later. I wouldn't stop for lunch if I were you, you've got some catching up to do. Don't call us because we may have a little nap after lunch, we're both a bit fatigued by the morning's efforts.' They could all hear Michael's final reply as she switched the handset off.

'How is he?'

'He said it was just as he had expected. Any fool knows that the fish run up the left bank at this height of water. He was surprised that we hadn't caught more. The rest of it you heard. He doesn't change.'

Genia had been putting the final touches to the salmon and, when his preparations were complete, he handed the women their plates. Steam rose from the cooked salmon, which was almost rare where the flesh had joined the spine. He passed them a container with salad that Bumble had prepared and another with

158

her own hand-made mayonnaise. A glass of burgundy from the bottle in the cooler completed their lunch.

'You sure how know to do it! This makes a change from a piece and a Scotch egg.'

'Yes, you can't see Wee Donny doing this, can you? Genia, this looks delicious. Do you want to fish or eat with us?'

He would usually have eaten with them. He got on well with Ginny, but Jody's presence unsettled him. He elected to fish.

'Use my rod if you like. It looks a bit longer than Ginny's and it might suit you better.'

He walked about two hundred yards upstream of the fire, where Jody had already fished. He waded a few feet out from the bank, the water lapping around his knees. He looked back at the women who were happily engrossed in conversation.

'I'm sorry Greg couldn't join us. Do you think he would be enjoying it?'

'I guess you already know the answer to that question, Ginny. He tries to enjoy fishing, but he's not cut out for it. There's not enough action in it for him. He hasn't got the perseverance to become patient, if you see what I mean. Or should it be the other way round?'

'I know what you mean. I only started because of Michael and I certainly had my frustrations in the early days. Now we just love fishing together. None of my girlfriends can ever understand what I see in it. It's something you can't really explain unless you've done it. Those who try to understand say that it must be a good time to think things through. The truth is, that I never think of anything really when I'm fishing. It's like being in a waking dream, the time flies. The same thing happens when you're driving on a motorway, when the miles click by but you aren't really aware of them. Then suddenly, it's junction fourteen and time to turn off! How do we ever react so quickly when we see brake lights in front of us, when we are in another world?'

'I know, time just flies.'

'It's good to see you enjoying yourself. We were worried that you might regret coming by yourself. We're a bit of a mixed bunch.'

'Ginny, let's just say that it came at the right time.' Jody made her answer deliberately short.

'I wasn't meaning to pry, but you know how fond Michael is of you. He just wanted to make sure that you are happy.'

159

'I know, and I appreciate it.' She forked some mayonnaise-dipped salmon into her mouth and savoured the flavours before swallowing. 'My, that's good. I defy any restaurant to come up with something like this.'

'It sounds strange, but you'll want to eat sandwiches by end of the week. Too much of a good thing – you know. Well, anyway here's to us, our first morning on the Volna and the happy thought that Michael and Steve are thrashing the water to a foam trying to catch up. Men are so delightfully predictable. I do wish that I'd told him we had caught seven. That really would have got them going.' They both raised their glasses.

Jody watched Genia fish. He stood close in to the bank, fishing quickly and delicately. She noticed that, unlike her, he would spend several minutes at one place repeatedly casting over it, sometimes at the recommended forty-five degrees and at others almost at right angles to the bank. Each cast presented the fly differently. Sometimes slow, sometimes fast; sometimes deep, sometimes shallow. Then instead of working his way down the pool, he would move thirty yards before repeating the procedure. He caught two fish in half an hour.

'Aggravating, isn't it?' Ginny disturbed her thoughts.

'Well, he sure knows what he's doing. I guess he knows the river.'

'It's strange really. When we first came here, Genia hadn't fished at all. He just couldn't understand what all the fuss was about. You know, us coming all this way to stand in the water to catch fish and then release them. Michael showed him the basics and gave him his rod at the end of the week. When we came back the following year he had mastered the art. He's even developed his own cast. Have you seen it?'

'Yes, I noticed it just now. That loopy roll he does.'

'Get him to show you. It's a great way of getting the belly of line upstream.'

'I may just do that later on. I'm still feeling my way at the moment. What's his story? He seems – I dunno – out of place. A teenager in a kindergarten – too good to be just a guide.'

'I've never worked it out. I'm sure there's a story there, but we've never got to the bottom of it. He's told Michael that he trained as a doctor before going to Afghanistan as a medic, but there the trail ends, apart from the fact that he spends most of the winter up here by himself. He's got a divine little hut upstream. There's nothing we girls like better than a bit of brooding mystery is there? Michael's very fond of him, but then he has a natural affinity with big men. He never really trusts short arses, as he calls them, which is really rather unfair.'

Jody thought of Greg as she watched Genia fish for a while.

He was fishing without his hat and in shirtsleeves, despite the coolness of the day. His hair curled over his upturned collar. A few days of sunshine had replenished his tan and concealed the darkness under his eyes. The hairs on his arms had bleached to a light biscuit colour; he exuded well-being. He was the first Russian man that she had known and his sense of humour had taken her by surprise. She enjoyed the grain in his voice – his easy masculinity. She was particularly taken by the kindness in his eyes. She had enjoyed her morning with him.

She poked the fire with a stick, pushing glowing twigs and log-ends into the flames to burn. The billycan of water that he had left was steaming on the embers and she set about making coffee. He walked towards them unaware at first of the women looking at him but ran his hand over his head when he noticed them.

'Do you want a cup?'

'That would be lovely, thank you,' Ginny replied as she produced another box with some fruitcake in it. 'Some traditions never die,' she added passing a slice to Jody.

'Let me help.' Genia had joined them.

'No, I'm OK, let me make myself useful. I'm afraid some ash has blown into the water, but it won't do us any harm. Pull up a chair and join us.'

Genia laughed as he sat down on a log opposite them, picking up a plate and unwrapping one of the parcels as he did so. Jody stifled a yawn with the back of her hand.

'I feel sleepy. It must be the jet lag kicking in. And I don't normally drink wine at lunch. I can see I'm going to have to pace myself with you guys. I may take a nap in a while.'

'Genia can take you back to your hut if you like.'

'No, I'll be fine on the bank. That mossy patch over there seems to have my name on it. I'll only sleep for a short while. It's not going to rain is it?' Dark smudges lined the base of the clouds, which had grown in size throughout the morning.

161

'Four seasons in one day, that's the Kola. It is always safe to say "yes it will rain today", but I think it will be dry for a few hours yet.' Genia ate his salmon and watched as Tim's boat came speeding up to them. Pana re-emerged from the woods barking as Tim moored the boat and walked over to the group.

'Good afternoon. How did you get on this morning?' His own good spirits were marred by the sight of Genia enjoying his lunch with a glass of buttery wine. Tim's nose was showing the first signs of sunburn, his pale skin reacting to the thin Arctic air.

'Tim, have you eaten? We've got plenty here if you'd like some,' Ginny offered.

'I'm afraid I haven't got time for that at the moment. I was wondering if I could beg a favour? We've got a slight problem in the casting department downstream. Sandra's struggling a bit and I was wondering whether I might borrow Genia for a while. I've spoken to Michael on the radio. He says it's up to you.'

'Oh the poor thing, she can't be having much fun. Of course she can have him, she'll be delighted.'

Genia stood up, wiped his hands on the grass and emptied his glass. 'Tim, why don't you stay here and I'll look after the others this afternoon? If you want to change over later then we can talk on the radio.'

'Yes, I was about to suggest that.'

The two men walked over to the boat followed by Pana. Tim checked that they were out of earshot before saying, 'That Australian woman hasn't got a clue and she's very rude. Mind you, her husband's no better. You're welcome to them! I'll see you later.'

Chapter Fourteen

Fergus and Simon were the first to return to the camp. They stood next to the rod racks by the river. Fergus held a cigarette in the corner of his mouth as he tied a new fly to the end of his line; Simon cradled a puppy in his elbow.

Through clenched teeth and a cloud of smoke, Fergus said, 'I'm tempted to have one last flick before dinner. You haven't got your eye on the *Camp Pool* by any chance?'

'I've done my bit for the day. It's all yours. I'll go and have a shower while there's still some semblance of calm in our hut.'

'Ah, the mark of a true friend Si! I can barely fit into that bloody shower, and even if I do it either freezes my *cojones* or singes several layers of skin. I tend to leave it until the last possible minute, when complaints have developed a uniform ring to them. Do borrow my shampoo if you can find it. So I'll see you later then. One more before dinner would make Fergus a happy bunny!'

Fergus had reason to be pleased. The pool would not have been fished for over a day and if any salmon were holding, they would have been undisturbed. Two more boats returned, reuniting Michael and Ginny who sat on the bank watching Fergus as he fished his way down the pool. Soon, Steve appeared from the camp hut with Bumble, who was carrying a tray.

As she handed glasses to Ginny and Michael, the sound of the last boat could be heard as it returned from downstream. The boat slowed as it passed the *Camel's Humps* and then stopped altogether. The passengers could be seen moving around the sides of the boat. After a few moments, the boat gently accelerated towards the camp and, when it was about fifty metres from Fergus, roared to full throttle. Passing perilously close to him, it pushed up a wake that all but submerged him, flooding into his

163

waders and leaving his ever-present cigarette smouldering in his mouth. Gary's hoarse laughter could be heard as he steered the boat past the beleaguered fisherman.

Tim turned to see what was happening and, assuming that Genia was at the helm, let out an astonished cry. 'What is that bloody man up to? I'm sorry Michael, I'll tear a strip off him later.'

'You may get more than you bargain for. I think you'll find that Gary is used to doing as he chooses. If he has broken camp rules, it may be better if I have a word with him.'

Michael's rebuke rendered Tim awkward and embarrassed, his cheeks turning the same colour as his newly-burnt nose. His only reply was a nervous titter that was ignored as the people on the bank watched the boat swing round for a second pass. Fergus's growl could just be heard over the approaching engine. Sandra sat upright in the bows with her hands over her eyes. Genia could be seen urging Gary to slow down. Common sense prevailed and the boat veered as it lost speed.

'Good evening, Gary. Had a good day?' a waterlogged Fergus asked from the river, determined to appear unaware of the discomfort that the cold water was causing as it wallowed around his nether regions. He cast his line powerfully across the receding swell.

'It's been a ripper Ferg! I do hope we didn't wet you. Had a bit of trouble with the old throttle here.'

'Oh well, these things will happen,' came the reply, although revenge was already uppermost in his mind.

Tim walked down to the water's edge to see if he could help Fergus. 'I say, do you want any help? You must be drenched.'

'No. Sod off Rudolf! You'll frighten the fish with that hooter of yours,' was the abrupt response.

'I was only trying to be helpful...'

'Well, don't,' Fergus fumed.

The party sprawled across the bank exchanging news about the day's fishing. Jody was still laughing as Sandra sat down next to her. 'He'll never grow up.'

'So how did it go today?' Jody asked.

Sandra's answer was made in a whisper that was audible to

Tim, standing a few yards behind her. 'Well, it picked up in the afternoon, if you know what I mean. All that that Pom did was confuse me. Your fella was great, though. He got me casting and I caught my first salmon.'

'Such a relief,' said Gary as he joined them. 'At lunchtime I thought we'd be packing our bags. Next thing that happened was I had to drag her out of the water. How did you get on Jody?'

'Terrific! We had nine between us and lost a whole heap more. Did you eat one for lunch?'

Gary stretched and yawned. 'Fantastic, just the best! Well, I'm going to grab a shower, San – how about you?'

'Yeah, might as well. Oh bugger! I knew I'd forgotten something. I've gone and left my fishing bag at that last pool. Tim, do you think someone could go and get it?'

Tim said, 'I'd go myself, but it's most probably best if I get Genia to pick it up for you. He'll know where it is.'

Jody watched Genia prepare to leave. She had slept well in the afternoon, but had awoken with a headache and did not relish the prospect of drinking more before dinner. 'Do you mind if I hitch a lift downstream with him? I'd love to have a look at the *Lunch Pool* you've told me so much about,' she asked Michael.

'Why of course, my dear.'

Jody skipped down the bank to the boat. She laughed as Pana pushed past into the boat before her. The engine kicked into life and the boat sped downstream.

Fergus stood at the top of the bank, releasing the straps of his waders and peeling the rubber to below his knees. His wet jeans and shirt were glued to his skin, and he looked forlornly at a wet packet of cigarettes. For solace he grabbed a glass of champagne from Bumble's passing tray. He took a large gulp, belched and exclaimed, 'Nectar. Pure nectar. What a day, what a glorious sodding day! In spite of being drenched to the skin. I think I must have died and gone to heaven.'

'You'd better get inside or you'll catch a cold,' his sister chided.

'I'm fine where I am thank you. Why don't you run along to the kitchen. I'm sure you have more pressing duties to perform.' He waited until Bumble was out of earshot before whispering to Michael, 'Now then, which is Gary's rod? I have a little skulduggery to perform. Can I enlist our leader's assistance?'

'No. And don't go too far, Fergus.'

'What do you mean? He not only bloody well near drowned me; he also ruined a whole packet of fags. Ha-ha! Revenge will be mine.' He rubbed his hands as he looked at the rod rack. 'You could at least keep cave for me in case that old dingo emerges from his pit.'

'You're on your own – I'm leaving you to it.'

'How big a problem are the poachers?' Jody asked, as she shuffled some rusting tins into a pile with her foot.

They had found Sandra's bag and were now walking beside the *Lunch Pool*. Genia had been surprised when she had joined him in the boat, and at first felt his shyness reappear. He now had the opportunity to admire her as she squatted by the remnants of a poacher's fire. Her high-necked sweater accentuated the cleanness of her chin. She moved nimbly under the loose material of her waders. She was at home on the river. Her interest seemed genuine. He found his confidence return.

He scratched the back of his neck as he replied. 'Most of them come for one or two days, either from the army camp or from the village. It's a holiday for them. They'll fish a bit and drink a lot. The main damage they do at this time of year is leaving all this mess behind them. Look, this is one of their fishing rods. It can't be a good one or they wouldn't have left it.' He picked up a tin can with a long length of fishing nylon wrapped around it. At the end of the nylon was attached a home-made spinner, a large arrowhead of rusting steel, with the ends bent in alternate directions. Dangling from the tip was a large, barbed, treble hook.

'How the hell do they make that work?'

Genia unwound some of the nylon and, swinging the tin in a circular motion, released the nylon; it uncoiled from the tin drawn by the weight of the spinner. The metal splashed as it plopped into the water, some twenty yards away. He was left holding the tin to which the last strand of nylon had been tied.

'What happens if they catch a fifteen pounder on the end of that contraption? You'd need a strong pair of hands and a lot of patience to reel it in.'

Genia laughed. 'They don't bother playing the fish. The poacher just runs up the bank and tows the salmon out of the water.

Most of the fish are foul-hooked. They throw the spinner upstream and drag it fast across the pool, hoping it will snag on the fish's back. Their most important piece of equipment is a thick pair of gloves: nylon cuts like wire and a foul-hooked salmon will run straight back to the sea if it can. It doesn't look much now, but in a month's time when the river is much lower and the pools are full of salmon, it can be very effective. That's when the commercial boys turn up with their nets.'

She had listened and smiled encouragingly as Genia stumbled over some of the phrases. 'It happens back home, but the equipment is a bit more sophisticated. Can I keep this? I could have some fun with this on the Miramichi with the boys. We could have a casting competition.' Genia handed it to her and Jody started to rewind the nylon onto the tin.

'You should have some practice first or you will hit one of your sons. It's not that easy.'

Jody paused for a moment, and then smiled. 'No, I haven't got any kids. I was talking about my brothers. We always refer to them as the boys. How about you? Do you have any children?' As she spoke Pana brushed himself against her, his tail wagging.

'No, I haven't married.' Genia looked upstream. It was getting late. 'I think we should go back.'

'Yes, I suppose so. Pana seems a good dog. How old is he?'

'Eleven, maybe older.'

She pulled the dog to her and spread the fur over his wound. 'Ouch! How did he get that?'

'A bear.' Genia knew what the next question would be and decided to explain. 'We hunt them for their skins. One way is to use dogs. Pana was hurt a few years ago. I go out alone now.'

Jody didn't reply at first, instead she ran her hand along the even scar. 'Did you have to stitch it?'

Genia nodded, not knowing what her reaction would be. Some of the Americans he had met found it distasteful that he killed bears. He was relieved to see her soft smile and hear her reply, 'Well, it looks like you did a pretty fine job.' She ran her fingers through the heavy fur. 'Doesn't he get hot with all this?'

'If he does, he just goes for a swim. You'll often see him swimming across the river. He has a good life out here, and he is company for me. We have a good relationship: I talk and he listens. Only rarely does he disagree!'

'Ginny told me that you live out here all the time. Don't you get lonely or bored?'

'I find it peaceful. It's the life I choose – not many people from Murmansk have that. I breathe clean air, eat good food and,' he pointed at Pana, 'I enjoy good company.'

'Are you kidding me?'

'Not at all. It's how I see it.'

'There must be more than that, surely?'

Genia shrugged and smiled and, holding the fishing bag in one hand, gestured to the boat with his other. 'Jody we should go back. Dinner will be waiting.'

She frowned. 'OK. But I'm not sure I should let you get away so lightly. Come on, then, let's get back. Can I drive? I love these things!'

Genia laughed and took her hand as she boarded the boat.

The blue swirl of cigar smoke hung over the table as dinner came to an end. The guests had broken up into groups. At one end of the table Gary was coming to the end of a joke and at the other Tim, his face shiny with after-sun, was expounding his theory of the use of the riffle-hitch as opposed to the bomber. Michael strained to keep his eyes from closing and stifled a yawn.

Gary had reached the punchline, '...and then the Padre says, 'Don't worry little fellah – I got him with the door!'

Fergus exploded with laughter, his head rocked back and from his mouth came a noise like leaking bellows. Others within earshot laughed, while Jody shook her head and looked over to Sandra. 'You were right about the chest hair. That's outrageous. He wouldn't get away with that story back home.'

'I hate to say it, but that was mild. The stupid thing is that half our stockmen were aboriginals, and they thought the world of the old bugger, although we had a pretty high turnover.'

'I tell you what, how about a game of backgammon? I have a feeling we won't contribute much by staying here.'

'Yeah, good idea. I'll grab that box of truffles, too, before they all disappear.'

Jody walked over to Michael and put a hand on his shoulder. 'Michael, I'll take you up on that offer of a cigar if I may. They smell delicious.'

168

'But of course. Tim be a star and pass the box, will you?'

Tim leapt up and took the box over to Jody, who picked a cigar and joined Sandra on the sofa, who had started setting up the board.

Tim asked Michael, 'Do you know if anyone wants to fish tonight? I thought I'd take a party across the river if anyone would like.'

'I don't know, let's see.' Michael tapped his knife lightly against a glass and the hubbub moderated. 'Right, anyone for a fish this evening? Tim's offered to take people across.'

Fergus was about to say something disparaging but saw a better opportunity and looked at his watch. 'What time is it? Ten thirty. Mmh – I might be on actually. How about you Gary?'

'Yeah, why not? But I see me having a crack at that *Camp Pool*. You've been hogging it since we got here.'

'An excellent choice for a duffer like you. Come on, get into your waders and I'll bring the decanter. I may just watch for a bit before heading downstream. Bumble, why don't you join us? Gary can show us how it's done. Besides I've hardly spoken to you since we got here.'

'I'll just go and grab my jacket. Bring my glass, will you? I'll see you outside.'

'What about you, Steve?'

'I've got some calls to make, but I may join you later.'

Simon was reading the fishing record and shook his head at his father.

'Well, it looks like you haven't got any takers at the moment, Tim, but thanks for offering. Oh by the way, I've arranged for Genia to take Jody and Simon upstream tomorrow.'

'Wouldn't you like me to take them?'

'That's very kind, but Jody is keen to learn that cast of his, and he does know that bit above the junction better than anyone. I'm afraid I've committed him. I'm sure you won't mind.'

'Oh no, not at all.'

Bumble and Fergus sat on the bank watching Gary fish his way down the pool. The sky was overcast and there was a steady upstream wind that delivered strong irregular gusts. They both smoked cigarettes and gossiped.

169

Fergus asked Bumble, 'Why didn't you put your waders on? I'd hoped we could have gone and had a fish together.'

'I don't really feel like it. Maybe tomorrow.'

'Don't be such a bore! I drag my way out here especially to see you, and you won't even pass the time of day with me.'

'Ooh, poor Ferg! No one wants to play with him!'

Fergus grimaced and stuck out his bottom lip, but his mood changed when he saw the bend in Gary's rod. 'This should be fun. Go and get Michael and the others. Be quick!' He stood up and yelled at Gary, 'Go on. Give it some stick you big poof. Show him the butt!'

Gary did as he was told and the fish responded by fighting its way into the middle of the stream, jumping twice as it did so. The rest of the party soon lined the bank to witness the tussle and give words of advice, all of it conflicting.

Fergus put his arm around Simon's shoulder. 'Tell him he's being too hard on it. Get him to let it run.'

'Gary, be more gentle with it. Give it some slack or you'll lose it.'

Gary gingerly lifted his hand from the rod to wave in acknowledgement, swiftly returning it to the cork grip. Soon the metallic clicks of his reel could be heard as the line was pulled from it. The fish jumped one more time and pulled hard, the reel screamed and then the fish was gone. Gary slapped his rod against the water in disbelief and then lifted to check what had happened. He saw that the line had broken free from the backing. The fish had escaped with forty yards of line attached to its mouth.

Fergus bellowed, 'Oh, bad luck Gary! It must have been a monster.'

Bumble realised immediately what had happened. 'You didn't, did you?'

'I don't know what you're talking about.'

Jody asked, 'What's happened? I don't understand.'

'My darling brother has only cut the join between the line and the backing.'

Jody and Sandra nodded at each other confirming their dissent at such puerile behaviour while Gary waded out and joined them shaking his head. 'Well, I'll be buggered! I've never had that happen before.'

'That really is too bad. Are you sure you checked it before you went fishing?' Fergus asked innocently. 'Oh well, these things will happen.'

'Of course I bloody checked it! I checked it before we started this morning. It just doesn't make sense.' Realisation began to dawn. 'Wait a minute. You wouldn't. You did. You bastard!'

Fergus's face was the picture of innocence. 'I simply don't know what you mean, old thing.'

'You cut my line. Do you realise it cost me over $150?' Gary was furious.

'Well, I'd have a go at whoever spliced the line. You could do without that happening when you're into a big one.'

'You wait, I'll have you, you flabby faced drongo!'

Fergus beamed a warm smile and offered his hand. 'What do you say we call it quits, *pax* and all that?'

'No way! This is war! Keep an eye over your shoulder, I'll have you!'

'What about the poor fish? It'll be swimming around with all that line attached to it.' Sandra was concerned.

Michael thought it was time to intervene. 'It's a good point Sandra, but the fish should detach itself – the hook was not barbed. It's still not a clever thing to do. Gary and Fergus, as you are both my guests and in the interests of harmony and safety, I would appreciate it if you would draw a line under this before real harm is done.'

Tim, with cigar in hand and with his confidence swelled with alcohol, added 'Yes, quite right Michael.'

Fergus muttered to him, 'Who rattled your cage?'

Jody had seen enough. She walked over to Michael and kissed his cheek. 'I think I'll call it a day, my book beckons. Thank you for a great day.'

'Jody, bless you. Sleep well. You should have an interesting day upstream tomorrow.'

Chapter Fifteen

The river was a sombre reflection of the sky, which hung like a grey curtain to the horizon. The monotony was only broken by the bouncing flashes made by a pair of Arctic terns, as they skimmed the surface in search of salmon par. The wind had dropped during the night, leaving a humid morning to greet the anglers as they left the camp hut after breakfast. Slowly, they paired up with their guides and prepared to set off in the boats for the day's fishing. Simon was yet to appear. He had missed breakfast and Michael was about to go to his hut to wake him up, but Jody intervened.

'Let him be, Michael. I heard those guys banging around at three o'clock this morning. Let him sleep it off. I'm happy reading here for a while, and as long as its OK with Genia, I don't mind if we get up river later.'

'I've never known breakfast so quiet.' Michael was concerned. 'What were they up to?'

'Drinking vodka with the guides. Gary bet the guides that he, Simon and Fergus could drink them under the table and it looks like Simon bit off more than he could chew. The other two aren't looking that great either.'

'Well, that's their look out. We are heading off and should all be in for a great day's fishing. The water's dropped overnight and I recommend a floating line. Make sure Genia stops at some of the glides – you can catch 'em on a dry fly there. He knows the drill. But remember, if you're fishing on the surface you must strike. Don't ask me why, but there it is. As for my son, if he's not out in half an hour give him a good uplifting kick. That usually does the trick. Tight lines – we'll see you this evening.'

'Tight lines. See you later.'

The sound of the boat engines faded into the distance, leaving

Jody to read on the bank. She undid the braces on her waders and peeled off her sweater; the humidity was increasing. She sat for nearly an hour, before Pana walked over to her, followed by Genia.

'Good morning. How's your head?'

'I wasn't with them last night. I was upstream with Steve and Tim moving some people on. Looking at everyone this morning, I think that the river was the best place to be. Michael told me you wanted to wait for a while.'

'How long will it take us to get up there?'

'About ninety minutes, and then we fish our way back down. We should get going soon or we won't fish all the pools.'

'Yes, there's no point us sitting here all day. I'll go and see what Simon's up to.'

She pulled her braces over her shoulders, wrapped her sweater around her neck and half walked, half skipped to Simon's hut; in the way Genia had seen her, when she first arrived. She was only with Simon for a few minutes before visiting her own hut and returning to Genia on the bank.

'Well, it's just you and me, I'm afraid. He's in a bad way. He says he'll fish the Camp Pool after lunch if he feels up to it. I hope you don't mind. Let's get out of here fast – I don't want that Tim hanging in with us. If you've got your rod, let's pack up and go.'

Genia looked at her as she pulled her hair through a rubber band and planted her cap on her head. The sun had melted her freckles into a healthy tan. He breathed in her freshly applied scent; it hung around her in the moisture-rich air like a fine scarf. He carried her kit to the boat and it was in a silence of anticipation that the two boarded the boat. They sped their way upstream, Jody in the bows with an arm around Pana, while Genia stood with one knee on the thwart and one arm tucked into the braces of his waders at the stern.

After a while, Genia slowed the boat down and they nosed against the current. Jody turned to see if there was a problem and saw Genia pointing to a clump of fir trees.

'Can you see the eagle's nest? The female is with her fledglings, you can see their heads.'

Jody scanned the trees, failing to see the eyrie. She was looking for something far smaller than the huge raft of twigs and branches that had been woven into a platform which would be capable of bearing the birds' weight and withstanding the ravages of wind, ice and snow.

'I can't see it. I must be blind or something.'

'Look at the top of the middle tree. You must be able to see it.'

'Golly! Now I've got it! She's got a white streak and there are two fledglings. I thought the nest would be much smaller – it's huge!'

'She's been here for the last five years. We may see the male when we come back this evening.' He accelerated away.

As they passed Genia's hut, Pana barked out of habit expecting to have a few happy hours mousing under the boards, but they swept on upstream for another mile to some rapids. They negotiated these carefully, before turning the corner into a short bend. The bend opened to reveal a high, grassy bank. The water flowed gently and a breeze that had developed under the cloud riffled the draw towards the tail of the pool. Genia steered the boat into the bank and helped Jody ashore. Pana had already disappeared into the willow scrub.

Jody looked admiringly at the river. 'It's just like a Scottish river. I feel I can work out the water here. Come on, let's get going. You go down in front of me – no arguments! I hate being watched.'

Genia opened the palms of his hands to her. 'Jody, *Pazhalysta...*'

'*Pazhalysta, shmyhalysta!* Do as you're told and don't get all uppity with me! Let me see what you can do.'

'OK, Jody, but we've got a lot of fishing, all the way back to camp, so use your eyes and pick the best places. If you find somewhere good, stay there for while. Try to fish the fly differently, don't just fish like a robot. Do you want me to show you where is good?'

'Purlease!' She made a look of mock horror and waved him away to walk further downstream. She waded into the water with a determination she hadn't known in years. Above the noise of splashing she could hear his laughter.

They fished the pool for an hour and both caught salmon. Jody whistled to Genia when hers took, and he turned around and gestured to her that she would have to land it herself.

He waved for her to come and join him by a smooth glide,

where the river ran fast and evenly over a level bed. From time to time small boils would occur where the bed had indented, causing turbulence that sent small bodies of current to the surface. Any salmon here would be running, and it was a matter of chance whether fish would be there.

'Let's fish the surface, before the wind picks up too much. Have you got a floating line on?'

'You bet. Come on!'

He took her rod and bit the nylon that joined her fly to the line and pulled it free, leaving only a short strand. He replaced it with a long-tailed fly from his tobacco tin and tied the nylon around it in such a way that it would waggle on the surface of the water.

'There, try that.' He handed the rod back to her. 'Stand here on the bank and cast across the current, almost upstream, and let's see what happens.'

She loosened some line from her reel and cast at right angles to the bank. The fly fished through the surface film leaving a wake – a small water-vole swimming across a pond. They both watched the ripples, twin Vs, created on the surface, as at first they accelerated and then slowed down as they swung downstream. She cast again, further this time. The fly pushed up water in front of it like a billiard cue through baize. Suddenly there was a pronounced swirl as a fish swam a figure-of-eight around the fly. Then they could see the salmon's tail slapping and splashing water onto it.

'Holy cow! What do I do now?'

'Be patient, he'll come again.'

The fly wallowed for a moment in a small back eddy and then the salmon struck again, this time fully lifting out of the water and crashing down in an explosion of spray, taking the fly into its mouth.

'Strike! Strike now Jody!'

She lifted the rod-tip and the fish was on and swam away out of the flat water and down into the rocks and shallows below. Her line sheared through the water lifting a corona of spray, which misted the surface. Within seconds it was lost. Jody grabbed Genia's arm.

'What was that all about?'

'I think you made him angry.'

175

Genia looked up at the sky. The wind was increasing, the limpid grey of the morning was now looking bruised and menacing. 'OK. A few more casts and then we'll go downstream. There are plenty more pools to fish.'

Jody caught and landed a salmon and returned it to the river, while Genia whistled for Pana so that they could return to the boat and head downstream. The first heavy spots of rain were falling. He started the engine. It masked the rumble of distant thunder.

Jody waved him on past the next pool, urging him to find the next place where she could fish the skated fly.

'But this is a great holding pool, Jody. We'll find sixteen, seventeen pounders here. Are you sure?'

'Sure I'm sure. I want more of that riffle hitch business.'

He looked across the river and saw that longer gusts of wind added to the unevenness of the surface, already pockmarked by large, infrequent raindrops. He steered them downstream to his hut at the junction.

'There is a good place about a hundred metres upstream around the corner. We can have lunch here in the hut, if you like. We might be glad to be inside. It's going to be very wet in an hour.'

'Well, I'll get going then. Are you happy to cook lunch again?'

'Sure.'

'If you catch a fish we might be guaranteed a feed. I haven't mastered this technique yet. I'll come back in say an hour or an hour and a half. Can I take Pana with me?' Genia smiled and nodded, but she had already whistled and the dog was following her as she walked away into the scrub.

Genia was glad to be back at his hut and he set about opening the shutters and preparing for his guest. The crackle of kindling brought life to the stove as he set about catching a fish for lunch. He returned shortly afterwards to find steam swirling over the simmering pot. He had brought batteries with him and the sounds of Alfred Brendel playing Mozart issued from his machine, through the open door and out over the river, where they were lost in the gathering storm. A blast of wind slammed the door shut, bringing Genia's reverie to an abrupt end. The weather front was on its way, and in the distance, there was a hazy flash of lightning, followed nearly a minute later by a brooding roll of thunder.

He went outside and noticed that the wind direction had changed, the storm was being blown towards them. He made everything safe in the hut and brushed past Pana, who was seeking sanctuary, before loping up the path to get Jody. As he went, the heavens opened and delivered a downpour of warm heavy drops which splashed on the metallic surface of the water. Another flash of lightning lit up the river and, in silhouette, he could see Jody still fishing, her rod in the air. The rain now puckered the surface of the river like ostrich leather, the drops forming tiny mercurial balls, which rolled across the surface before being absorbed. Then, only thirty seconds later, there was a loud clap of thunder. He motioned to her to get out of the river. She waved back, unaware of the danger.

'Get out of the water! Get out, Jody!'

Genia's shouts reached her and she began to understand the seriousness of her predicament. She turned to walk to the bank. No further prompting was required as another flash of lightning rent the air above her. She stumbled in the water, still holding her rod.

'Drop it. Drop it!' Genia almost screamed. 'Leave it, Jody – just get out!' He was with her now, pounding through the water. He snatched the rod from her hand and hurled it at the bank. His hands looped under her arms as he hauled her back onto her feet. She said something, but her words were lost in the next flash, which was followed seconds later by a thunderous explosion. It shook through their bodies. The storm was nearly over them.

'Where do we go?'

'Get up on the bank and lay flat in the open.'

She was too exhilarated to be scared. She kept hold of his hand and threw herself on to the grass dragging him with her. Her cap had blown off and her face shone as the next flash briefly illuminated the drops that clung to her skin.

She shouted to the sky in defiance. 'One Mississippi, Two Mississippi, Three Mississippi, Four Mississippi, Five ... Holy shit! Did you hear that? And it's still five miles away. I guess me standing in the water fat, dumb and happy with my rod in my hand wasn't the right option?'

He laughed. 'No, the worst. You rod's made of carbon fibre. You would have been safer holding a lightning conductor.'

They both lay on their backs, the warm rain splashing on their faces, Jody counting the seconds between lightning and thunder. The storm reached its climax with a tumultuous flash and explosion; it shook the shallow valley and made her squeal with delight. Genia could only laugh at her reaction, he had seen men cowering at the first glimmer of lightning.

She stood up and pulled him up with her. 'Come on, let's get back to your hut and dry out.'

'Let's just wait a bit longer, it's still very close.' Genia was still wary.

'Come on, we can get the rod later. Don't be a sissy!' He didn't know what the word meant.

The temperature dropped as the front passed through and the rain intensified. The hut door swung wildly in the wind behind Pana, who had ventured out onto the top step to greet them. Genia stood at the bottom of the steps and gestured Jody to enter his home.

'My...' she exclaimed, as she peeled off her wading jacket and wriggled out of her waders. She walked into his hut wearing silk longjohns, a T-shirt and a fleece – seemingly unaware of the consternation it was causing her host. He walked in behind her.

'Hey, take those boots off – we don't want to mess it up in here!' she said, turning to the stove.

Genia took off his jacket and waders leaving him in a shirt, shorts and his woollen socks. Pana curled up in front of the stove.

'Its gorgeous! Ginny said it was. And I didn't expect it to be so tidy. Hey, and flowers too!' He had collected a few large buttercups from the river and put them in a bowl. The small table was set for two. 'And all these books!' Her gaze took in the contents of the hut. 'I'm not sure about this though.' She pointed to the bearskin that lay over the bed.

'Jody, it keeps me warm.'

'You must remember I'm a woman. We have God-given right to take a peek into everything. OK, I'll overlook poor Yogi over there in exchange for the Mozart and a glass out of one of those bottles we brought up with us.'

She spoke quickly and he was finding it difficult to keep pace with her humour. He found himself on the fringes of irritation.

'I now remember why I like being here by myself. Jody, why don't you bring those wet clothes inside? Please take the cork out of the bottle and let me finish cooking lunch.'

'Just because you live up here alone doesn't mean you should have forgotten how to entertain a lady. And besides, do you normally meet and greet in your underwear?' She pointed at his legs.

Had he been wearing boots, his heels would have clicked together but his threadbare socks gave an adequate impression of a military man. '*Touch the Wild* insists that all members of staff will wear company uniform at all times,' he quoted ironically. 'It's one of the reasons I'm stopping at the end of this year.' He reached for a battered pair of jeans hanging from a hook and put them on. 'There, now I'm ready to cook lunch.'

'Good, and I can have a look at your shelves. Oh great, photos too! Take your time.'

Shaking his head, he set to work and they both busied themselves as the rain rattled on the roof and the thunder rumbled. The tape came to an end with a hiss and a click. Jody turned it over without comment and sat back on the bed. She rested her head against a pillow which she propped against the log wall, took a glass in one hand and a book she had picked from the shelf in the other and curled her legs underneath her. She would have preferred to ask him more questions that would have provided answers to the clues she had found on his shelves. The last thing she wanted to do was to read, but he seemed easier in the silence. She half looked at the pages and half watched him as he prepared lunch. It was peaceful and cosy; even the coarse softness of the bearskin felt good.

Genia prepared two plates of salmon and rice that steamed as he set them on the table. He raised his glass.

'*Dabro pachalovat ka mnie*'

'I hope that means I get to eat this.'

He laughed. 'It means welcome to my home.'

'*Na zdorovye!*' she nodded graciously and raised her glass to his.

'*Na zdorovye,*' Genia responded.

'Hey look, I'm sorry if I was a bit pushy earlier. I could sense I was getting on your nerves. I'm sorry.'

He smiled a warm open smile. 'Don't apologise. I speak enough English so we can communicate well. But your mind works very quickly. Sometimes you speak too fast.' He paddled his hands to illustrate what he meant.

She laughed and forked some food into her mouth, was about to say something, but let him speak. 'I think maybe we are both shy, but we have different ways of showing it.' Her face set. She was about to retort, but he didn't let her speak. 'It's just what I see, I don't mean to be rude.'

She thought for a few seconds. 'I do tend to overcompensate. It's a fishing thing. I'm usually the only woman in a fishing party. I suppose I try and do my female version of male affability. It doesn't work, huh? Can I ask you some questions though?' He had just swallowed a hot forkful and tried to create a facial gesture that expressed the simultaneous messages of agreement and encouragement, without opening his mouth.

She smiled. 'I was looking at your shelves. Pictures, books, religion – a lot of religion, and philosophy. You served in Afghanistan. How come you don't have any ... I don't know – souvenirs is the wrong word – but every soldier I've ever known, old or young, always holds onto something – even a trophy. It's such a big thing in their lives.'

'I did hold on to things for a while – but the war was bad for me, and a while ago I decided to wipe it away. Erase it.'

'But what about friends, comrades? You guys always seem to hold on to all of that.'

'I had to let it all go. I burnt everything – my uniform, my diaries, my photos. Everything. Do you really want to know?'

She sat upright, put her hands together and rested them on her lap. 'Yes please, I would like that very much.'

'I left the hospital to join the Army; because of my training I became the platoon medic. I didn't have it any better or worse than any other soldier. I was injured when our helicopter was shot down. I was rescued and healed by an old man, Salim. He saved my life and cared for me. I hid with him in the hills for several weeks away from the war, away from the world in a cave, high on the Pakistan border.'

'A bit like here?'

'Yes, a bit like here.'

The wind had dropped and the sky had lightened. There was silence in the hut.

'What happened next?'

'Well, he knew we could not stay there forever. We agreed that we would set out together to try to find some Russians for me

180

to join. We did, only they were being chased by some Mujahideen. Salim and I agreed to split up, and return each to our own people. Mine welcomed me. Salim was shot.'

'Did you get sent home?'

'No, I was kept on a field hospital until the end of my tour. We were either patching people up or tending to the typhoid and hepatitis sufferers. When we weren't doing that, we were trying to stop orderlies selling patients' urine to soldiers who wanted to contract an illness and be sent home. It was madness. The surgical spirit that should have been used for cleaning wounds was mostly sold to be drunk – we had to use petrol as a disinfectant.'

'I didn't realise all this was going on.'

'No one did. At first, soldiers' parents were told their sons were being sent to reinforce the border. One hundred thousand soldiers to patrol the border...' his voice tailed away.

'It sounds like Vietnam in the early days.'

'Afghanistan was our Vietnam. When I was in America last year I watched a video – *The Fourth of July*. it was a powerful film. When I finally got home from the war we were sent to schools to talk about our gallantry out there. If I was Tom Cruise in my wheelchair, I would have ignored instructions and told them the truth. But I was Genia, so I got drunk and lied. I would walk into a classroom reeking of vodka, in my pressed uniform and white belt, a paratrooper, a hero, an *Afganits*, a *Zinky Boy*... Pitiful!' He paused before continuing, 'It was the simple things I remember. You lose common courtesies – please, thank you, I'm sorry – don't exist in the army. I was only twenty-four, but I saw how easily the eighteen-year-olds found it to kill. They had no...' he searched for the word, 'no compassion. Salim said the war broke my ... he used the word heart. I think that is what they say in his language, but it had broken my spirit. I lost my sense of decency and, later, with the drink, my self respect.'

He was still looking out of the window. Jody had moved back to the bed where she sat listening.

'So, Genia hides in the forest, not using his skills and not facing up to reality. That is what my father says – but it is only part true. Russia, my mother country, has treated her sons badly. It's not just about the war. It's about the recent changes and their effect. Decent people playing by the rules don't stand a chance, corruption is everywhere and it will take more than my lifetime to sort itself out.' He turned towards her. 'I live the life I choose. I take strength from my belief in God, comfort in my solitude and fulfilment in the enjoyment of simple pleasures.

'So there you have Genia – you have his life. You can put it in a bottle and take it home with you.' He laughed softly. 'I didn't intend to make a joke, but that would be a good place to keep it. Our country still drinks over four billion bottles of vodka a year!'

Jody said nothing for a moment, then asked, 'What is a *Zinky Boy*?'

'Ah, the *Zinky Boys*. The coffins that were used to send the bodies back were made of zinc. There were thirty thousand, forty thousand, fifty thousand of them – who knows? They were sent home and most were buried discreetly with few military honours. They were the true *Zinky Boys*. I was lucky. I lived, my body came home walking, but I left my soul in Kabul.' He smiled.

'Hey, enough about me, what about you? That's a phrase I heard a few times in the United States. You most probably want to fish. Hell, it's meant to be a holiday for you.' His tone was turning sour.

'I don't want to go fishing just yet. Can I ask you some more?'

'Jody, it's very nice that you show an interest in me, but maybe we should go fishing.'

'I know, but you can't get to talk to too many people like this. I'm genuinely interested. Tell me about Salim. How did you know the gunfire you heard was him being shot? It could have been anyone. How did you get from drink-blasted veteran to being out here? And most important of all, is this a no smoking room?'

'I'll get you an ashtray.' He found a small painted saucer and put it by the bed. He started to clear the table as she found her cigarettes in her fishing jacket.

'Do you mind if I tidy up?' he asked.

'Not at all. I'm not very good at all that. Do you want one of these?'

He declined her offer, and went on. 'In my heart I knew about Salim immediately. The platoon commander sent out a patrol to investigate. The Mujahideen had returned to the valley, the patrol found his body. They brought me his prayer-beads. They're there on that hook.' As he spoke, he reached up for the amber beads and handed them to her. 'When I got home and did my

182

propaganda visits I was restless. I had no inclination to go back to medical school. I was fighting with my parents, my friends, myself. I was in a sorry state, but no worse than hundreds of others. We would meet at the comrades' club and drink. We had a reputation to keep up. Some went back, some went into crime. I went to sea on the trawlers. I spent six years in the Barents Sea. These are my souvenirs of that time.' He showed her his roughened hands. 'I wound up working on a boat owned by the Collective that owns this river. The boss was a man called Sergei. You'll see him tomorrow. He found out I could speak English and they needed someone to work here. I was tired of the boats, so here I am with you in this hut. Genia in a nutshell.'

She ran the well-worn beads through her fingers. 'I still don't get Salim's importance.'

'He told me many things when we were in the cave. At the beginning I was either mad with pain or my head was full of hashish. I think he gave me opium at one time too. When I left him, I didn't immediately say, 'Yes, you are right old man. I'll change the way I live my life.' I just buried that experience with all the other experiences and tried to forget. What you will find hard to understand is that, here, in Russia, I was brought up without religion. No concept of God. No life after death – just this life. As a child at school you were taught Communist Citizenship. A key part of my degree course was Scientific Communism; fail that and you fail the degree. It was one of the reasons I dropped out, as you say.

'When I was first with Salim and he started telling me about God and explaining his simple faith, I argued against him with everything that I had ever learned. He would get angry. 'If you cannot believe in God, then there is no point in life. You are just as you appear to be – an ant crawling over the sand, your coming and going will not even leave a mark. I will still heal you, but the sooner you leave the better.' He would then stalk out of the cave and leave me to stew.'

Jody nodded. 'We used to talk about all this stuff at college. We were usually on dope at the time as well. It sounds like we had more fun, though. How weird to think when I was there with my roommates, you were hunkering down with that old man. But if he was a Muslim, how come he took drugs? I thought they were against all that.'

'He was a Sufi, and Sufism is as much a way of life as a religion. Sufis come from all religions. They believe that, because God created everything, then everything on this earth is here for a reason including alcohol, drugs, sex – whatever – can be enjoyed, as long as they do not get in the way of our relationship with God.' He paused and looked at her. ' Do you really want to hear this?'

She imitated his plaintive gesture.

He continued, 'But religion, belief, personal things... Do you want some coffee? I learnt how to make it the cowboy way – gunpowder coffee.'

'Please, don't change the subject.' She saw that he was becoming distant again. 'OK, give me one thought to take with me and then we'll have some coffee.'

'Find God in everything you do and in everyone you meet. Delight in simple pleasures and happiness will follow.' He suddenly felt self-conscious. The words seemed naive and facile in front of her, as they had to him all those years ago.

She sat and thought as he looked out across the river to the scraggy wilderness beyond. After a few minutes, she stood up and went to find the provision bag. In it she found a container that held the ground coffee, with it were slices of cake, moist and crammed with fruit. She broke a piece off one of the slices and nibbled it, before offering some of it to Genia. He was in the process of pouring the boiling water into a metal pot; both his hands were occupied. She fed the cake into his mouth, and wiped a crumb from his chin. She smiled shyly, before returning to her place on the bed, seemingly unaware of the effect that this simple act had on both of them. For him the softness of her skin on his lip. For her the bristle of his chin on her fingers. Two distinct and contrasting sensations created one identical response. Sensual tension hung in the air like a sustained note.

Genia looked uncertainly into her eyes. A frown formed between her eyebrows. Neither wanted to disturb the weight of their silence. Slowly, a smile broadened across her face; a thought came unbidden and expanded with that smile. It was Jody who spoke first.

'Why don't we stay up here tonight? We can go back tomorrow in time for Michael's birthday lunch.' The words were said without a shred of embarrassment or fear of rebuttal. 'And, before you say anything, I'm not feeling pity for you. But I like it up here. I can do without the whole fishing party thing for an evening. So, why don't we stay?'

'Jody...' He shook his head sadly.

'Genia, hear me out, *Pazhalysta*. This is how we do it. You've got that communications thing. We call Steve and I get to talk to Ginny. I explain that this is my idea and it's what I've decided. She'll put it right with Michael, and Tim will do as he's told. Hell, you'll be the man who persuaded me to stay here. It's my reputation not yours...'

'But you know it's not like that.'

'If it was like that, I wouldn't have come up here with you alone today. I'd still be reading my book, waiting for Simon to wake up. Let me tell you something. We both are going through unsettling times. I'd really like to stay; we can fish, eat, walk, talk and fish some more. We've got another bottle of wine. After all, we're both are as good as middle-aged; we are grown ups, we do what we please. I promise I won't pounce!'

He laughed and shook his head. 'Yes. I would like you to be my guest tonight, Jody. Please will you stay?'

'There ya go! Why, sir, I would only be too delighted.' She stood up adding, 'I don't want to seem indelicate, but where is the bathroom? I've got to tinkle.' She wrinkled her nose as she spoke.

Genia's face revealed the shock that her remark had caused, although his words seemed unaffected. 'Outside, under the trees upstream from the junction. There is some good moss there. That is my guest bathroom.'

'Great. And then we can go fishing. What say we go up to that holding pool that we went past and see if we can't catch some bigger fish? And how about some of that coffee before we go?'

She opened the door to reveal tentative rays of light appearing beneath the clouds. The air was colder, the humidity had disappeared. She picked up her clothes and sat on the step to get into her waders while he stoked the stove, relieved to have a few minutes by himself to collect his thoughts and regain his composure.

'It's going to be a great afternoon, I can feel it,' she mused as she walked up the bank, Pana following in her tracks.

Chapter Sixteen

The last traces of storm had disappeared, leaving a warm sun-lit afternoon. Genia sat on the bank watching as Jody played a fish, her rod glinting as it bent and shook with the salmon's efforts to free itself. Pana lay stretched out next to him, his head on his master's lap. She turned around, aware that he was look-ing at her, and smiled. The salmon splashed across the current and into the bank. She followed and bent to return it to the river. As she walked up the bank towards him, Genia anticipated her mood. The effects of the wine and the intimacy of the cabin would have worn off. She would want to return to the camp. It had all been a mistake. Salim's words which he had repeated to her now seemed shallow and pretentious. What could he have been think-ing about? She had just wanted to prove that she could attract a man. She had made her point, and now she would leave. 'Genia, you are a fool,' he told himself.

Pana lifted his head and trotted away down the path to greet Jody. She drew closer and swept her cap from her head. Genia squinted as he looked up at her, seeing her hair as a tattered halo against the sun, suspended in golden strands. Her mood was light as she talked to the dog, her words inaudible over the sounds of the river as it swelled against rocks, merging with birdsong from the trees. She stood next to him and put her hand on his shoulder.

'Genia, I've been thinking. Will you take me to your bed, please?'

Genia grasped her hand. 'Jody... Jody, we can't...'

'Is there something wrong?'

'No...' Genia looked into her eyes. 'No, nothing's wrong. It's not that. On the day you arrived, when the helicopter landed. I couldn't see you, but I knew that someone was looking at me. I had picked up some of the puppies. I didn't know who it was, but it unsettled me. I wanted to be there to see Michael, but I left. I saw you as you walked to the river that day, and again in the evening, you were standing behind the screen. And then we were together yesterday morning, and last evening...'

'Well, is that so bad?'

'I'm not sure...'

'Why?'

'Because to make love with you would be the best thing I can imagine. But then you'll leave me. What do I do then?'

'You'll stay. What will I do then?'

'Jody... I know I will miss you... I miss you already.'

'Genia, I've heard most lines in my life, and let me tell you, that one's not original. You don't have to say anything.'

'It's the truth. Maybe it's the first time someone has really meant it. Jody, I'm settled here. You will complicate things for me. You have already. Making love with you will make it even more complicated. I mean it. Look, stop me talking because this is not good for you or me.'

'Remember what Salim said? Take delight in the simple pleasures,' she raised her hands above her head, pouted and smiled, 'Well, *voila!*'

'You are not a simple anything, Jody. I think you know that.'

'I have really thought about this. Sure, we could let the moment pass, but I don't want to do that. You don't have to feel responsible for me. It's as much my choice as it is yours, more in fact.' Suddenly doubting him, she said, 'Maybe I've misread the way you're feeling?'

His look answered her question.

'Well then. Please – *pazhalysta!*'

He stood up and took her hand. He stroked the palm against his cheek and then kissed it tenderly. He was about to say something, but a finger across his lips and an admonishing smile stopped him. He walked with her back to his cabin. They walked in silence.

She stood barefoot on the floor. The wood felt smooth and welcoming to her soles as they enjoyed its latent warmth. She put a pan of water to heat on the stove, her white T-shirt inadequately covering her nakedness.

They had gone to the bed and made love. She had pulled Genia on top of her and had given herself to him. He took as she gave, selfishly and unashamedly, two people working away years of loveless passion. They had looked into each other's eyes throughout, the silence serving only to heighten the easy pleasure that their bodies felt. He climaxed before her and she held him in her. Her body arched, her face a picture of pleasure, bordering on pain, as she worked herself to pensive fulfilment against him.

Genia lay curled up under the sheets, he hoped for light-hearted words from her. But no words came. He was sobered by the intensity of their pleasure, and for the second time that day, he cursed himself for being a fool.

She was subdued as she watched the first bubbles form in the bottom of the pan and rise to the surface, wisps of steam forming on the surface. She was not aware that the pot had begun to boil; her mind was racing. She too had realised that something had been set in motion that would not rest easily. They had made love without precaution and when he was close to climax instead of pushing him away, she had clamped her legs around him and drawn the seed from him. For a flickering moment she had wanted to have his child. She wanted to tell him now – but she knew that she couldn't accept the way she felt herself; let alone share it with him. She was annoyed with herself. Whatever made her think that she could come out here, meet a man and make love to him without regard or care? The expression on her face betrayed her doubts.

'Will you come to back to bed and let me hold you?'

She nodded, pushed the pan from the heat and squirmed into the bed beside him. He kissed her and then rolled her over, wrapping himself around her. They lay together breathing in harmony. The sounds of the river filtered though the door into the room. She felt the weight of his body against her, the strength in his arm and nestled her face into the pillow.

'Is something wrong?' he asked.

She squeezed his arm tightly. 'No ... not any more.'

He kissed the fine hairs at the nape of her neck, inhaling her soft scent. They both drifted into sleep.

They awoke to the sounds of the walkie-talkie; a stark mechanical squawk, reality's wake-up call screeching into the hut. Pana barked. Genia kissed her cheek and grimaced as he brought life to his arm that had lain under her head. His back ached, but for once the pain brought a reminder of pleasure. 'I should have called Steve earlier. It's seven-thirty and they'll want to know if we are going to back in time for drinks.' It was a question he wanted the answer to as well.

'Tell him about the fishing, the storm and so forth, and then say I need to speak to Ginny. Unless you've changed your mind?'

He opened his arms and looked down his naked body to beyond his navel and smiled.

'Well, I guess not. Come on, let's get this call over with and then you can come back to bed. Here, put this around you, I don't want any distractions.' She tossed him his shirt which was lying by the bed, and he put it over his shoulders.

Genia stood on the steps and spoke to Steve. He told him about the storm and the fishing and then asked him to find Ginny, so that Jody could speak to her. He turned to pass the radio to Jody and she kissed him before pulling her hair from one side of her face and placing the handset to her ear.

'Ginny. Hi there, how'ya doin'? Can we talk?'

Out of habit, he went to check the boat. He leant against the metal hull and looked out across the river. During the last few days spring had turned to summer and the narrow valley had burgeoned into life. A large bumblebee flew a meandering course across the river, buffeted by the breeze, reaching the opposite bank through ponderous determination. Genia drew deep breaths; catkin pollen and wild herbs had sweetened the normal peat smells. He could hear Jody's voice. In his house was a woman, for the first time, a woman. In a week he would be sitting in this same position and she would have gone. How would he feel then? How did he feel now? He heard her feet on the steps and turned to look. She was holding two glasses of wine. Her legs were long and brown, her bare feet slapped softly on the stone, as she came to sit down beside him.

'Well there you go. I've arranged everything with Ginny, she told me she was "green with envy my dear", she'll cover it with Michael – and I've managed to stop Tim coming up here later to see if we're all right.' She squeezed his arm with hers. 'Genia, we have the most wonderful night ahead of us. Let's be sad when

189

we part, not before. I know what you said about missing me, and I don't know how it'll hit me yet. But why don't you listen to some of *my* homespun philosophy, for a change? Never anticipate an emotion. Hell, you may be sick of me by morning.'

He thought for a while and then smiled. 'Yes, I understand. I apologise for being so Russian! Jody – I am truly happy to know you. I'm sorry for being so ... so ... maudlin. Please, will you smile and kiss me?'

She put her glass on a rock, placed her hands to either side of his face, running her fingers through his hair to the back of his neck. She pulled his face towards hers and kissed his mouth, her lips partly opened. She sipped greedily. He ran an arm around her waist and pulled her tightly to him. With eyes closed they kissed for some time, until she finally pulled away. She took his hand and, opening the craggy palm, kissed it. Earlier, when they had made love she had to encourage him to touch her. He had been shy of the coarseness of his hands. She ran her tongue to the crook between thumb and first finger and bit gently.

'Now what's for supper tonight?'

'I will give you my trout rod and send you to catch some grayling. These I will serve with potatoes and wild garlic,' Genia replied with a flourish of his hand.

'I could get used to these simple pleasures of yours!'

Jody caught several small grayling and returned to the hut to find it restored to its original tidy condition. When she had left, the sheets had lain ragged on the bed, the bearskin pushed into the corner, her clothes scattered everywhere, with the smell of their sex fading in the air. All gone. She thought of Greg.

'Why did you tidy up?' There was an edge to her voice.

He turned to her. 'Habit, I suppose. I live here alone; when I was drinking Sergei would come here once a month and sluice the place out with a bucket of water. Why?'

'I don't know. It's like you've cleaned me away. I didn't expect that.'

'Come here, I haven't washed you away.'

She put the fish on the table and clung to him; tall as she was her head fell against his shoulder. She breathed deeply and squeezed him hard. 'Let's bathe in the morning, not until then. What do you say?'

'I'm a *Touch the Wild* guide. Personal hygiene is top of the list. We are given one can of deodorant a fortnight. Yet again I am risking my job for you!'

'I won't tell if you don't.' She pushed her hips against him. 'I'm not hungry yet and you look mighty sleepy. Come here, I want to tell you something.'

'What is it?'

'I can't possibly tell you standing up. Come to my office over here, and I'll tell you.' She took his hand and led him to the bed. 'Now, why don't you just lie down? And if you don't mind, can we point that bear's head the other way? It feels like there's three of us in here.'

'You don't have to worry, it was a female.'

'That says more about you than it does about me.'

He laughed and pulled her down on to the bed rolling her over onto her back. Pinning her hands above her head, he kissed her. He pulled back and gazed into her eyes, was about to say something, but knew it would be inadequate. She raised her head from the pillow and nibbled his bottom lip with her teeth and then bit. He recoiled.

'Ow!'

'Now do as you're told.'

Later, after they had eaten, they sat propped up against a rock, Genia with his arms wrapped around Jody who sat between his knees. They stared into the dwindling flames of their fire, and luxuriated in the warmth that brushed their faces.

'So, when Mom died I started fishing seriously to keep Pa company. He loved the boys, but he brought them up to be independent and, most importantly, men. He didn't want, in fact he couldn't, let them see just how much he had fallen apart. You know, I was the only one who cried in front of anyone? I talked to Pa about it and he said that they all grieved in their own way. He sort of told me off. He said it was "not a team sport" – he actually used those words. The boys were sad and would take me to one side to say things like "You know, Jody, I really miss Mom," as if it were some dark secret, like they were gay or something. All I wanted to do was cry and get angry for the injustice of it all. What happens to families here when a mother dies?'

'Our country is our motherland and our mothers are the focal point of our family life. We have rigid relationships with our fathers, but they would understand and expect us to mourn openly the loss of a mother. Which is what happened with Nadia and me.' He picked up his glass and passed it to her. She took it and sipped the wine before passing back to him as she continued.

'Dad really fell apart. It was like they were joined at the hip. I was working at the time for publishers, selling international rights. I was travelling – it was a good job. But I had to devote more and more time to him. We would sit there and he would get me talking about our old holidays and stuff, and I would see him looking at me. He was searching for Mom in me, you know, my laugh, my smile, a simple mannerism. It was like I brought her back to life. It was spooky sometimes because I found myself trying to sound like her; he was willing me to do it. It was about that time I met Greg.'

She paused. They had already talked about Greg but she had just said that it wasn't working out. She was about to embark upon a darker journey. He leant backwards to pick a log from the pile and passed it to her. She took it and prodded the fire with it, scraping ash and smouldering remains into the middle of the flames. Sparks flew upwards and their faces were illuminated against the night. She lay back into his arms and squeezed his arms more tightly around her body.

'There's no point in us talking like this is there?'

'It is up to you. It's good talking about you – it helps me understand. Perhaps it would be easier for me, though, if you said you were happy in your marriage.'

'What do you mean?'

'I mean, I could say goodbye and wish you well. I would know you were happy.'

'Won't you anyway?'

'Of course, but if you are not happy, I would like to offer you more. But I've been to your country, I have seen it, and so I know I have nothing to offer you. You don't know Russia – you don't know Murmansk. Your country club is not the same as our Seaman's Mission. Don't think that I'm ashamed. We are a good family, my father was a surgeon.' He found a hollow laugh to mask a deeper sadness. 'But maybe my pride is hurt. I'm sad that I can't, what's the expression? – sweep you off your feet.'

'But you have, you know you have.'

'It will be me who will fall the hardest.'

'Let me ask you a question. When you were in America, did you sleep with an American woman?'

Genia moved uneasily behind her and waited for a moment before replying. 'Yes, in Montana. She was a guide.'

'Was it like you and me? You know, the same sort of thing.'

'No, she was much more sexually experienced. She... Ouch!'

Jody hit him hard in the ribs, and rolled over as she turned around to face him. 'Say that again, you bastard, and you're a dead man!' He laughed and straightening his arms lifted her above him. 'Let me explain. I was out there and she was living with her boyfriend. But, he was away and we slept together – but it was not right. She said something like, "Relax, it's just a fuck – that's all. You don't have a limited supply." I told her that she was wrong and that every time a woman – I remember I used her own words – "fucked" someone they didn't love, they lost a part of their soul.'

They lay on their backs as they had earlier in the thunderstorm, but now the sky was clear, stars had started to show. It was still twilight but the fire made it seem darker.

'So, where does that leave me?'

'This is different, Jody. I didn't say *you* had lost part of your soul when you made love with me. You did just that – you loved! I can't explain it, but something happened in bed – I don't know what, but ... and that is why,' he faltered, 'why I know I will sit here next week and be very unhappy, as unhappy as only a Russian can be. I am not bitter, but I think that you will get over it. I truly hope you will. Now do you understand?'

'Yes.' She took his hand again. 'I feel like I'm betraying a whole nation of women when I say I don't want to talk about this any more. Take me to bed, lay me on that rug and make love to me like you did this afternoon.'

That night they slept as they had in the afternoon, Jody on her side and Genia wrapped around her, his arm cradling her head.

* * *

She held his hand to her breast as she lay sleepily awake, content to hear his breathing and feel its warmth on her neck. The night had been warm and dawn had brought a gentle breeze that crept in through the open door and riffled the edge of their sheet. The sun shone low on the river, sparking off reflections, which marbled the wooden ceiling. Pana lay across the threshold luxuriating in the early warmth, an ear twitching as he heard stirring from inside. Wagging his tail, he turned to greet Genia who had awoken. The dog stood expectantly, it was past his breakfast time.

They both lay in silence for several minutes, uncertain of the other's wakefulness, each enjoying the soft warmth that their bodies created. Genia began to ease his arm from under Jody's head.

'Good morning.' Her words were almost a purr, an appropriate complement to her feline stretch that pushed her buttocks against him. 'And where do you think you are going?'

He laughed, kissed her cheek, slid out of bed before she could stop him and, grabbing a towel left the cabin with Pana in tow. The word 'spoilsport' drifted behind him. She rolled on to her back and surveyed his work, for he had built this cabin – every log and plank; each nail and dowel all done by him. She noticed the neatly trimmed felt, packed between the logs for insulation, and tried to picture him alone, with the storm outside. She looked differently at the photos now, for when she arrived she assumed the woman would be a lover. She felt proprietorial about them now. She looked at her watch and counted the hours until they would return to the camp. It was still some time away but she knew that she had to think what to do – it was going to be complicated. She left the bed, and went to the door.

Genia was standing up to his waist in the water, with Pana swimming around him. Genia's torso was milky white against the mahogany of his face and arms. He sensed her watching and plunged his head under the surface, before wading back to the bank, where his towel lay waiting. He waved for her to turn her head as he climbed up onto the bank. Her response was to stretch her fingers across her eyes so that she could see easily.

He wrapped the towel around him as she giggled. 'My, that water must be cold!' He walked up to her and kissed her. She held him to her and licked the river water from the side of his bristled face; it tasted cool and fresh. 'Come on. I'll cook us some breakfast. What's on offer?'

'The choice is limited. It is too late in the season for eggs, too early for mushrooms. So, the choice is fish – fish with rice, fish with potatoes or fish with fish.'

'What about those cans, what's in those?' She pointed at a row of labelless tins on a shelf.

'Those are for when I am desperate. They are a lucky dip. The cooks sometimes leave food behind. I never know what's in them until I open them. On a bad day I can have a meal of soup and custard.'

She pulled a face as he left with the pail to gather water. She imagined him at the table with the kerosene lamp and the dog sitting by. She tried to picture the expression on his face as he opened the tins. She thought about the loneliness, the isolation; she looked at the bed where they had lain and pictured him alone and asleep.

'Two different worlds?' he asked.

'Oh – oh no. I was miles away. It must still be the jet lag. Perhaps I still haven't completely gotten over it.' Then she turned and smiling softly caught his hand as he walked past. 'No it wasn't that. I don't feel so brave this morning.'

'No,' he reached to stroke her face with the back of his hand. 'I was thinking the same. Now I can't imagine my home without you in it.'

'What do we do?'

'Burn it down?'

'No, what do *we* do?'

'Enjoy the days we have together, be honest with ourselves and...'

'Hope for the best?'

'Yes, you're right, hope for the best.'

They pushed the cloud of parting away and continued with the morning's activities like two children playing house. Jody bathed in the river as Genia heated up the stove. When she returned, she tied her still wet hair in a ponytail, before explaining her plan for the morning. She had cheered up completely.

'OK, I've got it all worked out. For breakfast we've still got those sandwiches that we didn't eat yesterday. Why don't we fry those up with some oil? We can wash them down with some

195

coffee. Sounds – let's play that Rachmaninov tape that we listened to last night – *Isle of the Dead*? It's lovely, though it's a bummer of a title. Then fishing. After breakfast we head back upstream with one rod and take it in turns to fish and ghillie. That leaves sex. We leave enough time to say farewell to your cabin before heading back for Michael's birthday lunch. What do you say?'

Genia shrugged happily. She held his face in her hands and kissed him. She wound her arms around his neck and arched her body against his.

'I think we are going to have change the order around a little here,' she whispered into his ear.

Chapter Seventeen

Michael sat on the bank, a telephone handset pressed to his ear. He talked as he scanned a spreadsheet through his half-moon glasses. Dressed in his waders and fishing clothes, controlling his world from a fishing camp, he was the very image of a happy plutocrat. Steve sat by, ensuring that the receiver resisted Michael's pulls on the handset as he emphasised a point. The small grey box looked more like a laptop computer than a satellite phone that could be used anywhere on the earth's surface.

Steve, too, was at his happiest, the factotum sharing his master's confidences.

Behind them, Bumble and the Russian girls were laying a celebratory table outside. Wine was being chilled, wild flowers put in vodka glasses at each setting and, as they busied themselves, even the sun was working to adorn the great man's celebration.

'Well, that's the last one. Look, give Pippa a call to make sure she sets up that trip and then we can call it a day.' Michael propelled his bulk upwards and, standing, put his glasses back in their case before buttoning them into his shirt pocket. His hair, which usually lay brushed and pomaded against his scalp, was now tousled by the breeze and dropped in strands over his brow. He looked several years younger.

'Right. I'm off to catch my birthday fish. Once you've got all this lot sorted out come and join me. Tight lines!'

'Yes, tight lines!' Steve put the files back into the briefcase and closed the lid of the satellite phone. He took his equipment back to his hut to recharge the batteries.

The sun shone and the wind proved an essential aid to comfort, for the first mosquitoes had begun to show. In still air they hovered in noisily, but the sharpening breeze would keep them away. The whine of returning boats disturbed the peace of the camp, and soon the sound of champagne corks and laughter heralded the start of the celebrations. Genia and Jody were the last to return. Their walk across the grass to join the group caused discreet but obvious curiosity, curiosity which was transformed to laughter by Fergus's loud bellow, 'Well done Boris!'

Genia squeezed Jody's arm and murmured, 'I'm sorry...'

She raised her hand to show him Salim's prayer beads, wrapped now around her wrist. Her eyes turned to meet his, their warmth and confidence held his as they walked.

Michael remained some yards away from the camp counting the number of returning boats. He had waved at Sergei who had come from downstream earlier. When he was certain that the party was ready to receive him, he walked with Steve following, up the bank towards the gathering. His arrival drew attention away from Genia and Jody. His opening remarks, 'Oh, you shouldn't have!' were accompanied by a rousing chorus of *Happy Birthday*. The whole camp sang and raised their glasses. Michael was touched for, although he had organised every last detail, their display of gratitude and friendship was heartfelt.

Sergei walked over to Michael who hugged him. Their two stomachs collided in their warm embrace; Michael kissed Sergei's proffered beard fondly. As they patted each other Sergei looked for Genia. Genia intuitively went to join him; his English would be required.

Sergei nodded a greeting, but his preoccupation in preparing his salutations brought a slight flush of embarrassment to the bearded cheeks. 'Genia,' he began in Russian, 'Please tell Michael that I am proud to be here to celebrate his birthday. My family and the Collective recognise the importance of his esteemed friendship.' The two men, with Genia's assistance, exchanged friendly formalities for some time, while Tim re-filled glasses and Bumble handed round blinis coated with caviar. The whole camp, guests, guides and staff alike, blended into one happy group on the bank. The sound of the river was lost in the burble of talk and laughter.

Steve was the first to notice a different sound, a sound that he knew only too well: the staccato blasts of a helicopter's blades. He interrupted his conversation with Sandra and peered downstream. The first thing he saw was a shadow, and then the

198

aircraft itself, flying low and fast along the river. It reared up over the party as it approached the landing area behind the huts. The downdraft caused chaos amongst the table decorations, and a long shadow fleetingly eclipsed the sun over the camp. Genia glanced questioningly at Sergei, who replied with a shrug: it was not unusual for fishery inspectors to make surprise visits. Steve put his glass down and loped off towards the helicopter pad. Genia was about to join him but Sergei held his arm. Michael had just finished a long sentence and needed help. Genia watched as the huge transporter hovered to the ground until he lost sight of its rotors behind the trees. He looked over to Jody who was talking conspiratorially to Ginny.

Genia was in mid-sentence when, looking over Michael's shoulder, he saw Steve returning from the helicopter, his hands on his head. He was leading a small group of men, all but one armed and wearing combat uniforms. Genia recoiled as he recognised their leader. It was Viktor.

A short burst of automatic gunfire rent the air and captured everyone's attention. Some ducked, some screamed, but they all focused on its source – a wild-looking soldier wearing a black bandanna and brandishing a Kalashnikov. The soldier pushed Steve forward to join the group and yelled at everyone to sit on the ground. Four more gunmen positioned themselves around them. In ones and twos the group sat on the grass, only Sergei and Genia remained standing.

Sergei was outraged; Genia had to restrain him from charging at Viktor. 'Sergei, I think maybe I should do this.'

'I'll kill them!' Sergei looked defiantly at his captors one by one as he spat the words, his whole body shaking, 'I'll kill you all!'

'Sergei, let me do this.' Genia paused, for he realised the impact that his next words would have. 'I know them.'

'What?' Sergei swung round and shouted at Genia. 'What?'

'Sit down. Please ... let me do this.'

'What do you mean, you know them? Who are these scum?' He pulled against Genia's restraining hand. Sergei thought of Kim, Oscar and the Moscow mob. Incredulity wrestled with his outrage. 'They can't be *Soltsevskaya* – we've done a deal with them. Genia, who are they?'

'Please, just sit down and let me handle this.' Sergei reluctantly complied, staring at his captors all the while.

Genia remained the only person standing and, as he began to walk towards Viktor, a gun was raised at him. Viktor waved a hand for it to be lowered. Genia walked slowly. He could feel Jody's gaze but could not turn to meet it. His eyes focused instead on his brother-in-law. Viktor looked tired and pale, a weak grin of greeting accentuated the sweat on his brow.

'Genia,' he offered his hand. It was ignored. 'I should explain.'

'I don't want to know. Go away. Just go away, Viktor. Whatever it is, it's not right. Take this lot, and go away.'

'I won't. I can't. Twelve hours or so and it'll all be over. Everyone will be safe.'

'You don't know what you're doing, Viktor. You don't know who you've got here.'

'We know exactly who we've got!' The gunman with the black bandanna waved the barrel of his rifle at the group sitting on the ground. Genia noticed that he was wearing a mixture of combat fatigues and designer label clothes. He was revelling in the control he and his gun were exerting.

'I take it these are not volunteers?' Genia said to Viktor, shaking his head in disbelief. He wanted to look at Jody, to go to her, to try and explain. But he was helpless. Viktor interrupted his thoughts.

'It is a well planned operation, Genia. Trust me. Just get everyone to do as they are told and everything will be fine. Twelve hours or so and they will be safe.' There was steel in Viktor's voice now. Genia responded to it.

'Viktor, stop it and stop it now! These things always end in disaster.'

The gunman intervened, 'Viktor shut him up. You've got to shut him up or I will. Come on, we've got to get this going. Go back and sit down with the others.' He prodded Genia with the barrel of the gun. Genia noticed that the safety catch was off. The solider was looking for an excuse to shoot. Any reason would do.

'Do as Igor says,' Viktor told Genia, who turned to join the others. He looked at Jody. She was scared and bewildered; she grasped Ginny's hand and eyed him questioningly.

Viktor addressed the group in English as they sat on the grass. 'You are the guests of World Environment Action and will remain so until we have completed our task. You will join us on a helicopter ride to Murmansk, before you are flown to Finland and freedom. We do not seek a ransom; we do not want violence, but these guns are here for a reason. Anyone who interferes will be shot.'

His words were received by a silent exchange of frightened glances broken by Michael, who ignored Steve's signals to keep quiet. Steve thought he had trained Michael to 'go grey' in a hostage situation. It was clear that Michael had not the slightest intention of following his instructions.

'Now look here! I don't know who you are, and I don't much care. You are not only ruining my birthday party, but you are also upsetting my guests.' He spoke as if he was addressing his local parish council. 'I suggest we draw this episode to a close before it gets out of control. I give you my word that if you leave now no further action will be taken against you.' The short speech had contrasting effects. Viktor appeared to be listening and bending to reason, while Igor was simmering, eager to make an example of somebody.

Steve recognised the imminent danger. 'For God's sake Michael, shut up or they'll start shooting!'

But Michael was not to be silenced. 'Look, if it's money you want that can be arranged too, but I urge you not to put us all in any further danger. What do you say?'

Igor was about to shout at him but Viktor held up his hand. 'What do I say, Mr Michael Cummings? I'll tell you what I say. I say how dare you patronise and insult me? We don't want your money. Now shut up, sit down and do as you are told!'

'Michael, please sit down!' It was Ginny's voice pleading with him now, making him see sense.

Genia recognised the Viktor of old. Viktor held copies of the guests' tourist visas, bought from the immigration staff at Murmansk airport. 'I want four of you: Michael Cummings, Virginia Cummings, Josephine Lucas and Stephen Newman. I know who each of you are, so come forward now!'

Steve stood up first. 'Right, we are going to do as we are told, aren't we Michael?'

Michael nodded in agreement and then added. 'Yes, we do as we are told. We take our lead from Steve.'

One by one, they stood up and walked towards Igor, who checked their identities against the visas before bundling them together. Genia stood up and tried to reason with Viktor in English.

'Viktor, this is crazy. It won't work. You'll all be killed – all of you. You know how mad the security forces are. They won't let you do it. They'll stop you, whatever the cost.'

'But Genia! It was your idea!' Viktor had been waiting to deliver the remark and enjoyed the impact it had on Genia.

'What do you mean?'

'Bring our cause to the top of the agenda. "Chain Tom Cruise to the railings" – don't you remember? It was your idea.' He pointed at Michael. 'He's older and fatter than Tom Cruise, but far, far richer. The world will want to know why we have taken him.'

'You're crazy Viktor. Think of Nadia.'

'Genia, you've seen your nephew die. You know what's going on up there. It's got to stop. It was your idea!' he repeated.

Jody half heard Viktor's words and put her hands to her head. Emotions flooded through her – betrayal, anger, fear, confusion, despair, hate. All met in two simple words, 'You knew?'

Genia was speechless and looked impotently at her as she raged. 'You bastard, you knew about this! You and me and the hut – and you knew about this? You bastard!' She was hustled with the rest of the guests along the path before he could answer. Jody yelled at the top of her voice, 'I miss you already – you bastard!'

The words were followed by a burst of machine gun fire directed at the ground near the remaining guests and staff, which had the effect of making them run off in all directions. The last Jody saw of Genia he was fleeing into the woods, his hands over his head.

Another short burst of gunfire found Genia flat on his face working out what to do. He stood and turned to be confronted by Tim.

'You traitor!' Tim savoured the words again. 'You traitor!'

Genia turned on him and grabbed him by the throat. 'Shut up! Just shut up. Where has Steve left his bag? He must have told you, where does he keep it?'

'I'm not going to help you get away with this,' Tim's face had contorted into a theatrical snarl.

Genia lifted him with one hand around his throat and squeezed hard. Tim's face reddened, his eyes wreathed in fear. Genia strained to keep his voice calm. 'I have to go, Tim. Where is the bag? Tell me, before it's too late.'

202

'In his hut.' The grip was released and Genia ran towards the row of huts. Tim rolled to the ground choking; the sound of rotor engines started to fill the air.

Genia pounded up the steps and into the hut where he found the black holdall. It felt reassuringly heavy. He lifted it from the bed and opened it. He found the satellite phone and unplugged it from its charger before dumping it in the bag. He was pleased to see a handgun and holster in the recesses. He closed the bag and swung it over his shoulder and darted back outside. Sergei was standing at the bottom of the steps waiting for him. He was wielding an axe.

'You're dead,' he said flatly.

Genia jumped sideways down the steps and flinched as he felt the rush of air from the swinging blade. He stepped backwards as Sergei swung again, this time at his legs. Sergei kept approaching, his face a mask of anger, his swings more desperate. Genia heard the helicopter blades and put an appeasing hand in the air.

'Sergei, it's not what you think. I didn't know. Trust me.'

Sergei swung again, narrowly missing Genia's pacifying palm. He was tiring, but these were potentially lethal blows.

Genia pleaded. 'I trusted you about the smuggling. Was I right?' The blade whistled, as it narrowly missed his shoulder. 'Was I right, Sergei?' Sergei stood panting, the axe raised for another swing. Genia continued. 'Let me go. It's the only way, I've got to try and stop them. Trust me.'

'All right. But you know what I'm thinking. I pray for you that I'm wrong.' Sergei dropped the axe to the ground.

Genia sprinted along the path to the helicopter pad. The blades were now accelerating. The pre-hover checks were completed as he left the path and ran through the scrub. He approached the helicopter from behind. He strode across the open ground with his head bowed, the bag over his shoulder. The downdraft nearly knocked him over as he leapt on to the huge fuel pod that was suspended below the aircraft. Man and machine lifted from the ground. He was relieved to find the handles that held stretchers were still in place. He hung on grimly, as the helicopter swung briefly backwards before accelerating ahead, climbing away over the camp, heading North towards Murmansk, and 69° North.

Chapter Eighteen

Admiral Bodanin was wearing the cardigan his mother-in-law had knitted him for his fortieth birthday. It had been several years since he had stretched the woollen material across his stomach to make the buttons meet their matching holes. But it was blue and, although the hem was frayed in several places, leather patches on each elbow made it serviceable for his last few weeks in command.

He had requisitioned a guillotine from the stores, and was aligning a photograph under the blade when the warning lights started flashing. He pushed a pile of clippings against the bulbs, and continued with his task. He wanted to have the choir's photograph album finished before he retired. During his thirty years with the Northern Fleet, he had kept copies of programmes, reviews and photographs, which he had edited and gathered into fat volumes. He was now working on the fifth and was determined to complete the task.

He laid out a selection of cropped photos in their proposed places and, after shuffling them into different positions, commenced the part that gave him most enjoyment – sticking them into the album. He reached for the glue pot and picked out the brush. It was coated with glue, both on bristles and stem. He started painting the back of a photograph when a phone, one of three on his desk, rang. His face registered his mild irritation, but he chose to ignore the ringing until he had pasted the photo into position. He put the brush back into the pot and, with sticky hands, delicately manoeuvred the photograph into place, the tip of his tongue resting on his lower lip in concentration. It was at this stage that the second phone rang. This phone had a more frequent and higher trilled ring which, the musical Admiral noted, played in counterpoint to the first. It was only when the third phone came alive, when the photo was safely in position, that the Admiral picked up the nearest handset.

'Yes, what is it?' An urgent voice at the other end of the line briefed the Admiral, who was now wiping a gluey finger on a cardigan sleeve. 'Well, where's the Captain?' As he spoke, footsteps hammered up the outside staircase, and the door was knocked upon and opened simultaneously by Captain Osipov.

The Admiral finished his phone conversation and pointed to the other two phones which were still ringing. 'Answer those will you?' Osipov saluted and picked up a handset.

'Yes, yes. I'm with the Admiral now. He was away from his office on a call of nature.' The other phone stopped ringing and the Admiral frowned at the Captain's indiscretion. He tried to make out what was happening from the half conversation he could hear. 'Are you sure it's not an exercise? Who else has been alerted...? How far away is it now...? We'll call you back!' Captain Osipov wiped his forehead with the back of his hand. 'There's an unidentified aircraft, probably a helicopter, which has left civilian airspace and entered our restricted zone. It's flying low and fast along the fjord. If it maintains the same course it will be here in a few minutes. The anti-aircraft battery has been alerted.'

The Admiral's expression strained to maintain calm despite the alarm that was rattling around his brain. He had witnessed the last exercise by the battery. A few conscripts had taken over ten minutes to get from their barracks and have their missiles ready to fire at the practice targets. 'I'm sure it'll be innocent enough. What about air support, have we got anything to scramble? What sort of helicopter is it? And keep the phone line open.'

'Air defences has been notified.' A phone rang. Osipov answered it. The Admiral went to the window, his hands clasped behind his back as if he were back on the bridge of the *Polyanaris*. His jaw dropped open as he stared to the horizon.

Osipov had more information. 'It's a tourist helicopter diverted from its course to Murmansk Civil Airport. It's an MI –'

'Eight,' the Admiral finished the sentence for him. 'The bloody thing's here already!'

This was one emergency that Admiral Bodanin would be able not to ignore.

* * *

Genia was wet, cold, tired and, above all, frightened. As soon as the helicopter had taken off from the camp it had banked hard. The slipstream had snatched his body and the weighty holdall and swung him from the fuel pod. He had dangled over the passing tundra for several moments while he struggled to lever himself back into a position that gave him a chance to stay alive. Initially, the helicopter flew at about 1,000 feet above the ground. It was a mild day so the ambient temperature was not a problem. But as they climbed over the mountains that lay between the river and Murmansk, they had passed close to two squally clouds. Rain had soaked his shirt and jeans, and the helicopter's forward speed of over 110 mph induced a biting wind-chill. He knew it was only a matter of time before exposure set in, that his arms would weaken and he would plummet to the ground and death.

His arms were wrapped around a narrow strut, and he had managed to tuck his hands into his sleeves to give them some protection from the wind; his eyes were shut tight against the blast. The straps of the holdall dug through the material of his shirt and pulled relentlessly at his shoulder. He growled from time to time when the pain became close to unbearable. He considered dropping the holdall, but did not dare to release his grip on the strut in case he lost hold completely.

From time to time the helicopter went through pressure pockets and would plummet fifty feet. As the pod dropped away, Genia would find himself lifted upwards, only to bounce down heavily again a split second later. More pain, more groans and he swore and cursed for all he was worth. He did not know what Viktor had planned, but he was certain that, one way or another they were all flying to their deaths. He thought of Jody, and the look on her face as she was taken away – it was the look of the betrayed.

From the cockpit, the pilot contacted Murmansk Air Traffic Control and told them that they were experiencing low cloud and needed to divert to the north-west. The controller, assuming that this was a standard fishing shuttle and having already been told of a tight connection time, agreed, without checking the weather radar to see whether the course alteration was necessary.

The aircraft banked and descended low and fast into military airspace – towards Andreeva Bay. They were now flying only fifty feet above the fjord and the temperature had risen. Genia's clothes dried in the warmer, drier air, and through a squinted eye he could make out the shape of the *Polyanaris* and her attendant submarines. He swore again – it wouldn't be long before they were shot down. He looked at the water below and decided he had no option but to hang on.

The helicopter came to a hover and Genia was able to open his eyes. He saw below him the deck of the icebreaker at the stern of the ship, and for the first time in an hour he was able to ease his grasp on the stanchion. His arms ached and his shoulder felt as if strands of muscle had been torn from the blade. The deck rose swiftly to greet the helicopter's rubber wheels, the hydraulic rams that supported the undercarriage squealed as the machine bounced to a halt. Genia rolled off the pod. He tried to stand up, but the combined effects of the downdraft and the lack of circulation in his legs made him stagger to the ground. He had no more than thirty seconds before the doors would open. He had to get off the pad. He had to hide.

He crawled along the rusted surface and, as circulation returned to his limbs, he was able to stumble to the edge. He looked back to the aircraft to see the door being lowered. He peered over the edge of the deck. There was a fifteen-foot drop onto a steel floor, covered with debris. He dropped the bag over the side, swore and jumped after it.

The Admiral's office now had several more people in it. Captain Osipov stood with binoculars to his eyes, commentating as the helicopter landed on the *Polyanaris*. He saw what he thought was a body drop from the fuel pod, but then lost it from sight behind the helicopter.

'What *are* they up to?' asked the Admiral. His attention was partly on the rating who had been ordered to clear the desk of his album work. 'Be careful with those things!' he barked, 'I don't want you getting them in a muddle.' He went to the cupboard in the corner of the room and retrieved his uniform coat, replacing it on the hanger with his cardigan. He looked at the mirror, straightened his tie and tidied his hair with the knuckles of his hand. Finally he reached for his hat, and holding the rim in both hands in front of him he inspected the peak for dust. Satisfied, he placed the symbol of authority on his head. He was now ready to command.

Another rating entered carrying a radio handset. 'Sir, we have them on an open channel. They have asked to talk to you. It is a man called Viktor Kharkov. He says he knows you.'

The two men had met frequently over recent years, Viktor representing Medina in negotiating safety measures for storage of nuclear waste. They had developed a mutual respect for each other.

The Admiral looked unfazed as he collected the handset. He squeezed the transmit button and asked, 'Viktor, you know where my office is. Is this a game?'

There was a pause, a crackle and then an answer. 'No, no – it's not a game, Admiral.' Viktor's voice was calm, almost sad. 'I must tell you that we have captured fishermen from the Kola. Amongst them is a senior figure from the world of global finance, Michael Cummings, and his wife. We also have a rich American woman. So please, before we go any further, use one of those telephones on your desk to call off any action against us. I'll contact you again to make sure that you have done this.' The radio fell silent.

The Admiral tried to contact him, but received no reply. He looked at Osipov who shrugged. 'We have a helicopter gunship on the way and the FSB have been notified. They'll be here soon.'

'I would have preferred to have kept them away from this.' There was a hint of admonishment in the Admiral's voice, but he realised that Osipov would have been obliged to notify the newly styled KGB the moment he was aware of a problem. He had his career to think of. The Admiral knew he had to buy time. 'Tell the helicopter gunship to circle wide around the *Polyanaris* before landing here on the quay.' Osipov nodded and passed the order over phone. 'Also get the FSB to come to this office. Let them know I have set up the Command Centre here.' He scratched the back of his neck and looked over to the *Polyanaris*. 'What is that man up to? Get the listening stations to monitor any unusual radio traffic. We will need to block anything they're sending from the ship. If this is what I think it is, our friend Kharkov will want to talk to the outside world.'

'What about Northern Fleet Command, Sir?'

'Inform them I have set up the Command Centre here, and

that I am in contact with the intruders and with FSB. And find out who the Duty Commander is.' There was chance that Bodanin would be the highest-ranking officer on watch, in which case he could maintain control. He would have to consider contacting Naval Headquarters in Moscow before long. He resolved that if this affair was going to interrupt his drift into retirement he was determined to be in command. He stood newly erect at the window and watched as the gunship circled high and wide around the *Polyanaris* before landing on the quay. It was joined by another helicopter that approached from the rear of his building. The FSB had arrived.

The four hostages had travelled in separate makeshift compartments that had been constructed in the rear of the helicopter. Each compartment had a plywood surround, clad heavily in black plastic material which in turn covered material which looked like heavy sound-proofing. Each compartment had a standard seat and a small freezer bin with a bottle of mineral water in it. They had each sat in noisy isolation during their one-hour flight. All four drank from the water bottles, partly to quench their thirsts, partly for something to do. All, including Steve, were frightened. The noise, the isolation and the shock filled them with dread. It also rendered them silent. On arrival on the *Polyanaris* they had been permitted to leave their compartments and sit in the main cabin.

Viktor addressed them from the front of the cabin. He held the radio handset in one hand and the back of a seat with his other. Over his shoulder his passengers could see through the pilot's cockpit the huge dockyard. From their windows was visible the mighty superstructure of the *Polyanaris* which dwarfed their helicopter. Alongside her were rows of mothballed submarines.

'We have landed on the former nuclear powered icebreaker, the *Polyanaris*. She is currently full of spent nuclear waste. Behind me in the Andreeva Dockyard is ten times that amount. Most of it is in secure containers and stable, but with time the situation is more dangerous. The last time I visited this vessel there were acceptable levels of background radiation. Let's see what we have today.'

He picked up a Geiger counter that was on the seat in front

of him. It crackled into life making its own sinister sound. 'Well that's interesting! You see, today we are reading 1GY. Now that is only partly good. Specialists recommend that a person should not be exposed to that level of radiation for more than six hours – I had bargained for longer than that. Time is not on our side.'

'What happens after that?' It was Jody who the asked the question to which they all awaited the answer.

'Radiation is a curious thing, Mrs Lucas. You can't see it, you can't smell it, you can't taste it and you can't feel it. But, as I'm speaking, it is already changing the structure of some of your cells. At the moment the effects would be no worse than a bad hangover. But as the seconds tick by, more damage will be done. If we stay here too long that damage will be irreparable.' Viktor's reply was matter of fact. 'Then we have the breakdown of the body's immune system. It leads to cancer of the bone, skin, breast...' Viktor recited the list, 'and, of course leukaemia. Yes, particularly leukaemia. We have a lot of that up here – we call it Murmansk 'Flu. So we have no more than twelve hours if we are not all to be at risk. I personally would recommend not more than six hours for absolute safety.'

Michael interrupted him. 'So what is it you want us to do?'

'It's what we would like *you* to do, Mr Cummings,' Viktor replied. 'A simple television broadcast. We have a satellite news system with us. We will shortly notify our colleagues in Finland that we have successfully landed here and they will contact the news agencies to let them know that you wish to address them in a broadcast. Once we have completed that and we have received certain assurances, then we will leave here and depart to Finland and safety for us all.'

Jody stood up. She still had her water bottle in her hand. 'Why us, for God's sake? We've got no connections to the nuclear industry or anything like that. How the hell can we help you?'

'In the immediate vicinity is nearly twenty per cent of the world's nuclear waste. Most of it is in an increasingly unstable condition. You all, I guarantee, will know of Chernobyl. The reason you know about it is because for the first time the west was threatened by peaceful release of radiation. The wind that sent the radiation to the doorsteps of its Russian neighbours also delivered the truth. It was a scientist, a prophet, and a poet, but above all, it was the truth. If nothing is done to

210

accelerate the reprocessing and containment of *this* waste then within a short time we will have a disaster on our hands that will make Chernobyl seem irrelevant. It won't be a meltdown – no, nothing as spectacular as that. But it will deliver slow lingering deaths to countless thousands of men, women and children, not just here in Russia, but whichever way the wind blows.' His voice softened, but his face retained its grave expression. 'Everyone says, "Why me?", Mrs Lucas – I've said it myself countless times. But it is you. It is now. And you are all going to help us.'

Nickolai Kosterov, Head of the Murmansk FSB Division, entered the Admiral's office without knocking. He had a striking, handsome face. He was tall and his head hung forward a little from his shoulders, as if to compensate. He was dressed in black from head to toe, the new FSB street-uniform.

'So where are the terrorists?' His question was addressed to the room but only meant for the Admiral.

Bodanin did not reply immediately, he fought instead to contain his irritation. He turned to face his younger counterpart, and caught a glimpse of a gold tooth behind half closed lips. 'Kosterov, you really needn't have bothered coming all this way up here. We have everything under control. We have an environmental group that is playing some form of stunt out there. We handle these sort of things ourselves.'

'You must have misunderstood me, Admiral. I said where are the terrorists? Our information is that these are Chechens. If that is the case, we have a national security situation on our hands. They have just entered a Restricted Area in the heart of our Northern Fleet. There is not a great deal of thought needed for a solution. We have a no-negotiate policy with terrorists. When does the gunship go in?'

The statement confirmed the Admiral's worst fears. In the mid-nineties the government tolerated the growth of environmental organisations, even to the extent of working with them. The arrival of Putin as President had brought about a stricter control on information and accessibility; he was after all an old KGB hand himself. The offices of several agencies found themselves being raided and members harassed, some to the extent of impris-

211

onment. The Admiral swiped the hat from his head and threw it onto his desk.

'It is you who must have misunderstood me, Kosterov! Sitting out there on the *Polyanaris* is Kharkov, the Medina representative in Murmansk, some British money man and a rich American. There isn't a Chechen rebel within a thousand miles of here.' He slapped the palms of his hands onto the top of his desk. 'There is no easy solution!'

'Maybe. But wouldn't it be more convenient if that wasn't the case?'

'No... No! Even if we did want to attack them, we couldn't just fire rockets at the *Polyanaris*. The ship is stuffed with nuclear waste. Any explosion would risk creating a dirty bomb and with the wind from the north, as it is today, you would cover Murmansk in radiation.' The Admiral was continuing his argument when Viktor's voice could be heard from the handset.

'Admiral, do I understand that you have ceased all aggressive acts against us?'

Kosterov reached for the handset but the Admiral's hand swept it from under him. 'Viktor, we are waiting to know what it is you want us to do.' He looked at Kosterov whose only response was to kick over the wastepaper basket, scattering clippings over the floor. 'As I'm sure you will understand Viktor, you and your companions have put yourselves in a very difficult predicament. There is only so much we can do to help. As you can see the gunship is safely ashore. I suggest you think hard before doing whatever it is you plan doing.' The Admiral gestured for the rating to pick up the wastepaper basket. 'Before you say what it is you want, I'll offer you a way out. You fly the helicopter off the *Polyanaris* and back to Murmansk. As long as your hostages are returned unharmed, then we can put this incident down to a navigational error and close the file on it. What do you think?' Kosterov was glowering at the Admiral.

'That's very thoughtful of you Admiral, but – no – we won't change our plans.' The Admiral tried to reply to Viktor, but the handset had gone dead. It was Kosterov who filled the silence.

'Right, I need a line to Moscow, now! I am not going to stand by and watch you play around with these people, Admiral. I have to advise you that I will be seeking a swift and final solution to this matter and that your approach has not in anyway helped.'

'Of course you will want to contact your superiors, that is only natural. But I must remind you that Andreevo is technically a ship and therefore under my command. Unless I am instructed otherwise, that command also includes you.' The Admiral returned Kosterov's stare as he spoke. 'Captain Osipov, please make your office available to our comrade from the FSB.'

Chapter Nineteen

Genia hid underneath the ledge of the helicopter pad as the noise of the rotors died away. There was no footfall on the steel deck: he decided that his presence on the helicopter had gone undetected. His jump from the landing pad had been higher than he anticipated. He had already commenced his roll to break his fall when he hit the deck – an action that saved his ankles, but winded him severely. He lay with his cheek against the rusting metal and allowed himself the luxury of a few minutes to catch his breath, as he worked out what to do.

He reached over to the black holdall that was beside him, the cause of so much pain, which had left a throbbing ache in his shoulder. Wincing, he unzipped the holdall and rummaged inside, his hand locating the pistol. The handgun was of a make he had never seen before. It felt lighter than he had anticipated. His inspection of the slot in the butt, where the magazine was normally held, elicited a groan – it was empty. He searched the depths of the bag, but to no avail. Steve had stored his ammunition in a separate place. He laughed hollowly – as much about finding a release from the fear of the last hour aboard the helicopter as about the humour of his predicament. He stuffed the pistol into the belt of his trousers; even unloaded it retained a latent potency. There was a mass of electrical equipment, chargers, wires and aerials, none of which made sense to Genia. The satellite phone was the only piece of equipment he recognised.

He heard the sound of footsteps echoing from the metal deck above him. Two seagulls dropped from the platform and flapped away to the stern of the vessel, squawking in irritation as they flew. Genia heard a voice. It was Michael.

'You'll have to be patient, old boy. The prostate's been playing up a bit recently. It sometimes takes me a while to get started.'

Genia walked under the lip of the pad to where he guessed the voice was coming from. Slowly he moved his head forward out of the shadows to peer upwards. Just as he was raising his head, urine trickled over the ledge and onto the deck below. The breeze braided the flow into several fine rivulets, narrowly missing his face. Genia jerked his head away, and retired muttering back to the darkness of the canopy. He peeled the hem of his shirt from his trousers and pulled the distinctive plaid material over his head.

'Hurry up, Cummings!' It was Igor. The voice sounded as if it was coming from behind Michael, but Genia could not be sure.

'I can't bloody well speed up. You'll just have to be patient.' Michael was clearly not intimidated by the soldier's presence.

Genia edged his hand holding the shirt forward, until it was in the open. But there was no reaction from Michael. Like most men, he adopted a vacant gaze into the middle distance while relieving himself. Genia's chance would come when it came to tucking himself back into his trousers. All men looked down at that moment, even for the most cursory of inspections. Genia slowly waved his shirt from side to side, upwind of the faltering stream. There was no response for a few seconds and then Michael could be heard saying, 'Sorry, not quite finished. Give me a bit more time will you?'

'Hurry up!'

Genia was confident that Igor was behind Michael now. He leant forward and turned his face upwards. If Michael was surprised to see the waving material or Genia's weather-beaten face emerge from the darkness, he hid it well. Genia was greeted by an avuncular gaze and the wink of an eye. In return Genia smiled encouragingly at Michael, relieved that Michael was not going to expose his presence to Igor. He pulled the pistol from his trousers. He pointed at the empty chamber to Michael, and made a questioning shrug before disappearing back into the shadows. He re-emerged to show the satellite phone before disappearing again.

'Well that's much better. Thank you. At least I can sit in that thing in comfort now.' Michael's voice trailed away as the two men returned to the helicopter.

They walked past Viktor who stood outside the helicopter, leaning over the technician who was trying to make their communications system work. They had now been on the

Polyanaris for over half an hour, and had reached the time for their first scheduled contact with Finland. The clock was ticking and Viktor's impatience was apparent.

Steve watched their captors as they argued about the equipment. He was glad to see Michael return safely from his trip to the edge of the platform. 'Everything all right, Michael?' he asked as Michael re-entered the cabin.

'Yes, fine.' Michael looked at the man who was left to guard them. He looked more like a student than a kidnapper. Michael nodded at Ginny and went further down the cabin to talk to Steve. 'You might want to "point percy" yourself in a few minutes. There's an amazing view from where I was standing.' Michael seemed to be blithely unaware of the danger he was in, and bending, he whispered quickly into Steve's ear.

'Shut up and get back to your seat!' The guard waved his gun but it was apparent to Steve that he was playing a role. He would be no problem when the time came. Igor and the two others outside presented more of a challenge. The pilots remained in their cockpit smoking; they were being paid a fortune for their day's work. Their job was to fly and they seemed detached from proceedings. They had the appearance of men who had spent a lifetime waiting. Steve could safely assume that they would fly for anyone who would pay them.

'Sit down and do as you're told! You'll get us all shot.' Steve prodded Michael away, noticing a relaxing in the guard's shoulders and a lowering of the gun.

'All right, all right,' Michael said as he returned to his place in front of Ginny, who was beginning to show signs of stress.

'Michael, please don't annoy them. We are in enough trouble as it is. God alone knows what's happening to us while we sit here on this wretched thing. I can't see how we are ever going to get off it. Please, don't make things worse for us.'

Michael reached over the back of his seat and held her hand.

'I'm serious Michael. All our lives are at risk, and this no time to be annoying them. I just want us all to get home safely.' There was a quaver in her voice.

Michael gripped her hand tightly. 'I'm sorry my darling. I won't do anything stupid, I promise.'

Jody sat behind Steve. She had her back to the window, bending her legs upwards and wrapping her arms around them. Her head rested on her knees. She chewed gravely on the corner of her bottom lip. She had been through the full gamut of emotions. Fear had initially replaced the raw nerve of humiliation. Now, she thought of betrayal. She thought of Genia and the hut – the words, the laughter, the tenderness, their lovemaking. The words again. Words – of love, of the future, of hope. She thought of his physical presence – the kindness in his face, the weight of his body upon her, the closeness, the sweat, the wildness in his eye, the harshness of his grasp on her flesh. She held her knees tighter and chewed her lip harder. She had seen him run into the forest. 'Bastard! Bastard! I'll break you. I'll destroy you.'

Kosterov returned to the Admiral's office. Bodanin remained seated and pretended to be unaware of the FSB man's presence but he had noticed a renewed calmness, nearing complacency, in the man who had become an adversary. He was not going to fill the silence and waited for Kosterov to speak first.

'Has anything happened?' came the question eventually.

The Admiral adopted a preoccupied expression. 'Mmmh? No, nothing so far. We'll let them sweat it out for a while. Viktor is more aware than anyone that he can't stay on that ship for ever.'

'Why don't we just go in and get them off now?'

'I've told you why. We haven't just got Russians out there, we've got foreign nationals.'

'And I've told you they are Chechen. You will soon hear the same from FSB Headquarters in Moscow. You know, if I were you I wouldn't be sitting here trying to pacify them. I'd be sending a squad in to get them off that ship. Dead or alive.' He then smiled, the first time Bodanin had seen him smile. 'Admiral, you retire shortly. In a few weeks there will be another man sitting at this desk. This will all be a memory. Think of your pension, a happy retirement; this isn't the time to be risking all that. And for what? No one will know what happens here today. Chechen rebels, a crashed tourist helicopter, whatever! You don't have to worry about it. Why bother?' The Admiral preferred Kosterov without a smile.

'Well, you're not me. And that's not going to happen while I'm in command.' The Admiral's cheeks flushed with anger.

'Have it your way. But you should realise that no one's getting off that ship alive.'

217

Viktor's educated voice boomed into the room from the radio. Bodanin said to Kosterov as he picked up the handset, 'Well, there's a Chechen, if ever I heard one.' He stood up and walked to the window.

'Viktor, I need a favour from you.'

'What is it?'

'I would like to see your hostages. I need to see that they are still alive. Will you line them up beside the helicopter for a moment?'

'They are safe. Their only problem is radiation, but hopefully we'll be away well before it reaches dangerous levels.'

'Viktor, please, I need your help now. There are those who feel that I should not be so tolerant of your predicament.' He eyed Kosterov. 'Listen to me when I tell you it is in everyone's interest that you do as I ask.'

There was a pause and then Viktor replied, 'They'll be out shortly.'

The Admiral reached for his binoculars and watched as the hostages were paraded beside the helicopter. He counted four, two of them women. This tallied with the report that had recently been received from the fishing camp. The colour in their clothes was in stark contrast to their captors'. They looked small beside the helicopter, which in turn was dwarfed by the *Polyanaris* and her submarines. And yet, he reflected, two of those people and their families represented more wealth than the entire Kola region.

By the helicopter it was Igor who was now venting his frustration at the malfunctioning communications equipment. The satellite camera unit had started service with CNN during the Gulf War. It had subsequently been acquired by Greenpeace who used it for a few years on their peace boat. Finally it was sold to World Environmental Action. Igor had supervised the testing of the unit, setting up links to their counterparts in Finland from various locations in the Kola, all without a problem. But now it was not working. WEA had planned for a broadcast that would feature on the lunchtime news across Europe and be in time for the breakfast bulletins in East Coast America. Their first broadcast would reach a potential audience of 500 million people. 'How much would McDonald's pay for an advertising slot like that?' he had joked with Viktor.

Despite the northerly breeze that brought cold air from the Arctic ice cap, the hostages were pleased to be in the open. The helicopter's cabin reeked of leaking aviation fuel and the ash-trays had been full of cigarette butts. Their warmth and shelter came at a price. Patchy clouds obliterated the sun from time to time, but the steel of the helicopter pad had accumulated suffi-cient warmth to compensate and keep them warm.

Jody was becoming increasingly impatient. Her anger at Genia had transformed into anger at herself for being so easily fooled. She felt isolated from the rest of the hostages. Leaving the fish-ing party for a night to sleep with one of the guides was bound to have caused a stir. But when that guide turned out to be asso-ciated with their kidnappers, the act could only cause a rift. Her fellow hostages were English and, as a result, nobody actually said anything to criticise. But equally nobody, not even Ginny, offered any words of comfort. She wanted to vent her anger on somebody else.

'So what have you got planned for us? We've been sitting here for nearly an hour now. If that Geiger counter's telling the truth, we will soon be damaging our bodies. What's the point?'

Igor turned from his work with the equipment. 'Viktor, tell her to shut up.'

Viktor walked over to Jody and looked down at her. She sat on the metal deck, her legs stretched out and crossed in front of her; her arms at an angle behind her acted as a prop for her body. 'Please, Mrs Lucas. Keep quiet. You will know soon enough.'

'Well, why not talk to us? You've obviously got yourself all worked up about something. Or are you just some sort of crack-pot?'

Ginny intervened. 'Jody, this isn't going to get us anywhere. Please, do as the man says and keep quiet.'

Viktor raised his hand like a conductor at the beginning of the slow movement of a concerto. 'No. No – I'll answer Mrs Lucas. She will shortly have to talk to people about her experiences here. She might as well know the truth now.' Viktor pointed around him as he spoke. 'What we have here is a small pro-portion of the Cold War's nuclear legacy. When we built all these nuclear warships, submarines and missiles, no one on

219

either side had any idea of how to decommission them. Even now, so many decades after the first atomic bomb, we are still wrestling with the technology. The sad truth we are learning is that you can't stop radiation. Its potency will fade away slowly. Very slowly. It will take over two thousand five hundred years. You can only neutralise it – not destroy it. That is the monster that our scientists have created. In America you have money. You treat your dangerous materials and bury them deep in the ground, but with time they will leak out and cause damage. In England, Mr Cummings, you wash your power station waste into the sea. The Kola River that runs past us contains salmon with minute doses of radiation. Nothing harmful as yet. Do you know where it comes from? Surprisingly not from here. Not now anyway. It is brought up by the Gulf Stream from your expensive treatment plants at Sellafield and Cap de l'Hague in France. Here, in Russia, we have no such luxury. As we enter this brave new millennium we are effectively broke, as you would say. The sailors on the quay over there haven't been paid for three months. They supplement the most basic of rations with surplus potatoes and dried fish, donations from a collective. There is no money.'

He pointed down the estuary to a tumble of buildings on the shore. 'Over there is a treatment plant donated by the west. It has never been commissioned. I fought for that treatment plant, but we were not given the funds to run it. Corruption in Murmansk and no long-term policies from America mean it will never work. It is rotting away as we speak.'

'That's bullshit!' Jody retorted, 'We do have long-term policies. Who started the decommissioning process? No one has fought harder for that than the US.'

'Your Presidents aren't interested in the long-term, they are only interested in the next term,' he replied flatly. He wiped his moustache and scratched his chin. He didn't want to argue; he wanted to explain. 'Do you have any children Mrs Lucas?'

'No.'

'Any nephews or nieces?'

'Four,' Jody replied.

'Well, you tell their parents all about leukaemia. More children die of this disease in the USA than of any other disease. Your President has just announced a twenty-five per cent increase in nuclear power generation. Your scientists refuse to make the link, too many vested interests. Do you want me to go on?'

'If you're so holier than thou, how come you use mercenaries and force? There must be a better way.'

'Mrs Lucas, when you are in the gutter you cannot choose your friends.'

'So, we take part in a stunt to help you. A television interview. A few minutes on television. You think that is going to change the world? You are so naïve if you think that is going to make one jot of difference. People won't remember anything past the baseball scores. You're wasting your time. But hell! If it makes you happy, let's get the cameras rolling. We'll say whatever you want and then let's get the hell out of here. What do you say Michael? This is easy.'

Michael was about to speak but Viktor answered, looking wearily at Jody.

'I must look very stupid Mrs Lucas, I apologise. Let me explain in a little more detail. I have told you a lie, but it is no worse than the lie that citizens of our countries are told. You see, I have lied about the level of radiation you have been exposed to. The Geiger counter tells the truth, Mrs Lucas, it tells us what is going on here. But remember you were each allocated specific seats on the helicopter? I see you have brought your water bottle with you. Hand it to me will you?'

Jody picked the plastic bottle off the deck and handed it to Viktor. He held the Geiger counter's sensor next to the bottle. The earlier test had produced a series of steady clicks. Now the clicks joined together into a high pitched screech. 'Here, lock this away with the other bottles,' he said to the youngest captor.

'The water in the bottles has been exposed to a high dosage of radiation for over a week. The four of you have all drunk from these bottles. I have to tell you that, as a result, the cumulative effect will be the same as exposure to 30, possibly up to 50 GY. That is a dangerously high dosage. At that level permanent cell damage is caused. The cells that die will do you no harm. The cells that change will give you cancer.' He paused. He had let his hands fall by his side now. He spoke softly. 'Yes, you will do our interview. You will say what you are told. But it won't be the end of the matter. It will be the start of a very public experiment – no, experiment is the wrong word – demonstration. Your countries will be able to monitor your lives and, over the months and years to come, witness the slow, but inevitable, drift into death. They will watch you battle with the disease. One or two of you will use, and be ravaged by, chemotherapy. The others will dabble with herbal cures. But you will not escape the simple truth, that you are going to die.'

There was silence from the hostages for a few seconds, and then Ginny let out a frightened sob. Jody stood up and approached Viktor. 'How could you do that? How could you do that to us? It's the same as injecting us with an HIV infected needle. You're lying. You wouldn't do that.'

'Mrs Lucas, it's the truth. It's not so bad. Statistically, at your ages, two of you will die of cancer anyway, one of you within five years. The percentage may be even higher. Perhaps, as your ill-ness will be so public, you will have time to reflect and use your money and influence to persuade people to look at the cause of all these cancers, and not the cure. For you know, even now, there is no proven cure. All we do is delay the inevitable. I urge you to do something in the time you have left. Not for this genera-tion or the next, but for the generations beyond. Now *that* is long-term thinking. Your media will love it and we will encourage them to. Think of it. "The Kola Martyrs". I think they'll put that story above the baseball scores.'

'No. They'll remember "The Kola Murderers". That's all you people are. You are mad.'

'You are very calm for a person has just been given a death sentence.'

'I'm not calm. I thought I was going to die the moment I got on that helicopter. I'm angry, angry and relieved. Relieved that I will see another dawn tomorrow. If you need us to live for a while, that's fine. And if it's OK with you I don't want any more sermons.'

Michael hugged Ginny. Jody walked around the deck, her hand in her hair. 'Oh, this just gets better. Thank you, God!' she mut-tered as she walked in a tight circle, 'Thank you very much.'

222

Chapter Twenty

A written transmission had arrived in the Admiral's office. Kosterov had delivered it himself. It was from FSB Headquarters in Moscow, instructing the Admiral to relinquish his command to Kosterov with regard to dealing with the terrorists. Kosterov stood at the Admiral's desk his arms folded across his chest.

'Well?'

'Kosterov. I am of course delighted that your superiors in Moscow take such a keen interest in what we are doing here in Murmansk. But, you must realise that I cannot respond to this. I report to Naval Headquarters not the Lubiyanka. Surely you know this?'

'You are only delaying the inevitable. Why? Soon you will receive a message from your superiors. It will say exactly the same. Why are you being so obstructive? It can't help your cause.'

The Admiral was thumbing through some old photographs, an act that created an impression of calm in the office and caused more irritation to Kosterov. 'My dear Kosterov. I assure you I am not obstructing you. This is my command. These are not terrorists. I too, have informed my superiors. I also have sent my recommendation for a negotiated and peaceful end to this unfortunate situation. I cannot and will not be blamed for acting inappropriately. Now, please leave my office. I will notify you when my orders have come through.'

Kosterov left the office in silence, but slammed the door.

'Look, I've got to relieve myself, if that's all right with you,' Steve said to Igor.

'Get behind the back of the helicopter, then.' Igor didn't want to walk to the edge of the platform again.

'It's a bit more serious than that.' Steve managed to look suitably embarrassed, and this had the desired effect.

'You take him over there,' Igor gestured to the young guard in the general direction of Michael's earlier visit.

Genia heard the pair drawing close. He ran the fifty yards or so to get to where he thought they would be. It was Steve's voice he heard this time.

'For God's sake! You don't have to bloody well stare at me! I'm not going anywhere with my trousers round my ankles.' Genia edged his head into the open, but pulled it swiftly away at the sight that greeted him.

Genia waited for a few seconds and when nothing fell from above, realised that Steve had come for another reason, and that the guard must have turned away. For the second time he emerged from beneath the deck. Steve nodded curtly, pointed to his watch and then raised the palm of one hand with his fingers spread open. He mouthed the words 'five minutes' before pointing to the helicopter.

Genia looked at his watch and marked the time, although he wasn't entirely sure what he was going to do in five minutes time with an empty gun and a bag of electronics that he could not work.

One guard watched the captives, while the rest of the kidnappers were huddled around the various bits of equipment. Steve looked at his watch and eyed the edges of the helicopter deck, alert for any sign of Genia. The seconds ticked away. One minute to go and he still hadn't formulated any plan. Jody was sitting next to Ginny with an arm around her comforting her; 'It'll be OK, it'll be OK.' Steve had managed to let Michael know that he had spoken to Genia but had not told him what he planned to do – for the very good reason that he didn't know. The interest being shown in the equipment presented his best opportunity. If only Genia could appear from behind, then it would be easy. His experience told him that nothing was as simple as that.

Five minutes came and went, still no sign of Genia. 'Russian watches...' thought Steve to himself. Then he saw the unmistakable mop of Genia's hair rise above the side of the heli-copter pad, from an angle that would be visible to their captors. Steve acted swiftly.

'Have you got any idea what you're doing with that equipment?' he shouted. His captors turned to face him as he moved round to address them. Igor stayed crouched on the ground. 'Shut up and sit down, or you get it!'

'It seems to me that you haven't a clue what you're doing there.' Genia was in the open now and running the fifty metres towards them – low and fast. All eyes on Steve.

'It'll never work. They'll have jammed the signal.' All eyes still on Steve. Genia was thirty metres away now. 'We might as well use semaphore!'

Igor stood up, he had a pistol in his hand. Genia was now twenty metres away, his face set. His target was Igor. He was going to break his neck. Fifteen metres. Jody saw him and turned to face him. Ten metres. She saw him running. She thought he was going for Steve. She yelled 'You! What are –'

Igor turned and crouched in the same movement. He aimed and fired a shot that hit Genia, knocking him sideways. He landed on the deck, sliding along the steel surface to bring him to Igor's feet. Igor stamped heavily on Genia's face.

Steve dived at Igor. In spite of his 12 stone weight, Steve's attack unbalanced Igor, who rolled to the deck. Both Steve's hands grasped Igor's wrist and levered hard. The gun fell to the ground before Igor's wrist broke. Steve grabbed the gun and rolled onto his feet. He turned and fired two shots into Igor's chest. The shots lifted Igor backwards and away from Genia. He was dead. Ginny screamed. Genia groaned and rolled over, his face bloody from Igor's boot. He coughed. He was alive. Steve fired two fatal shots at the young guard who was still fumbling with his Kalashnikov. A muddled expression crossed the young boy's brow, before death clawed him away.

'Genia, pick the fucking thing up! Pick it up!' Steve barked, pointing at the Kalashnikov. He turned. 'Michael, go to the pilots! Do a deal – any deal, do it. Now! I'll cover you.'

Genia hauled himself from the ground and plucked the Kalashnikov from the young guard's hands. He could only hold it in one hand. Viktor had found his handgun and raised it at Michael who was climbing the helicopter steps.

'Here, swap.' Steve grasped the machine gun from Genia and sprayed bullets at Viktor's feet. 'No!' shouted Genia, 'No!' Bullets sparked off the steel surface ricocheting wildly into the air. One tore into Viktor's stomach. His scream was lost to the echoing metal and Ginny's persistent wailing cry, 'Stop it! Stop it, all of you. Stop it!'

Steve was now yelling at the two remaining captors to lie down. Somewhere in the melée he had lost his glasses. He screamed like a drill sergeant into their ears. 'Move, and I'll kill you! You fucking move a muscle and I'll kill you!' The effects of the adrenaline easing with each shout, Steve was breathing heavily. He panted to Genia, 'Where's my bag? Where is it?'

'Over there,' Genia pointed at the rim of the helicopter pad, 'where I came from. There's a ladder...'

'OK. Get that man's gun and give it to Jody. Jody you stand behind them, and if they move shoot them.'

Steve loped off, returning soon afterwards with his holdall. He found the satellite phone and started pushing buttons.

Jody looked at Genia. A stain grew on his shoulder. First it had appeared like a map of Australia and then, as gravity took control, it formed the shape of Africa. His left eye was part closed, his cheek battered. His upper body was slowly rocking forwards and backwards. He reeled like a sailor after a long night ashore.

'You OK?' Jody asked.

'...mmh.'

'How did you get here?'

No words came, but a grunt as he lifted his good arm, and pointed across his blood-stained shirt to the helicopter.

'How?'

He smiled and shrugged as best he could. He blinked slowly, a giraffe in the noonday heat.

There was a long pause.

'Did you know?' She pointed at the carnage that lay around them.

Still no words, but a shake of the head and an expression that said it all.

She was about to say something humorous but the trauma of the last few hours took over. 'You don't know what we've been through. What they've done to us.'

A questioning look. Genia was in a daze.

She turned away. He could see her raise a hand to an eye. She turned to face him again and smiled. 'You look like you could do with some patching up.'

'Yes. That would be good.'

Michael returned to join the group. 'Well, I am now the owner of a particularly ugly helicopter and a crew for the next three years. Steve, come on, let's get on this thing and away from here.'

Steve was talking on the phone. He held his hand up to prevent the interruption. When he had finished his message he pushed a button that scrambled his words in a short burst to Wilton, the headquarters of the British Army Land Command.

'It may not be as simple as that, Michael.'

The telex in the Admiral's office rattled into life. A sheet of white paper was drawn from the feeder and the sound of the cartridge running to and fro across the page filled the office. The Admiral raised himself from his chair and stood over the printer. No one in the office, other than he, could see the contents of his orders. He read impassively and then smiled.

'Just as I thought!'

He took the piece of paper and placed it in the top right-hand drawer of his desk.

'Admiral, there's shooting on the *Polyanaris!*'

'Get that radio. Try and raise someone.'

The Admiral watched the events on the *Polyanaris* unfold through his binoculars. He was joined by Kosterov.

'Well that's two dead and two down. If they carry on like this, we can all go home in an hour or so.'

The Admiral chose not to reply.

'They've got someone good out there, that's for sure. We had better watch him. Have your orders arrived yet Admiral?'

'Nothing changes, we seek a peaceful resolution to this matter.'

Captain Osipov moved uneasily behind the Admiral. He had seen the orders arrive. Kosterov noticed, and repeated the question.

'So, no orders have been received?'

'Kosterov, I have given you my reply.'

227

Steve's voice could be heard on the radio. 'This is Major Newman, formerly of the British Army. I am responsible for the security of the members of the party who have been captured by the environmental group World Environmental Action. We have regained control from our captors, and we seek clear air space for our helicopter to the Finnish border. We will leave our captors on the ship for your authorities to deal with.'

'I'm sure that can be arranged. It will take a short while though. As I'm sure you will understand, we are at a state of high alert as a result of your unplanned arrival at a secret location,' the Admiral replied.

'I understand. But I should tell you that I have notified UK Land Command of our predicament and our request. They will be in contact with your Naval Command shortly.'

Kosterov whispered to the Admiral. 'He's bluffing. He can't have got through. We would have known. They are isolated. Let's go in now and finish the job, then we can all go home.'

Genia leant against a helicopter wheel. Beside him lay Viktor. They had both received treatment from the helicopter's first aid box. The box had been packed at the same time that the helicopter had been commissioned, some thirty years earlier. The bandages and dressings were pale and musty, but served to staunch the flow of blood from Genia's shoulder. Viktor's wound was bleeding so heavily that the rudimentary dressing could not keep up. Jody had tended to Genia. Viktor noticed the intimacy between them and smiled. Steve had done his best to bind Viktor's wound, but the bullet had splintered as it entered his body, causing mortal damage. The loss of blood and the effects of shock and pain weakened him by the second. Viktor spoke in Russian.

'I feel you are about to ask me why, Genia.'

'No, I know why. My question perhaps would be, why now? But it has happened, there is no point.'

'Why are you here? What's your reason?' he motioned to Jody with his head. 'The American woman? Is there something you want to tell *me*?' Viktor was trying to make light of his suffering. 'She is a handsome woman. Rich. Your passport from Murmansk. Is that why you're here?'

'We are close, but, no. It wasn't only that. What you were

trying to do was right, Viktor. The way you were doing it was wrong. But you don't need me to tell you that. Middle age isn't that bad, there are other ways to fight it you know.'

Viktor tried to laugh, but could only cough.

'Is there something you want to tell me? They say that you have poisoned them. That doesn't sound like you.'

Viktor smiled. 'Genia, our Genia... What would Nadia say? "So sensitive. He sees everything".'

'Well, tell me.'

Viktor shifted his weight, trying to find a comfortable position. As he moved, blood pooled between his legs. His words were softly spoken and punctuated by small sighs. 'It was another of your ideas. Or at least prompted by you. Do you remember going to the library all those months ago? For Volodia. I was late and you made a fuss. Do you remember? You said something. "I am sorry if I made you *think* that you looked a fool, that is far worse than actually being a fool".'

Genia smiled, '...and, so it is with illness?'

'Just so.' Viktor smiled a thin smile.

'But you convinced them?'

'The Geiger counter – the water. I pushed the test button. Strange isn't it, Genia? People wanting to believe they are going to die.' He smiled, was about to say something, but coughed again. His body shook. Blood trickled from the corner of his mouth. There was fear in his eyes now, pain on his brow. 'Hold me, Genia. Hold me...'

Genia slid down and lay next to Viktor. He hugged him to his chest. He murmured 'I'm here, I'm here...' He stroked Viktor's hair until his last breath had been drawn. He kissed his friend's cheek and closed his eyes. He whispered 'Goodbye my friend... *prachay.*'

'Genia?' Jody's voice was almost a whisper, 'We'd better get going. They are trying to get clearance. It may come at any time. Steve wants us on board. Here, I'll help you.' Jody gave Genia her hand, and looped an arm under his armpit. Genia stood. She looked into his tear-filled eyes. She touched his battered cheek, the lightest of touches. 'Come on my love, let's go home. It's been a long day.'

He took her hand from his cheek and brought it to his lips. He kissed the palm and mouthed into the soft, warm flesh. 'Yes. A long day. It's been a long day.'

Chapter Twenty-One

Genia stood in the clearing. It was a clear frosty day, the first day of spring. Snow carpeted the ground and hung heavily on the trees, bowing the branches of the fine-limbed birches. He made use of the clear weather to saw logs. He stood in his shirt-sleeves in the freezing forest, a pile of wood neatly stacked beside his saw bench. The forest floor had turned into a bed of sawdust around him. He stood for a few moments to catch his breath. He removed his fur hat and wiped the sweat from his brow, before replacing it on his head. He wiped condensation from his mous-tache; small ice crystals dusted the hairs beneath his nostrils. He touched his cheek and felt the uneven flesh where the sutures had been applied. Only three, but they had been administered in a hurry. They gave him sad comfort; it had all happened. It wasn't a dream. He breathed deeply and sighed.

Last year he was fitter. He could saw a hundred of these logs without pausing. Now the ache in his shoulder and lack of fit-ness conspired to tire him. No hunting for Genia this year. But, with the logging and daily walks, his body strengthened. With each day that passed the memory faded. 'Time will heal – time will heal,' he told himself, hoping that soon he would awake one morning and not have to say it again – ever. To one side, Pana lay on Genia's coat. Tormenting him was the puppy that Genia saved from last year's litter; a dog puppy, which Genia had called Kola, a welcome addition to his hut. Genia reached for his flask and gulped some water. He replaced the cork stopper. He shiv-ered. He must get back to work.

He placed a log on the bench and picked up his saw. He exam-ined the blade. It would need sharpening when next he stopped. Aligning the saw against the silvery bark, he pushed the blade across the branch with slight downward pressure. Flakes of bark were ejected at the top of his stroke. He retrieved the blade, pulling down hard against the wood. Golden sawdust was ejected downwards towards him – sparks from a grindstone. The fore-stroke now, with pressure and determination, a pause at the top and then the retrieve. He drifted into a rhythm; his mind went with him. He was the oarsman alone on the waves, he was the farmer scything hay, he was the man climbing a mountain. It was the rhythm. It was the breathing. It was the heart pumping, the blood pulsing, the sinews working. He was alive. He was well. 'Time will heal,' he said, in rhythm with his strokes. 'Time will heal.'

The hours passed, but he was unaware of time. His watch hung from a hook in his cabin. He had put it there upon his return, so many months ago, the hands and date frozen with the movement's last tick. On the shelf was the last carving he made for Volodia. Nadia had given it to him when he had gone to Murmansk to attend his father's funeral. Also on that shelf was a Christmas card from Michael and Ginny Cummings. A family photograph in front of a lodge in Scotland. 'Come any time. You'll find us pretty chaotic,' the message read. In his darker moods he could only ask if they had the slightest idea what the word meant. A card from Steve Newman, with a small parcel – an ammunition clip with a note attached saying, 'Look harder next time!' The writing was barely legible. A child's hand, the writing of a killer.

There, too, was the fragment of bullet removed from his shoulder, removed upon his return to Murmansk, now benign in a plastic bottle. Genia, alone in a ward with wheezing geriatrics and drunks. Nadia had visited. How could he explain? Who was responsible for Viktor's death? The man who fired the shot? The man who tried to stop him? Or was it the man himself?

There, on another hook, hung Jody's scarf. Jody's scarf... On some days he could pick it up, sniff the cashmere and imagine that it retained the last vestiges of her. How many times can a man relive a night of love? On other days, when the door of his cabin was open, the sounds of the river married with the wind to make the sound of her laughter, he lay frozen on his bed, hoping that her face would appear at his doorway.

'Let's go home,' she had said, 'let's go home'. The words he most wanted to hear. Such simple words; words that are part of man's common experience, in every tongue throughout the centuries. 'Let's go home.' But for them, words of polar meaning; for her America – for him this hut in the Kola. She asked him to go with her, but how could he? There was Nadia, his father – but more than that, he knew that it would not work. How could it?

'Maybe in the spring?' Maybe in the spring was the answer. It wouldn't work, couldn't work. But he loved her. That, amongst all the uncertainty, he did know. That one simple truth made all others irrelevant. But it was the hardest truth of all. For in his heart he knew it was a love without future. 'Time will heal – time will heal.'

She had written him letters full of candour and longing. The words stretched across the vellum in her long extravagant hand. Words laid down in turquoise. Candour about her marriage and the need to address the truth. Her determination to do something useful, but also her reluctance to be part of any organisation. 'I've got the time and I can be of help. The boys think I'm mad, though. We'll see!'

On the shelf, in a leather frame, was a photograph – a colour photograph. But, it was not the face he remembered. He had pored over the image, examining the features that he had come to know so well. The smile, the eyes, the teeth, the hair; all, in themselves, were as he recalled. But together, the sum of these features did not combine to create the face that he had known. He had seen her smile the most intimate of smiles. On his bed, in the half-light. Beneath him, her head in his hands, on the brink of ecstasy, her mouth parted, her eyes wild and demanding. His face so close to hers, breathing her breath, smelling her scent. That was the face he knew; a three-dimensional, vibrant, passionate truth. The image in the frame was a feeble likeness.

The silence of the forest was broken by the sounds of a motor in the distance. Genia stopped sawing to listen. Hunters, making their way back to camp along the frozen river. It was still light, too early to go back to his hut.

He had started tying salmon flies. *Touch the Wild* had provided him with a trunk load of equipment and materials. His hands took to the work easily, his eyes, less so. He worked now through half-moon glasses, glasses that he needed for reading as well. Most evenings he would tie ten flies. At $2 each, the winter evenings were well spent. At first he copied famous patterns, but

232

then created his own. The flies reflected his mood. Some nights they were dark and sombre, at other times bright and garish; all meticulous to the last detail. He mixed a varnish that was to become his own, an india blue, instead of the ubiquitous black or red.

One he tied. Deep red hackle, dark green body, black wing, whipped with gold wire. 'What shall we call it?' they wrote. *The Jody* he had replied. He had sent her one in a case. 'I'll treasure it forever,' she had written, 'it's far to good to be used.' He had replied, 'No, you must use it, Jody. You must!' He carved salmon for fishermen who wanted a trophy for their walls. He found that his hand coped easily with the painstaking task of painting so many scales. His final delight was found in mounting the fish on a varnished plinth. The simple inscription, 'Genia', written at the bottom right-hand corner in a cautious hand that gave a rare insight into the man to whom it belonged.

That same hand had written to tell of his love. He had told her of his hopes and his sadness in realising that they would come to nothing. 'Don't tell me that. You don't know, you just don't know.' He didn't know, and that is why he had to write it down. Their love deserved honesty of that calibre. He cursed himself for writing it a thousand times, but took solace in his honesty.

Dusk settled on the clearing. He stacked the logs onto the pile and draped his coat over his shoulders. 'Come on, let's go home!' He smiled as he called his dogs with those emotive words. He walked down to the river and the path that would lead him to his hut. He thought he could smell woodsmoke in the air. It must be an illusion. He rounded the corner and saw the light from his kerosene lamp casting a dim glow in the window. Pana raced ahead barking, Kola bundled behind.

Genia's mouth went dry. He walked swiftly, running as he neared the hut. He climbed the steps and stood still on the threshold. There, on the handle, hung Salim's prayer beads. Genia smiled a happy smile.